Pokémon™ X•Y

STORY
Hidenori Kusaka

ART
Satoshi Yamamoto

2

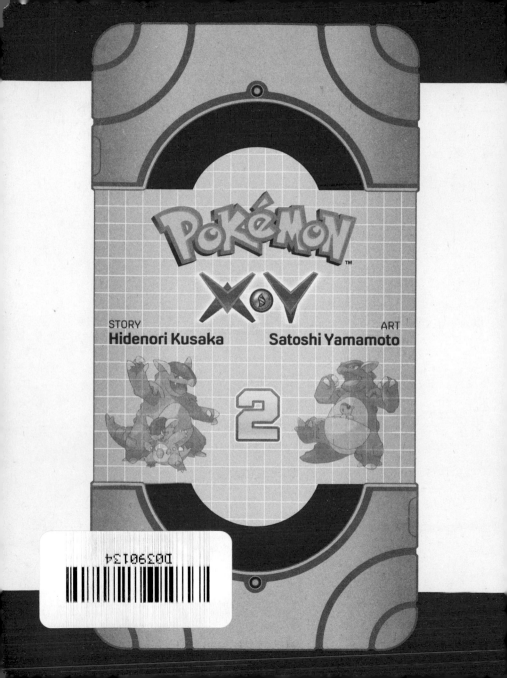

CHARACTERS

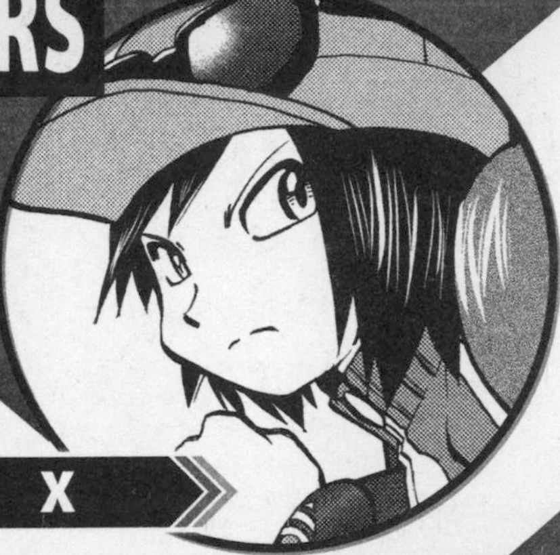

X

The main character of this chapter, and one of five close childhood friends. He was once a highly skilled Trainer who even won the Junior Pokémon Battle Tournament, but now...

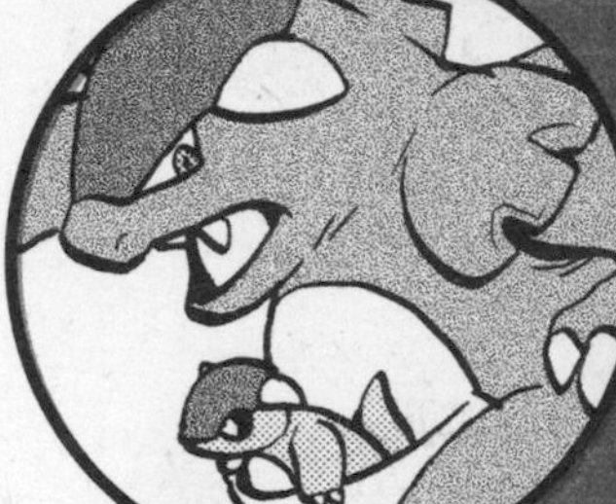

KANGA & LI'L KANGA

X's longtime Pokémon partners with whom he won the Junior Tournament.

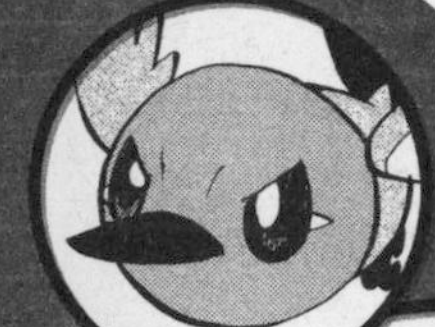

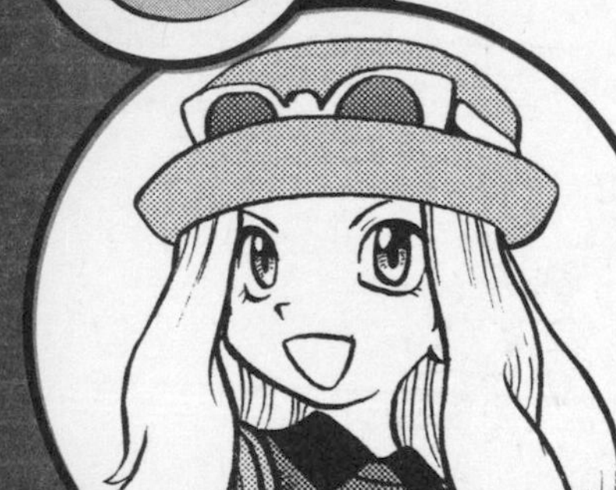

Y

X's best friend, a Sky Trainer trainee. Her full name is Yvonne Gabena.

MEET THE

TREVOR

One of the five friends.
A quiet boy who hopes
to become a Pokémon
Researcher one day.

TIERNO

One of the five friends.
A big boy with an even
bigger heart. He is
currently training to
become a dancer.

SHAUNA

One of the five friends.
Her dream is to become a
Furfrou Groomer. She is
quick to speak her mind.

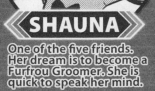

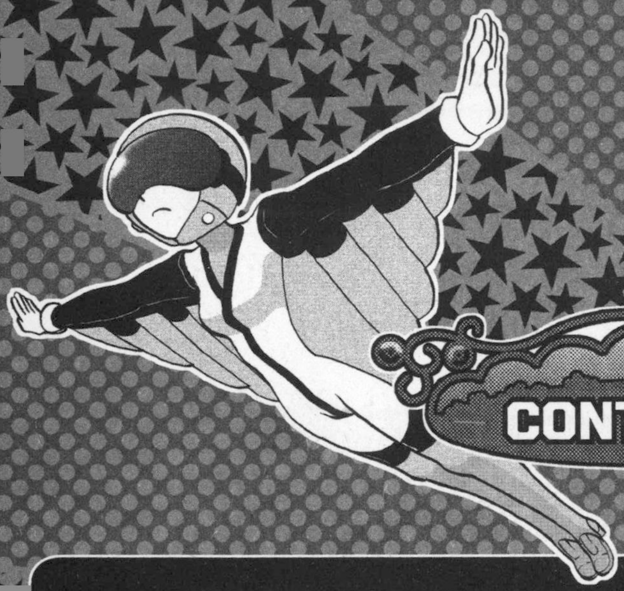

CONTENTS

Adventure 4
They Have a Flare for a Li'l Kanga-Napping

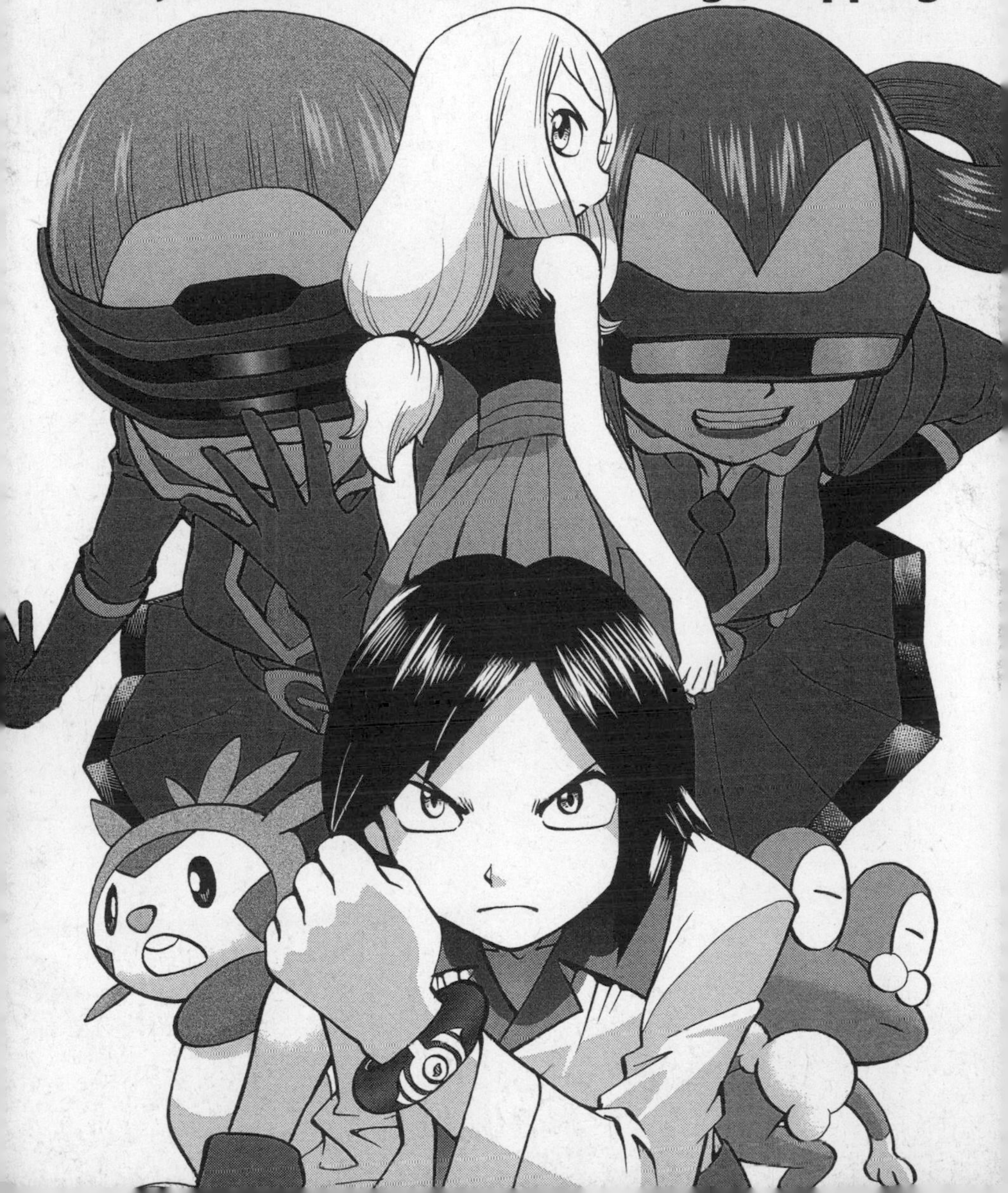

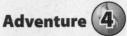

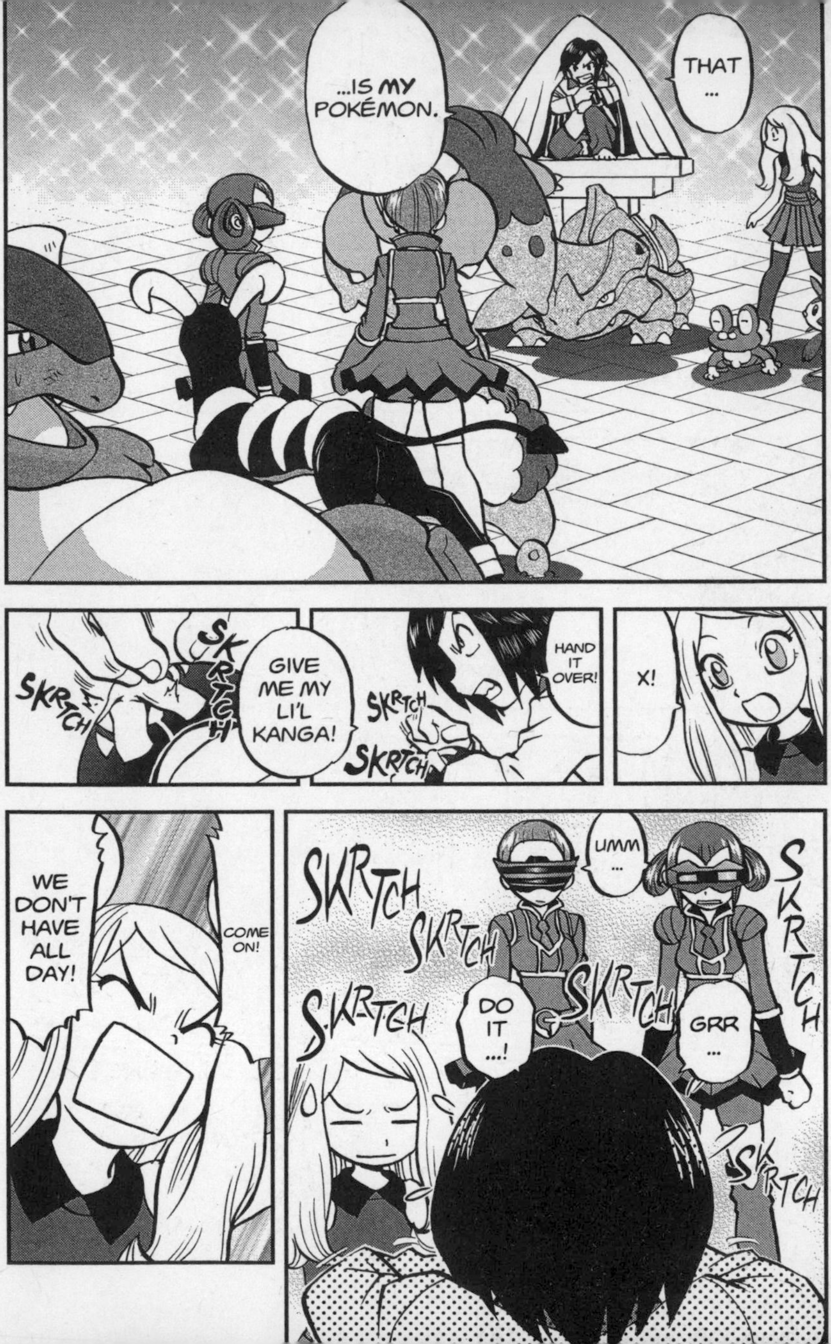
THAT ...
...IS MY POKÉMON.
X!
HAND IT OVER!
GIVE ME MY LI'L KANGA!
SKRTCH
SKRTCH
SKRTCH
SKRTCH
SKRTCH
SKRTCH
UMM ...
GRR ...
DO IT ...!
SKRTCH
SKRTCH
SKRTCH
SKRTCH
SKRTCH
COME ON!
WE DON'T HAVE ALL DAY!

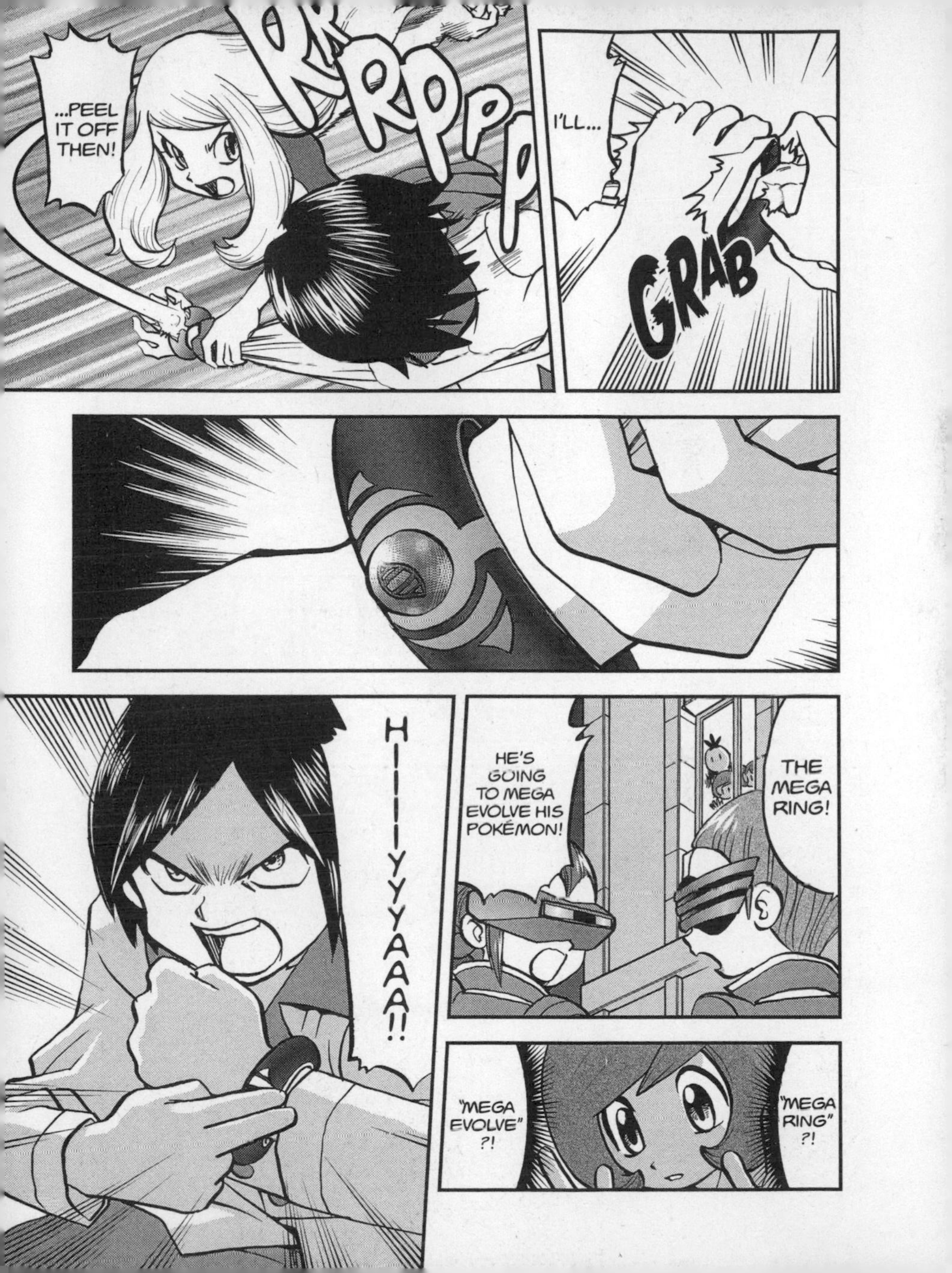
I'LL...
GRAB
...PEEL IT OFF THEN!
KRRPPP
THE MEGA RING!
HE'S GOING TO MEGA EVOLVE HIS POKéMON!
"MEGA RING"?!
"MEGA EVOLVE"?!
HIIIIYYYAAA!!

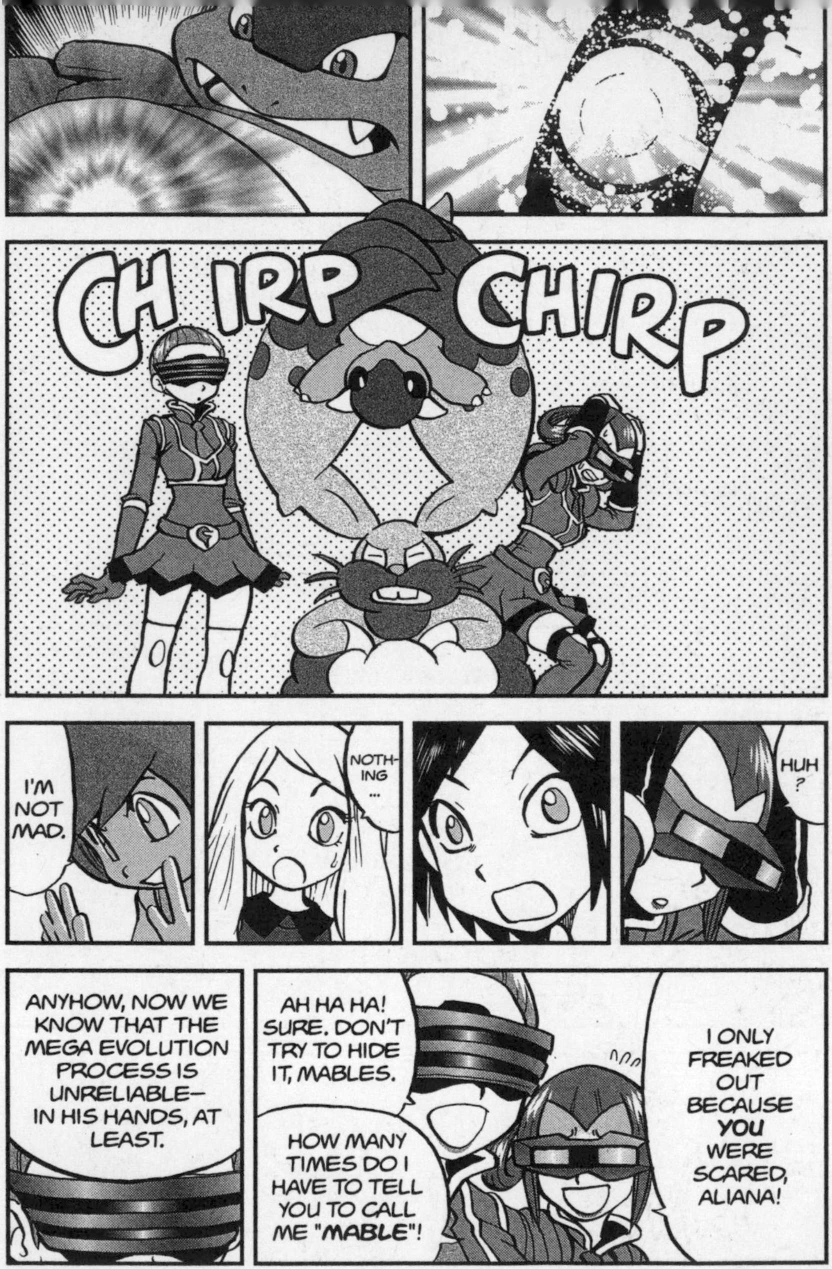

CHIRP CHIRP
HUH?
NOTHING...
I'M NOT MAD.
I ONLY FREAKED OUT BECAUSE **YOU** WERE SCARED, ALIANA!
AH HA HA! SURE. DON'T TRY TO HIDE IT, MABLES.
HOW MANY TIMES DO I HAVE TO TELL YOU TO CALL ME "**MABLE**"!
ANYHOW, NOW WE KNOW THAT THE MEGA EVOLUTION PROCESS IS UNRELIABLE—IN HIS HANDS, AT LEAST.

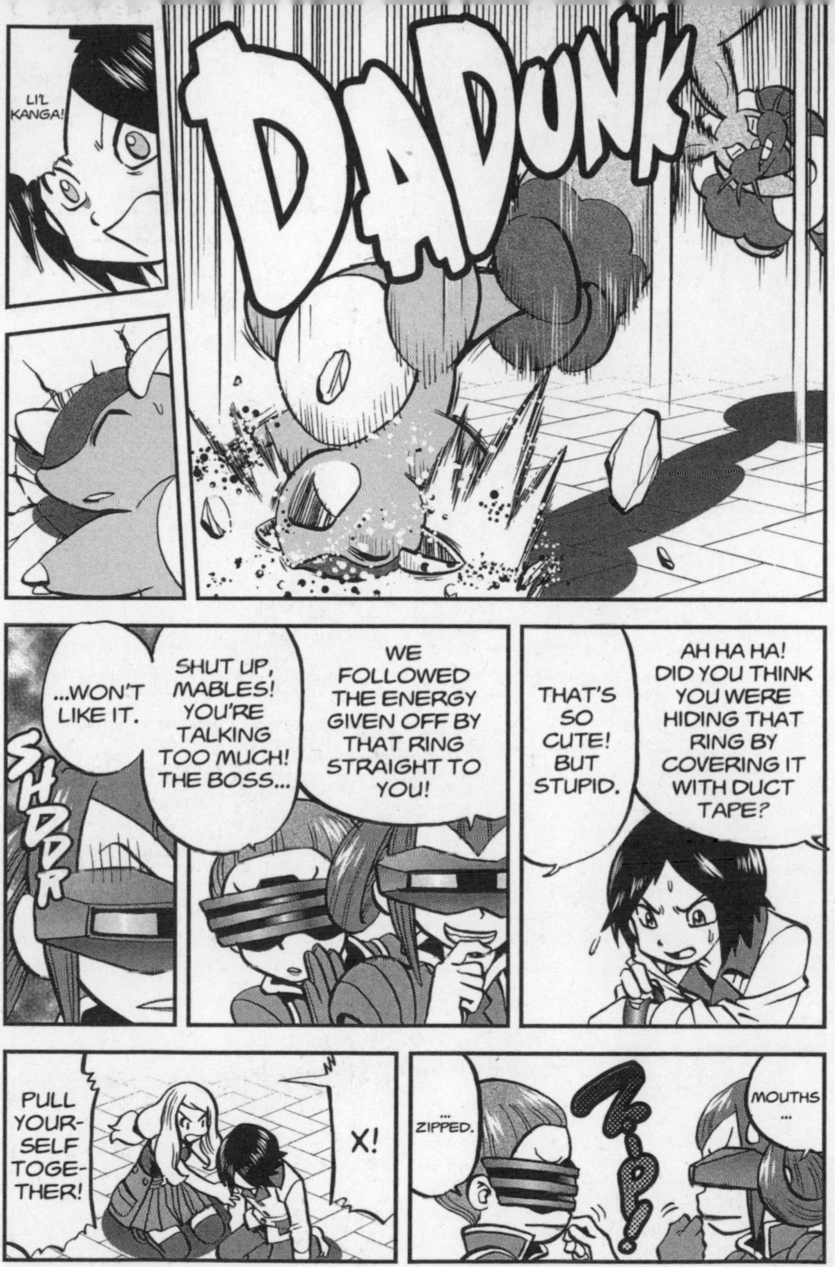
DADUNK
LI'L KANGA!
AH HA HA! DID YOU THINK YOU WERE HIDING THAT RING BY COVERING IT WITH DUCT TAPE?
THAT'S SO CUTE! BUT STUPID.
WE FOLLOWED THE ENERGY GIVEN OFF BY THAT RING STRAIGHT TO YOU!
SHUT UP, MABLES! YOU'RE TALKING TOO MUCH! THE BOSS...
...WON'T LIKE IT.
SHDDR
MOUTHS ...
... ZIPPED.
X!
PULL YOURSELF TOGETHER!

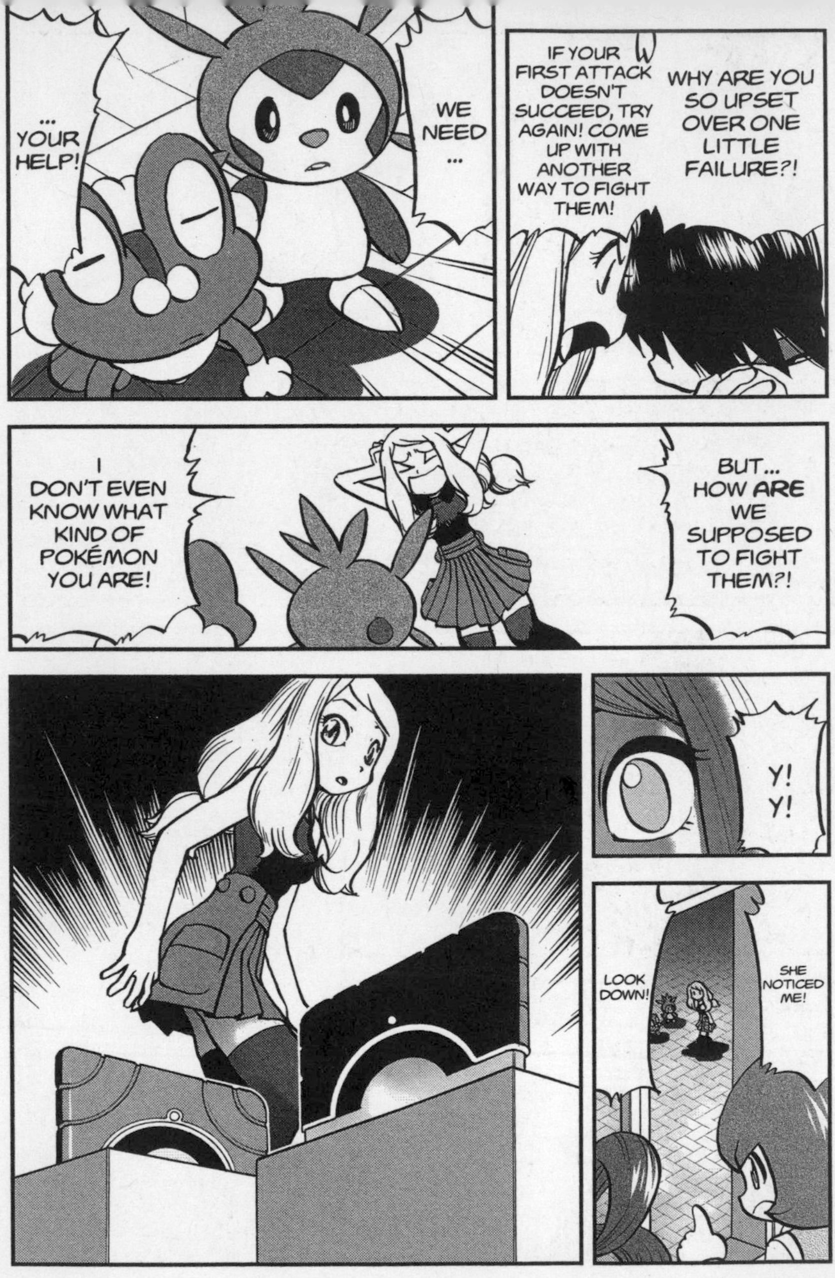
WHY ARE YOU SO UPSET OVER ONE LITTLE FAILURE?!
IF YOUR FIRST ATTACK DOESN'T SUCCEED, TRY AGAIN! COME UP WITH ANOTHER WAY TO FIGHT THEM!
WE NEED ...
... YOUR HELP!
BUT... HOW **ARE** WE SUPPOSED TO FIGHT THEM?!
I DON'T EVEN KNOW WHAT KIND OF POKÉMON YOU ARE!
Y! Y!
SHE NOTICED ME!
LOOK DOWN!

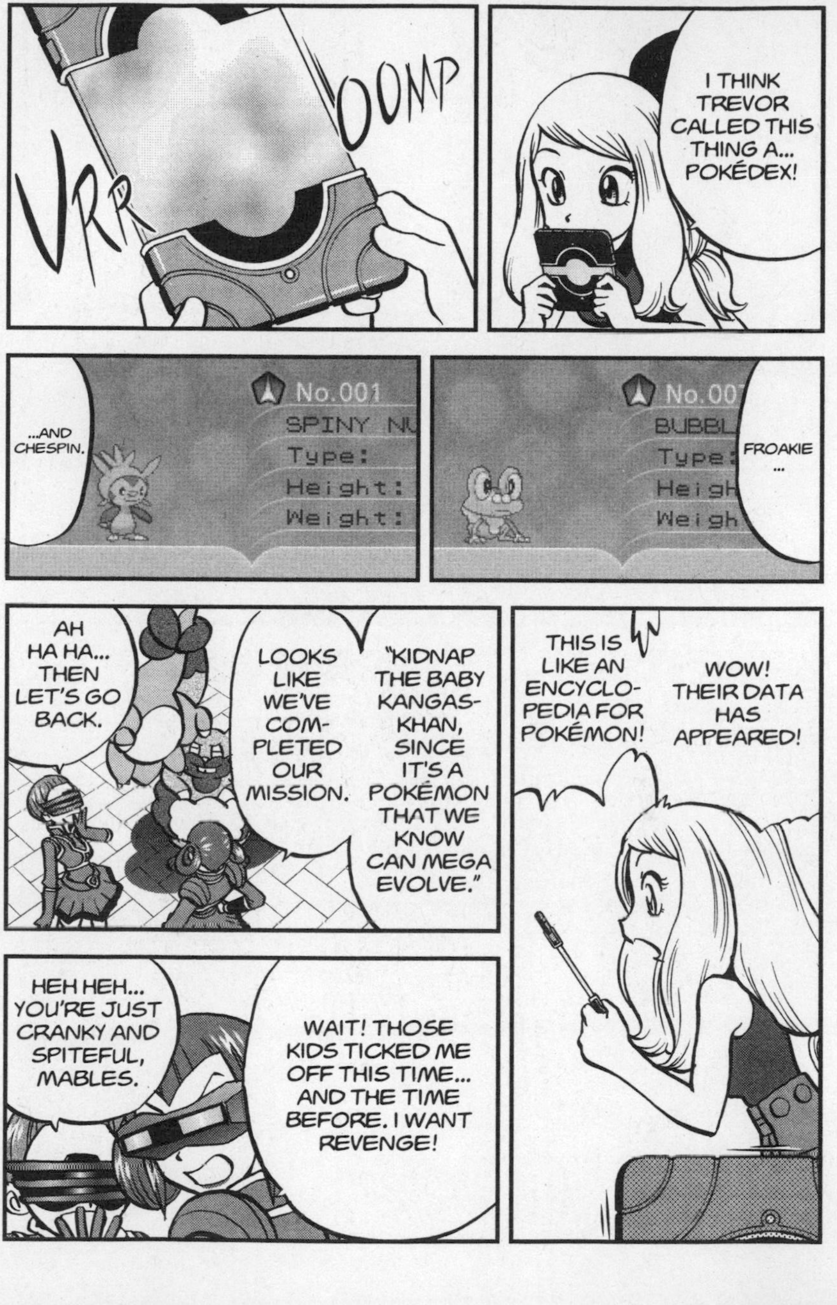
I THINK TREVOR CALLED THIS THING A... POKÉDEX!
VRR
VOOMP
FROAKIE ...
No.007
BUBBL
Type:
Heigh
Weigh
No.001
SPINY NU
Type:
Height:
Weight:
...AND CHESPIN.
WOW! THEIR DATA HAS APPEARED!
THIS IS LIKE AN ENCYCLOPEDIA FOR POKÉMON!
"KIDNAP THE BABY KANGASKHAN, SINCE IT'S A POKÉMON THAT WE KNOW CAN MEGA EVOLVE."
LOOKS LIKE WE'VE COMPLETED OUR MISSION.
AH HA HA... THEN LET'S GO BACK.
WAIT! THOSE KIDS TICKED ME OFF THIS TIME... AND THE TIME BEFORE. I WANT REVENGE!
HEH HEH... YOU'RE JUST CRANKY AND SPITEFUL, MABLES.

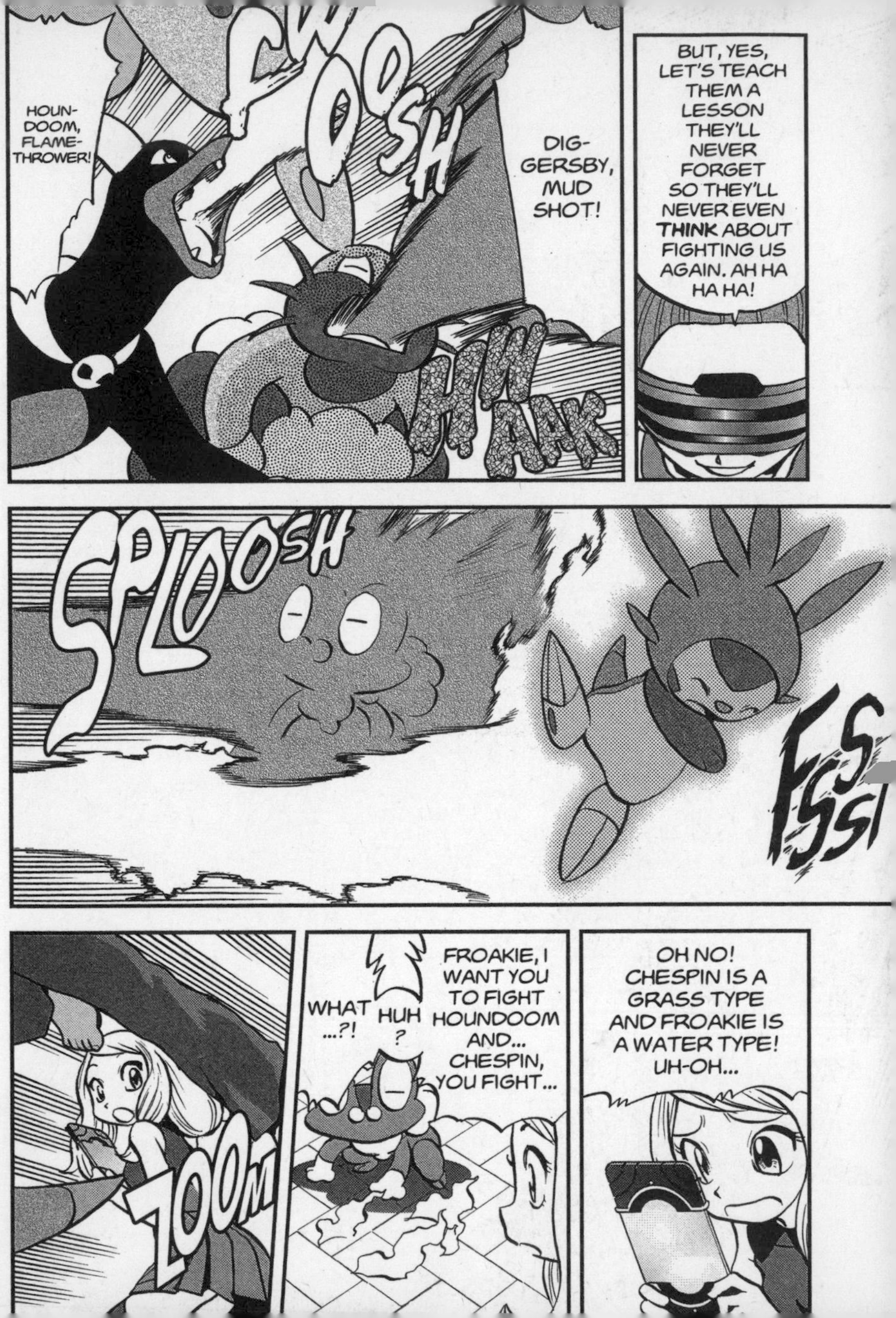
BUT, YES, LET'S TEACH THEM A LESSON THEY'LL NEVER FORGET SO THEY'LL NEVER EVEN **THINK** ABOUT FIGHTING US AGAIN. AH HA HA HA!
FWOOSH
DIG-GERSBY, MUD SHOT!
HOUN-DOOM, FLAME-THROWER!
WHAK
SPLOOSH
OH NO! CHESPIN IS A GRASS TYPE AND FROAKIE IS A WATER TYPE! UH-OH...
FROAKIE, I WANT YOU TO FIGHT HOUNDOOM AND... CHESPIN, YOU FIGHT...
HUH?
WHAT ...?!
ZOOM

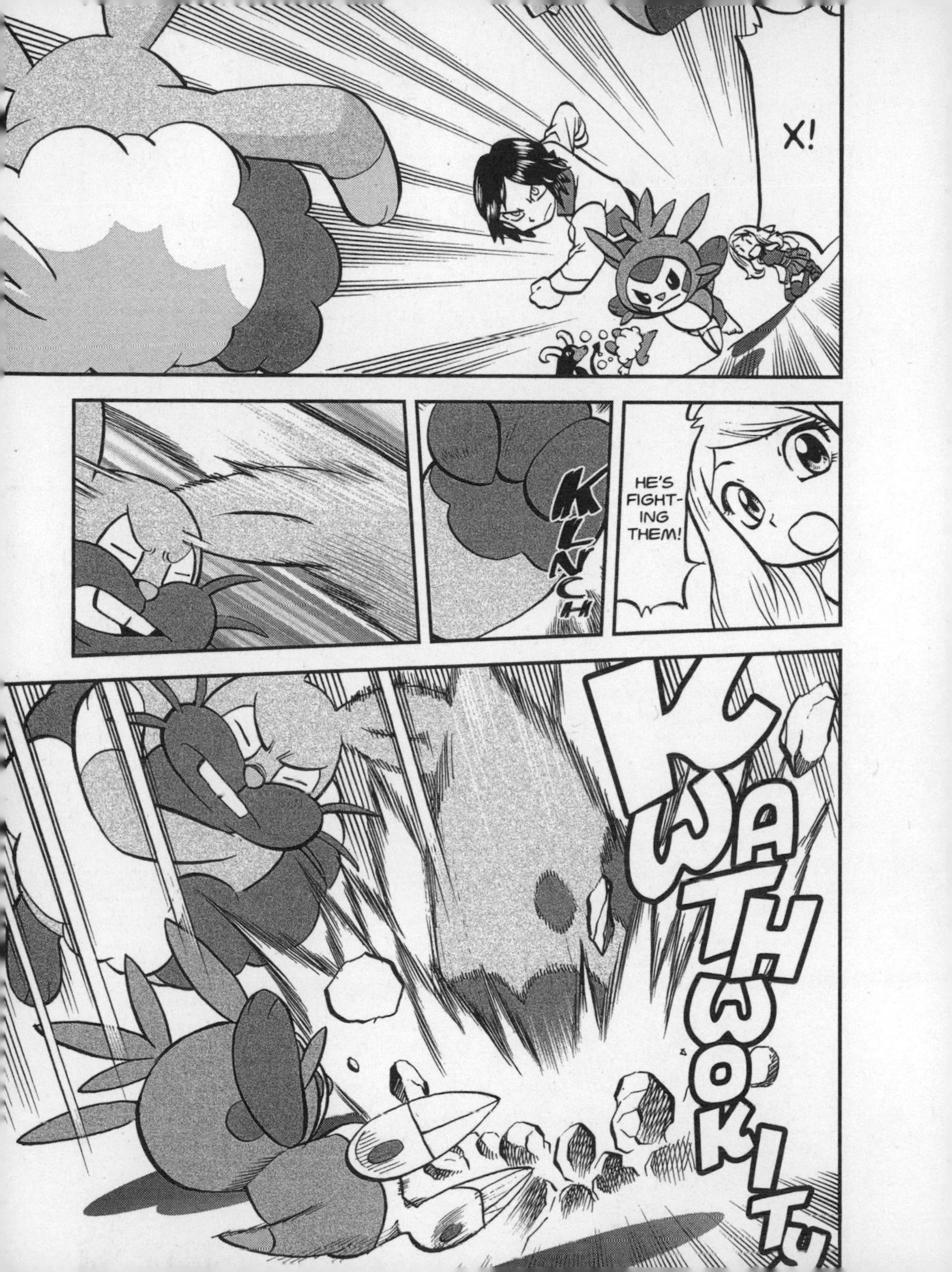
X!
HE'S FIGHT-ING THEM!
KLNCH
KWATHWOKITU

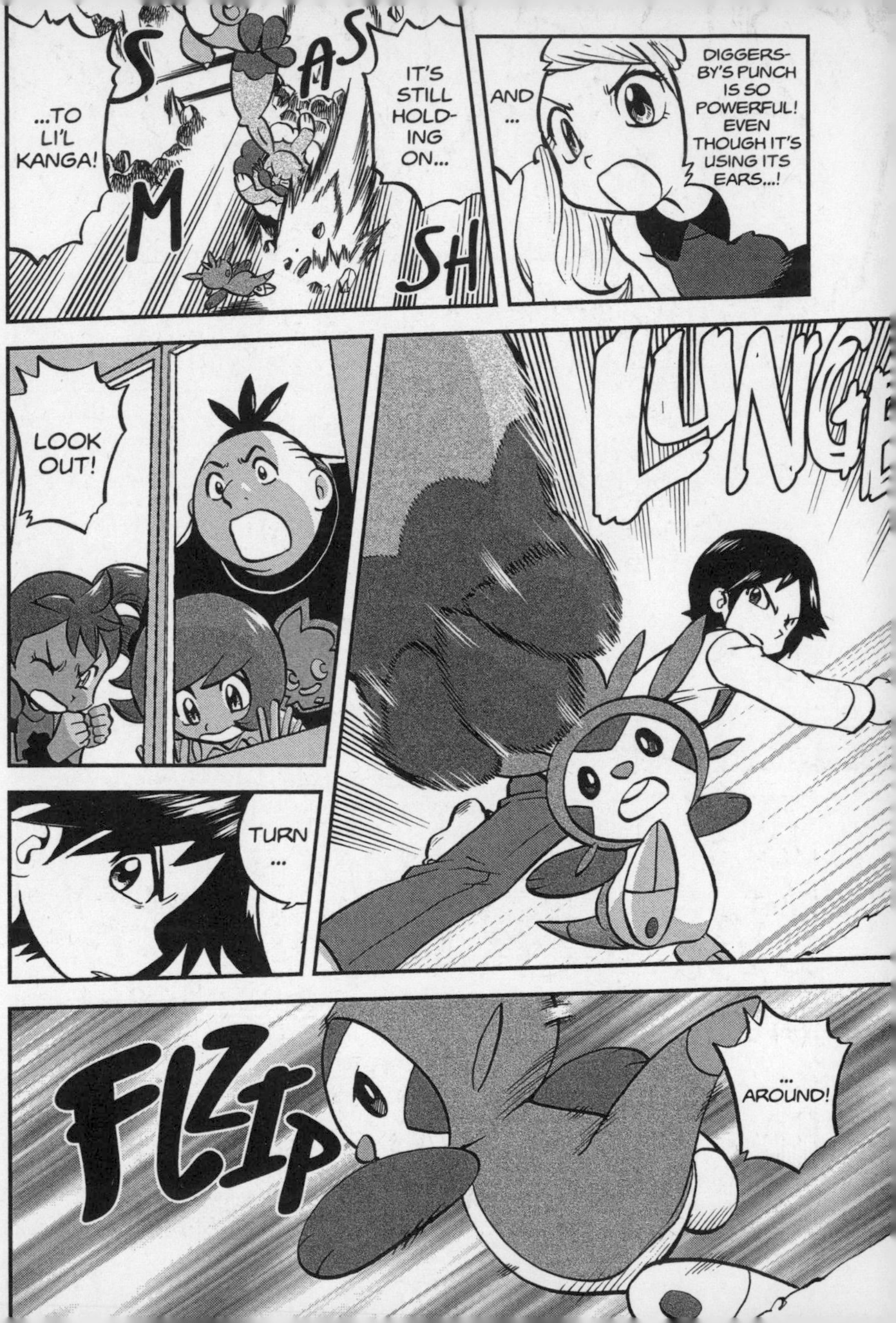
DIGGERSBY'S PUNCH IS SO POWERFUL! EVEN THOUGH IT'S USING ITS EARS...!
AND ...
IT'S STILL HOLDING ON...
SMASH
...TO LI'L KANGA!
LUNGE
LOOK OUT!
TURN ...
... AROUND!
FLIP

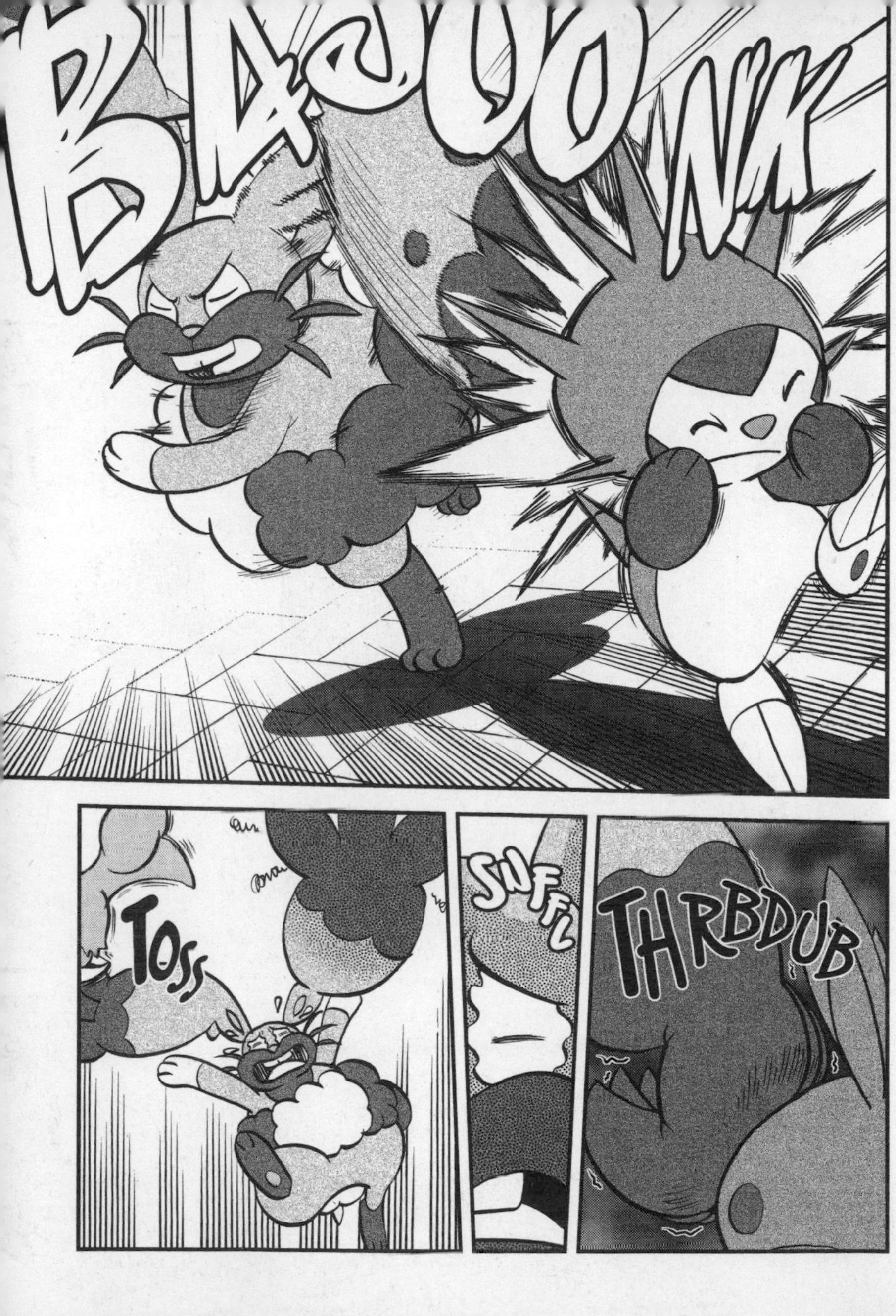
BAGOONK
THRBDUB
SNIFFL
TOSS

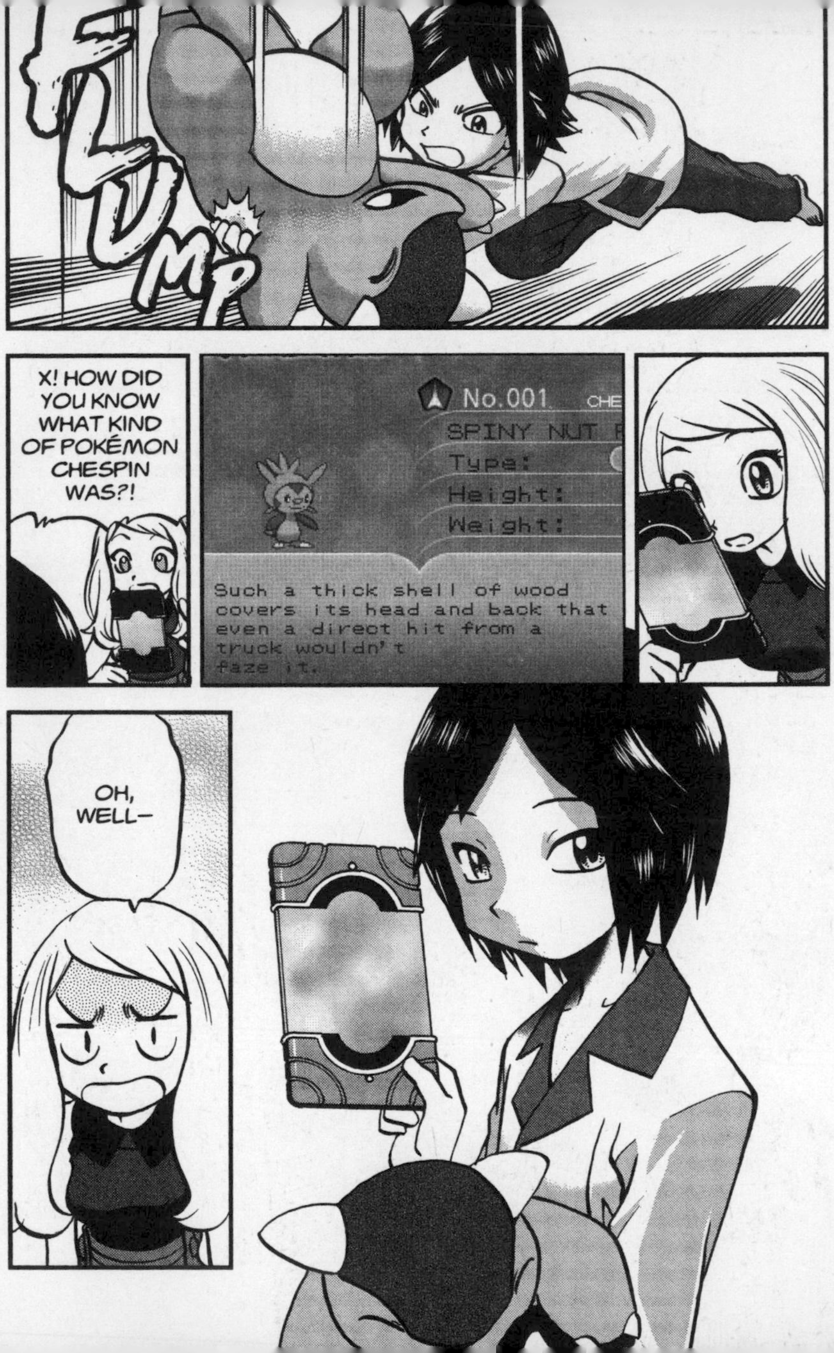
FLUMP
No.001 CHE
SPINY NUT P
Type:
Height:
Weight:
Such a thick shell of wood covers its head and back that even a direct hit from a truck wouldn't faze it.
X! HOW DID YOU KNOW WHAT KIND OF POKÉMON CHESPIN WAS?!
OH, WELL–

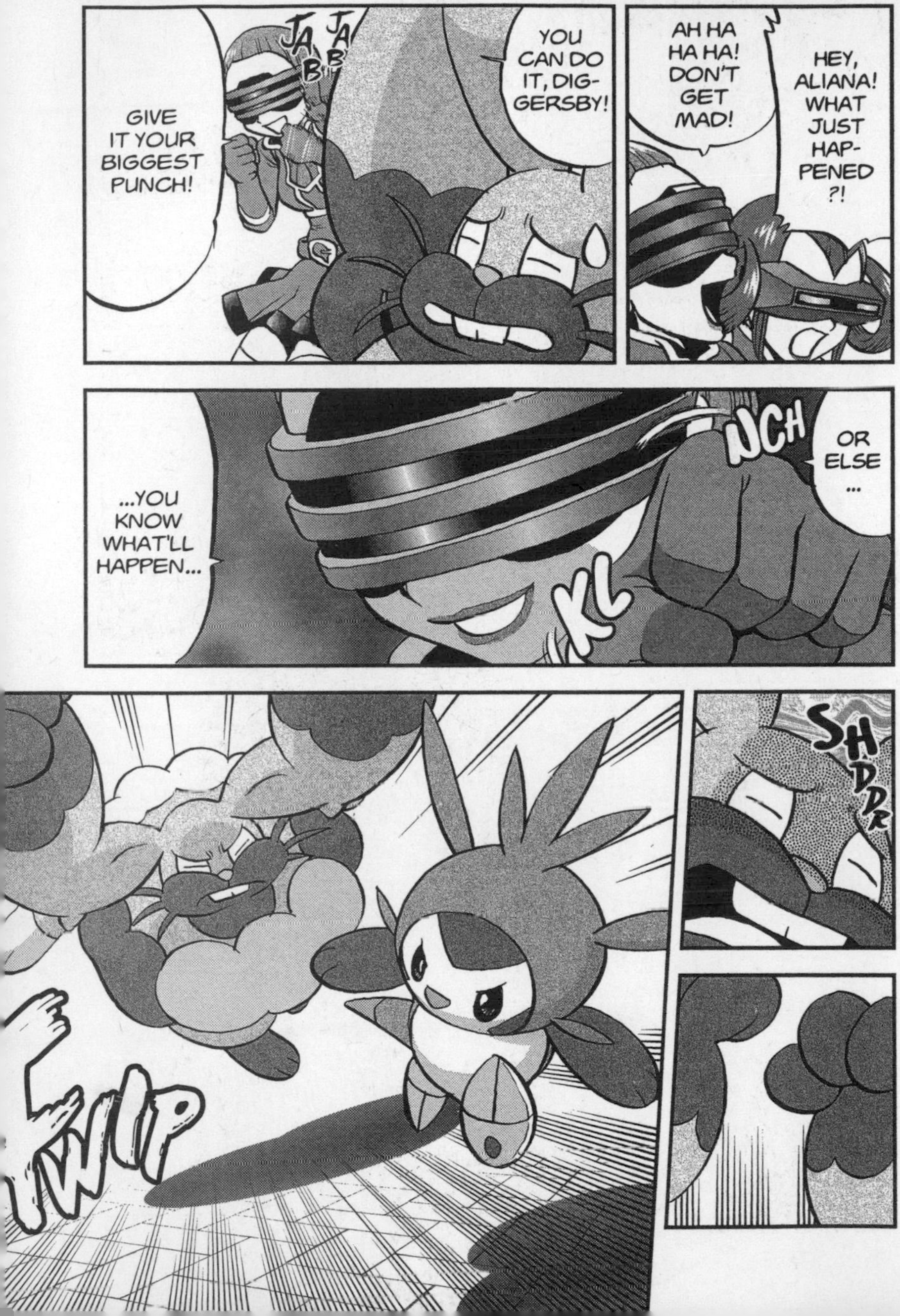
HEY, ALIANA! WHAT JUST HAP-PENED ?!
AH HA HA HA! DON'T GET MAD!
YOU CAN DO IT, DIG-GERSBY!
JAB JAB
GIVE IT YOUR BIGGEST PUNCH!
OR ELSE ...
NCH
KL
...YOU KNOW WHAT'LL HAPPEN...
SHDDR
WIP

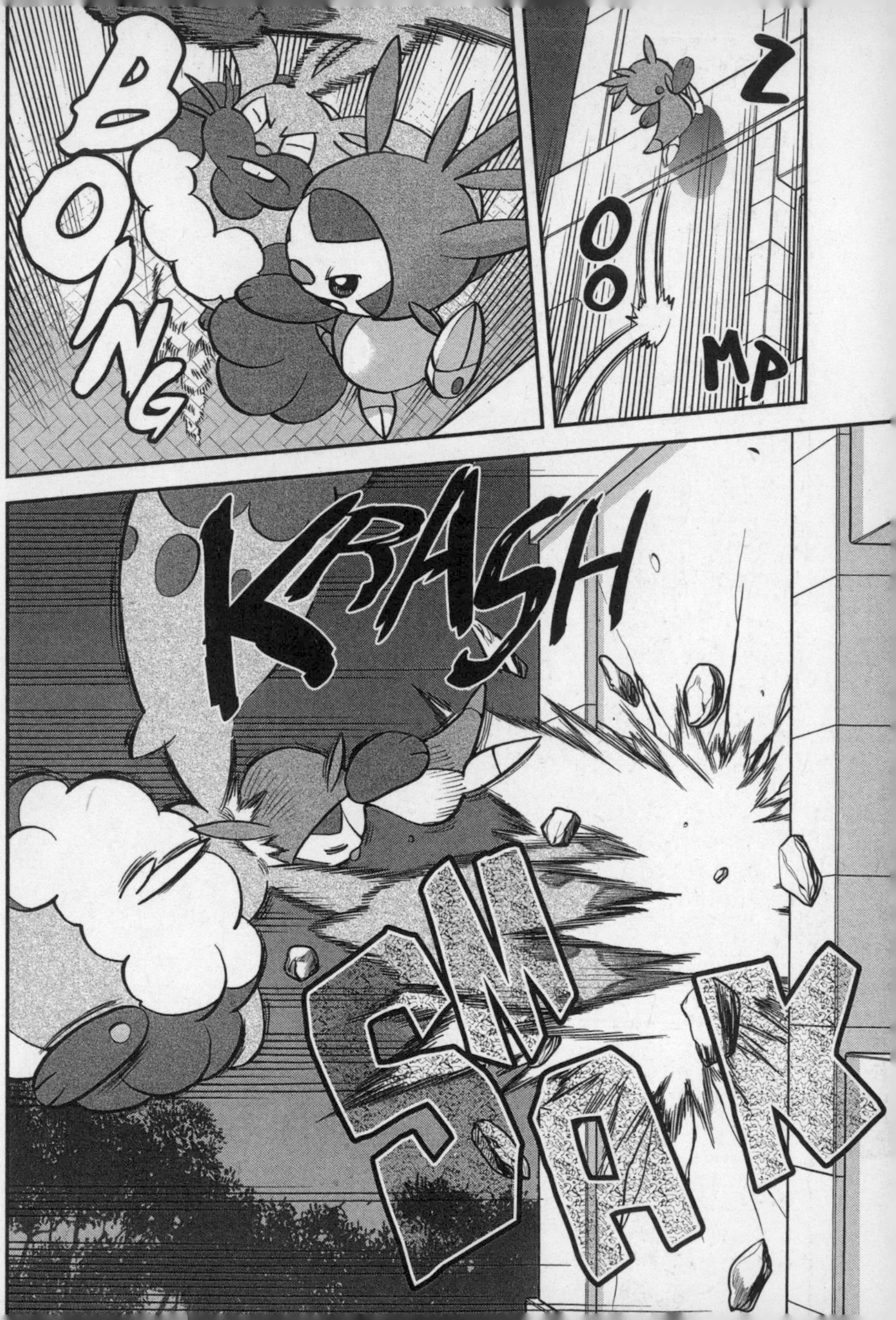
ZOOMP
BOING
KRASH
SMAK

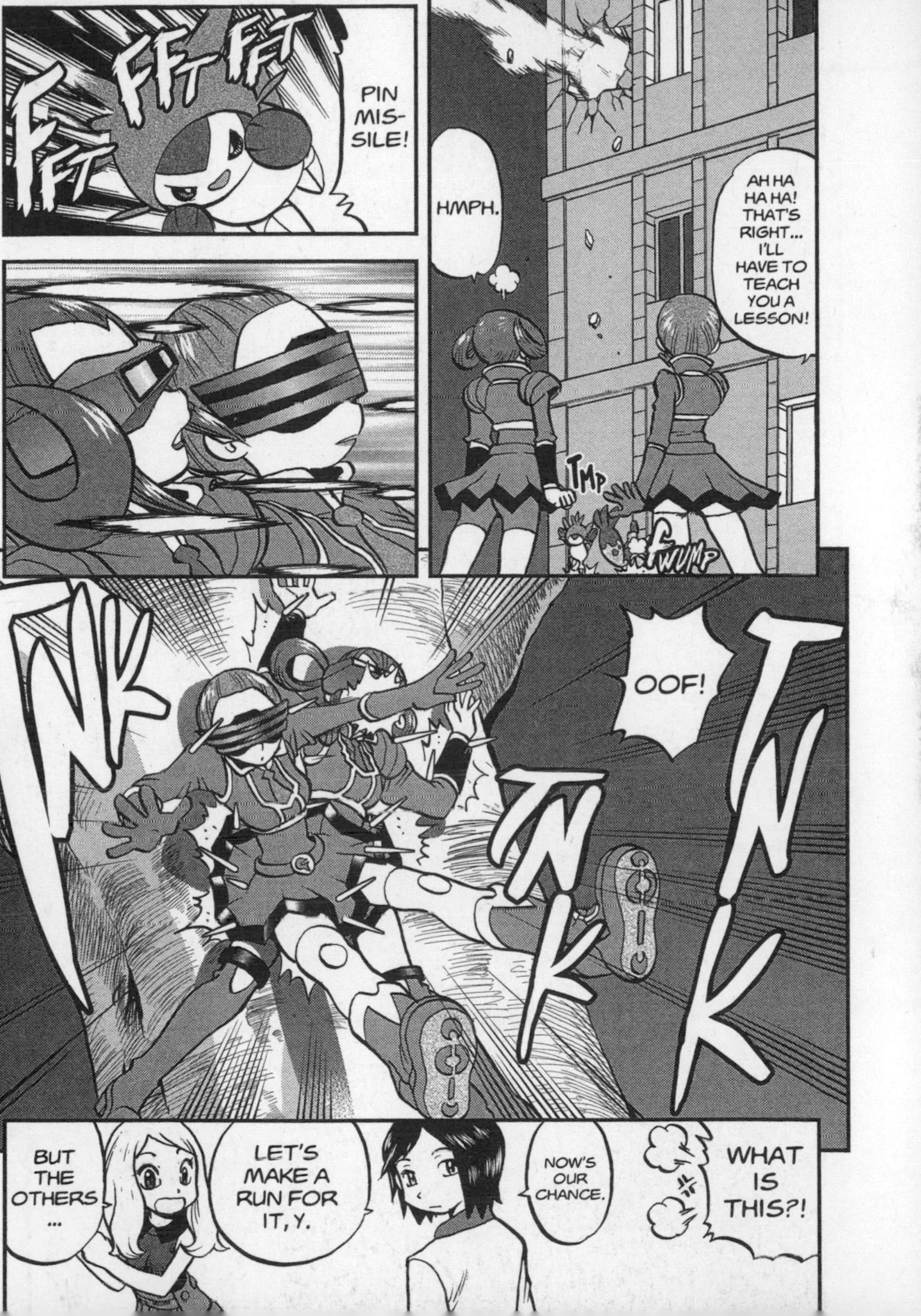
AH HA HA HA! THAT'S RIGHT... I'LL HAVE TO TEACH YOU A LESSON!
HMPH.
TMP
FWUMP
PIN MISSILE!
FFT FFT FFT FFT
OOF!
TNK
TNK
TNK
WHAT IS THIS?!
NOW'S OUR CHANCE.
LET'S MAKE A RUN FOR IT, Y.
BUT THE OTHERS...

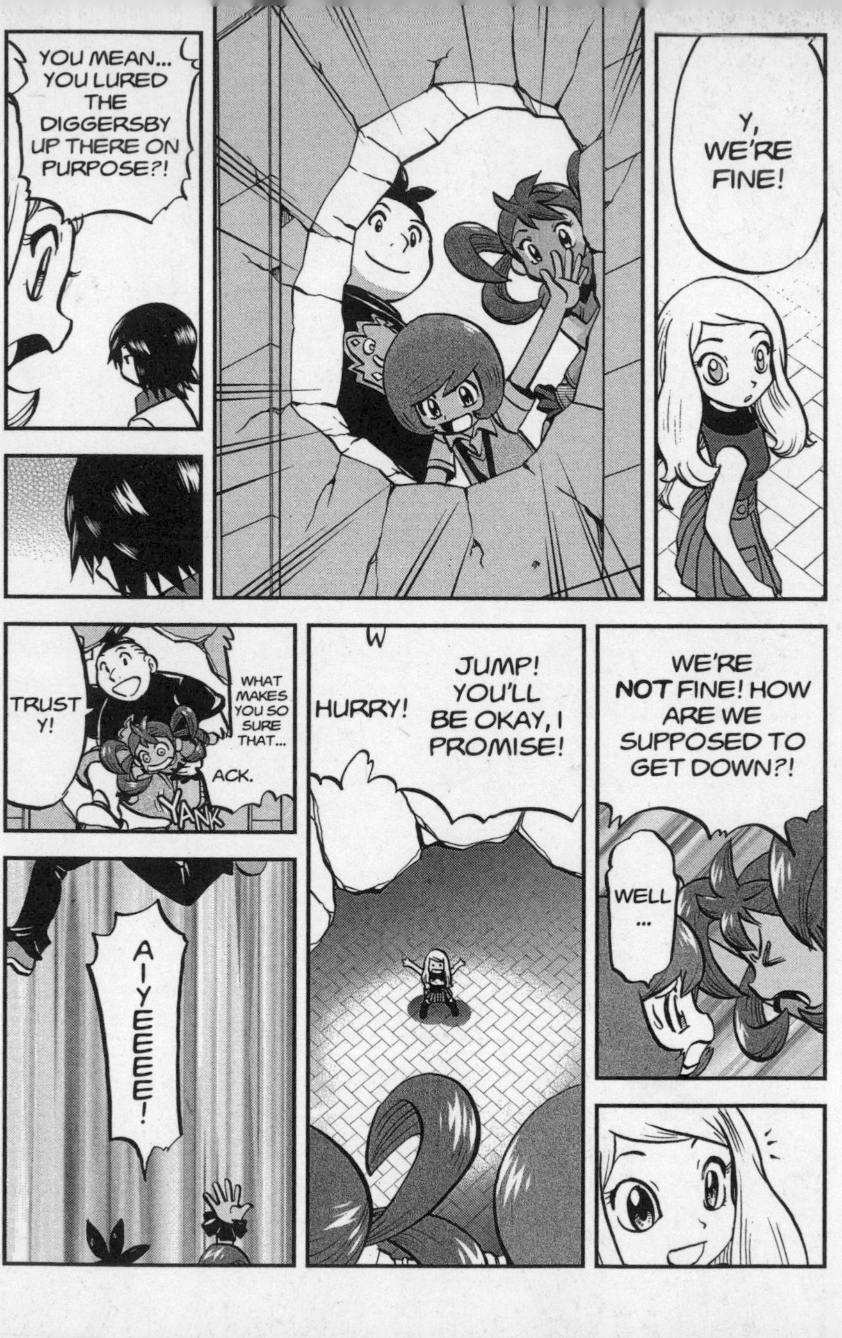
Y, WE'RE FINE!
YOU MEAN... YOU LURED THE DIGGERSBY UP THERE ON PURPOSE?!
WE'RE NOT FINE! HOW ARE WE SUPPOSED TO GET DOWN?!
WELL ...
JUMP! YOU'LL BE OKAY, I PROMISE!
HURRY!
WHAT MAKES YOU SO SURE THAT...
TRUST Y!
ACK.
YANK
AIYEEEE!

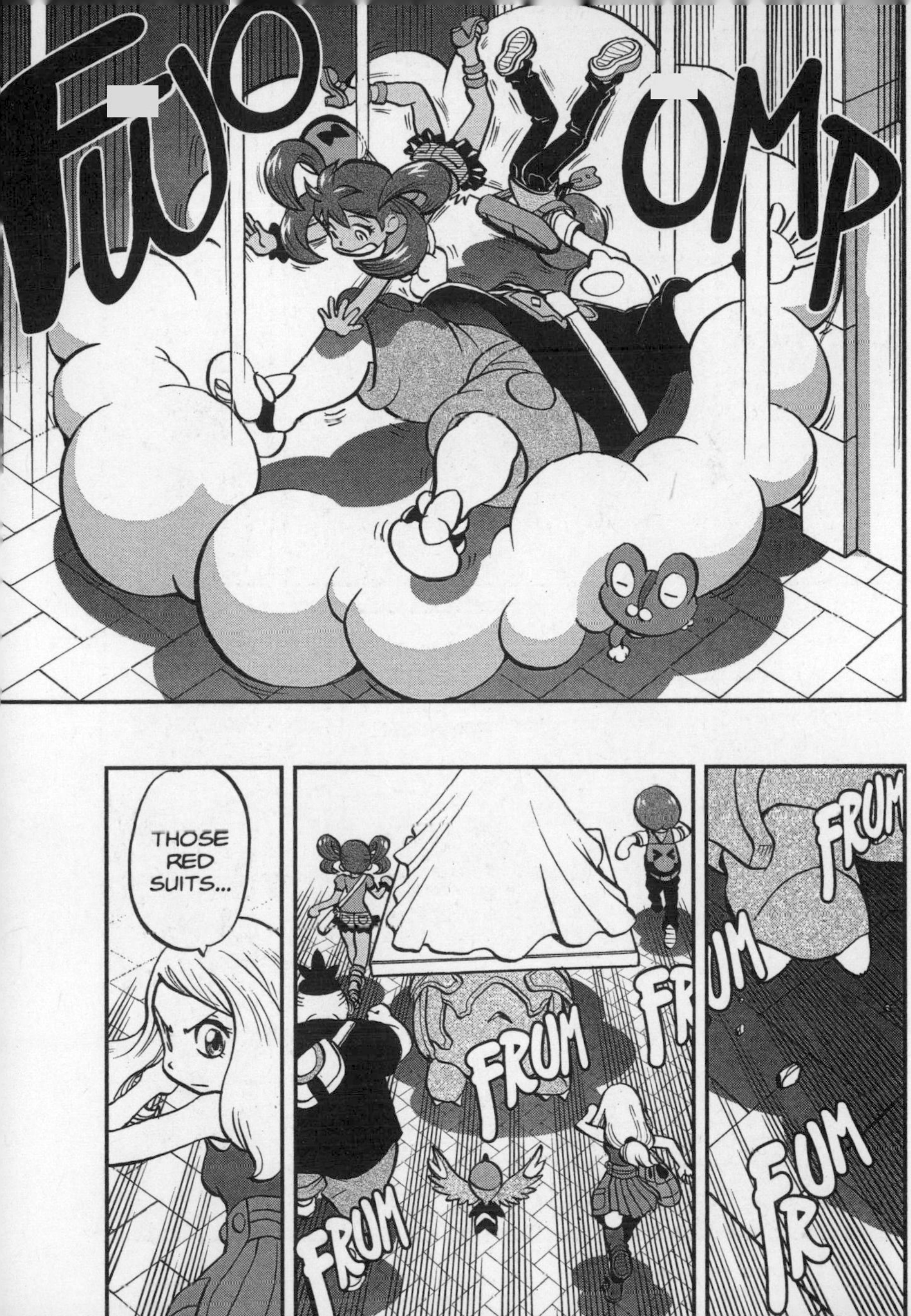
FRUM
FRUM
FRUM
FRUM
FRUM
THOSE RED SUITS...

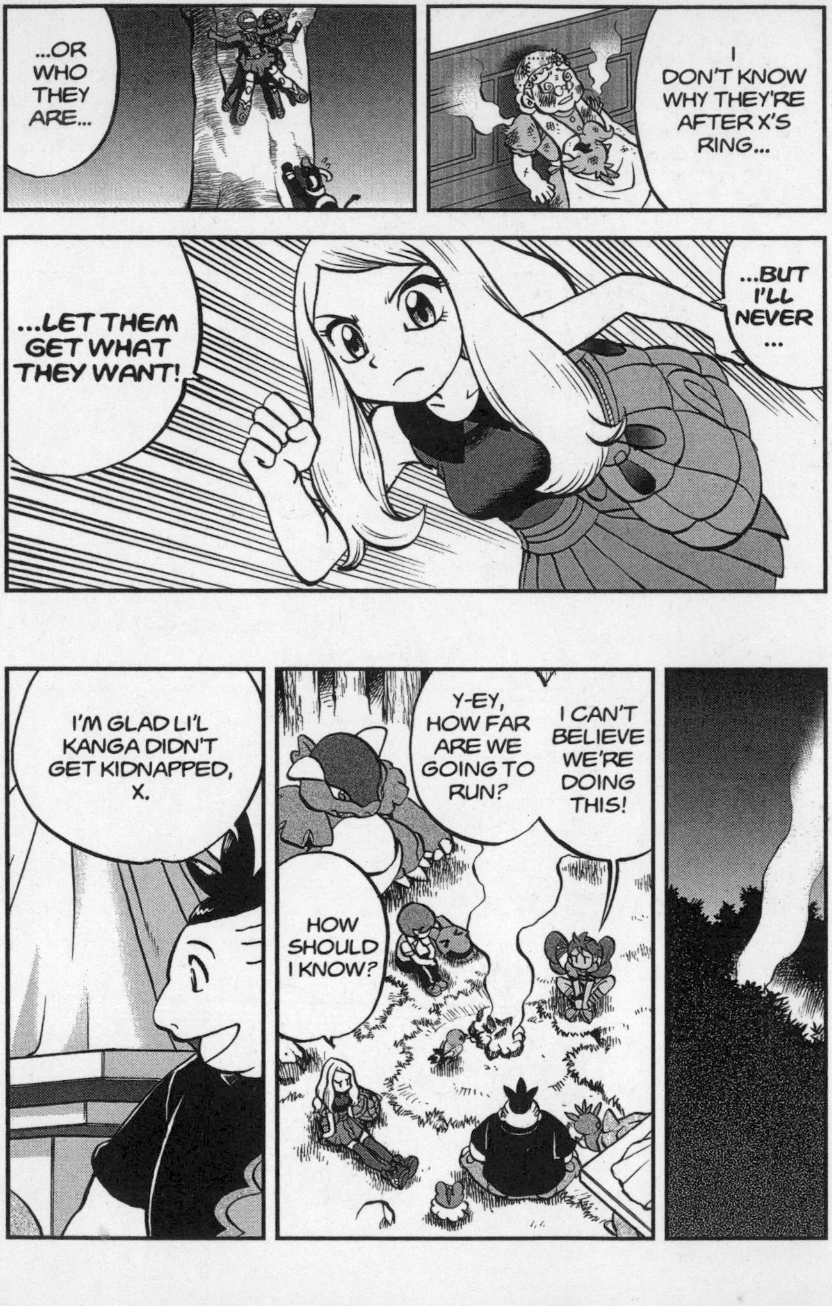
I DON'T KNOW WHY THEY'RE AFTER X'S RING...
...OR WHO THEY ARE...
...BUT I'LL NEVER ...
...LET THEM GET WHAT THEY WANT!
I CAN'T BELIEVE WE'RE DOING THIS!
Y-EY, HOW FAR ARE WE GOING TO RUN?
HOW SHOULD I KNOW?
I'M GLAD LI'L KANGA DIDN'T GET KIDNAPPED, X.

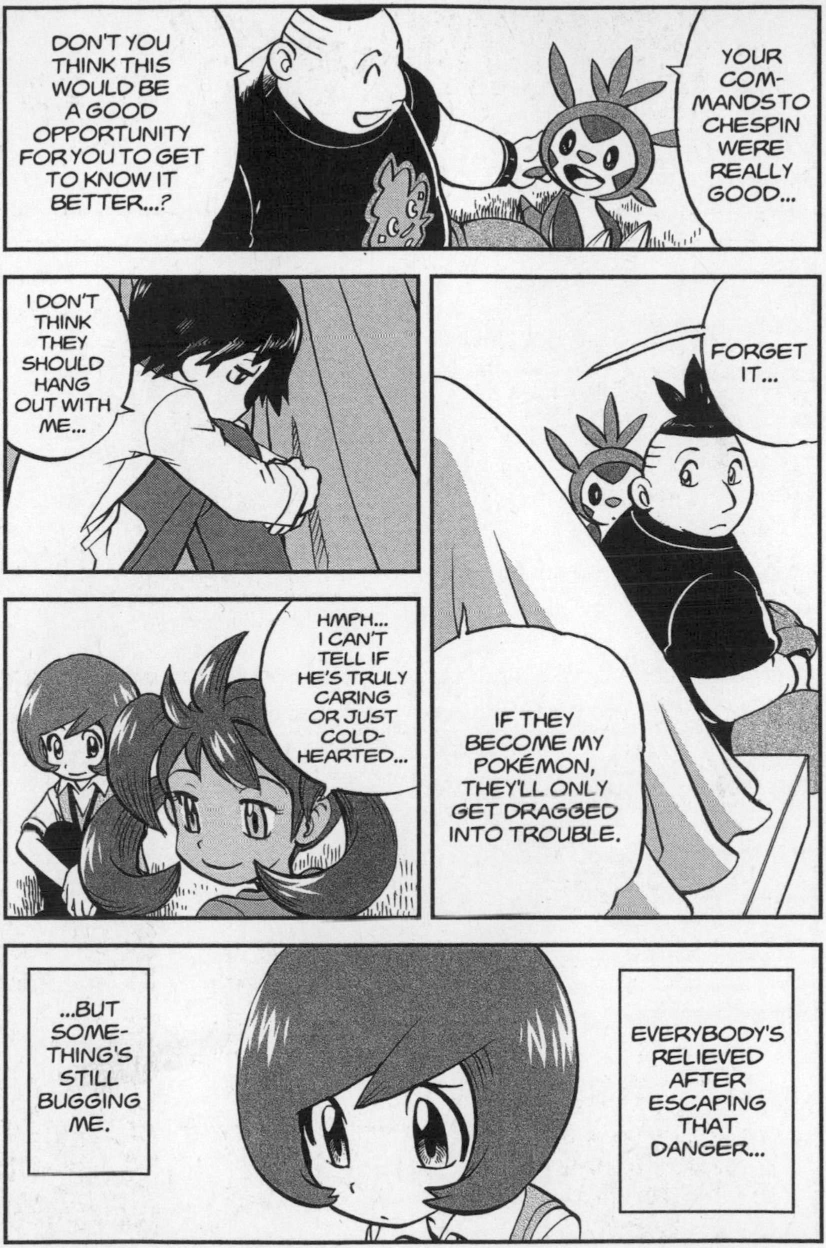
YOUR COMMANDS TO CHESPIN WERE REALLY GOOD...
DON'T YOU THINK THIS WOULD BE A GOOD OPPORTUNITY FOR YOU TO GET TO KNOW IT BETTER...?
FORGET IT...
IF THEY BECOME MY POKÉMON, THEY'LL ONLY GET DRAGGED INTO TROUBLE.
I DON'T THINK THEY SHOULD HANG OUT WITH ME...
HMPH... I CAN'T TELL IF HE'S TRULY CARING OR JUST COLD-HEARTED...
EVERYBODY'S RELIEVED AFTER ESCAPING THAT DANGER...
...BUT SOMETHING'S STILL BUGGING ME.

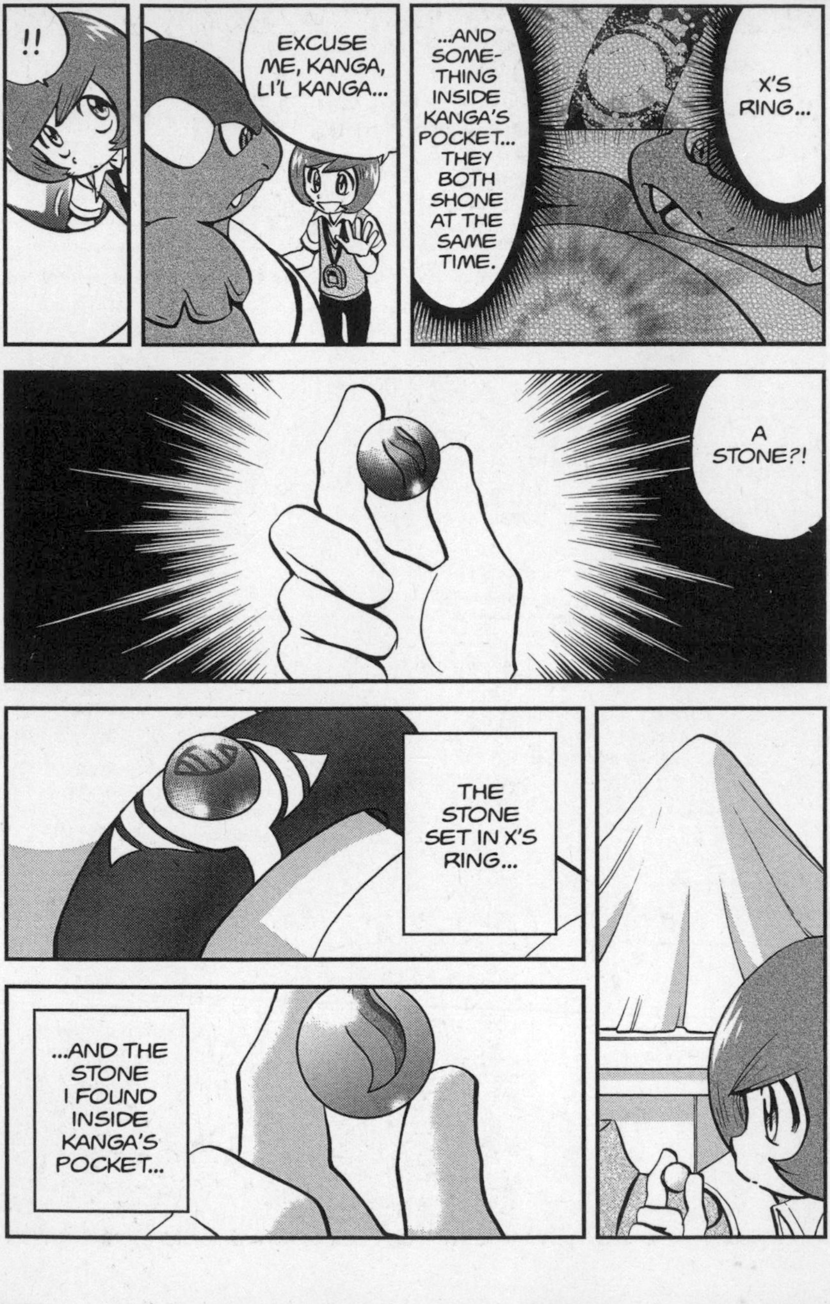
X'S RING...
...AND SOMETHING INSIDE KANGA'S POCKET... THEY BOTH SHONE AT THE SAME TIME.
EXCUSE ME, KANGA, LI'L KANGA...
!!
A STONE?!
THE STONE SET IN X'S RING...
...AND THE STONE I FOUND INSIDE KANGA'S POCKET...

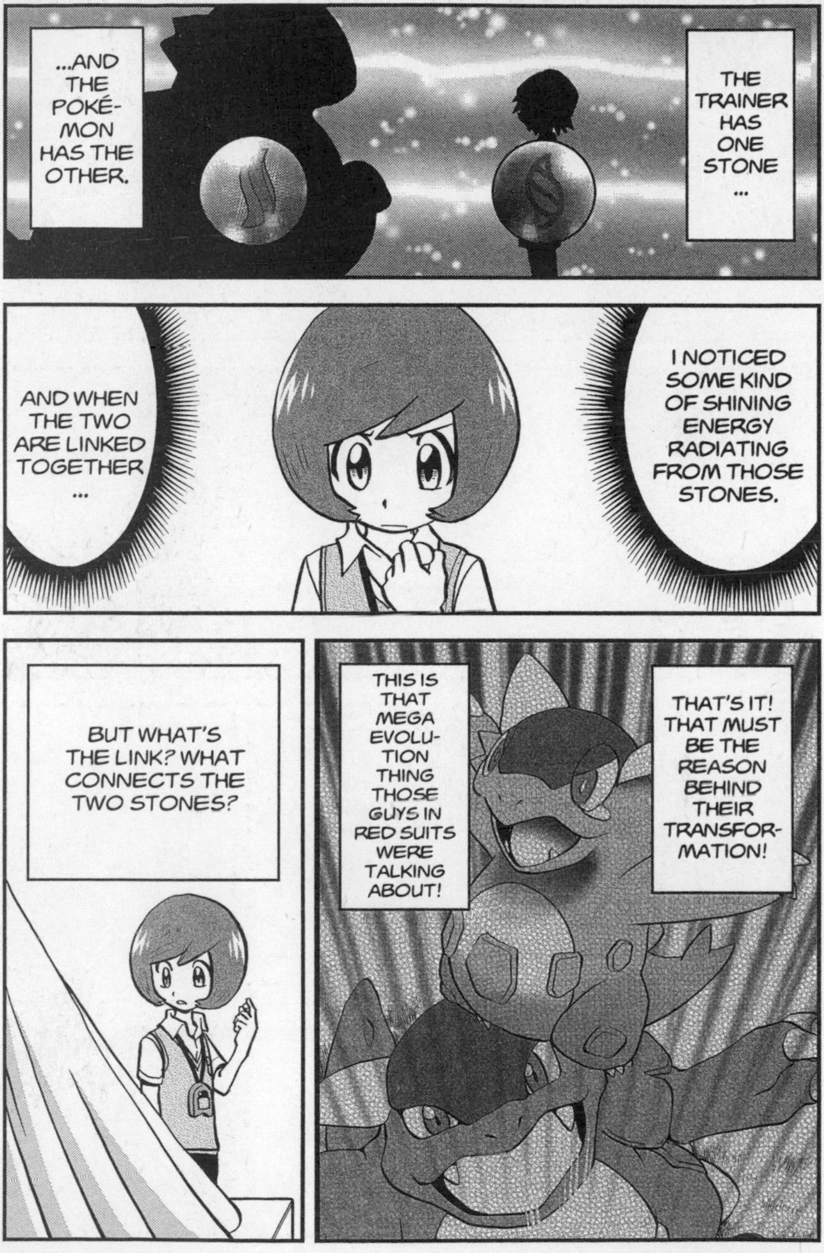
THE TRAINER HAS ONE STONE ...
...AND THE POKÉ-MON HAS THE OTHER.
I NOTICED SOME KIND OF SHINING ENERGY RADIATING FROM THOSE STONES.
AND WHEN THE TWO ARE LINKED TOGETHER ...
THAT'S IT! THAT MUST BE THE REASON BEHIND THEIR TRANSFOR-MATION!
THIS IS THAT MEGA EVOLU-TION THING THOSE GUYS IN RED SUITS WERE TALKING ABOUT!
BUT WHAT'S THE LINK? WHAT CONNECTS THE TWO STONES?

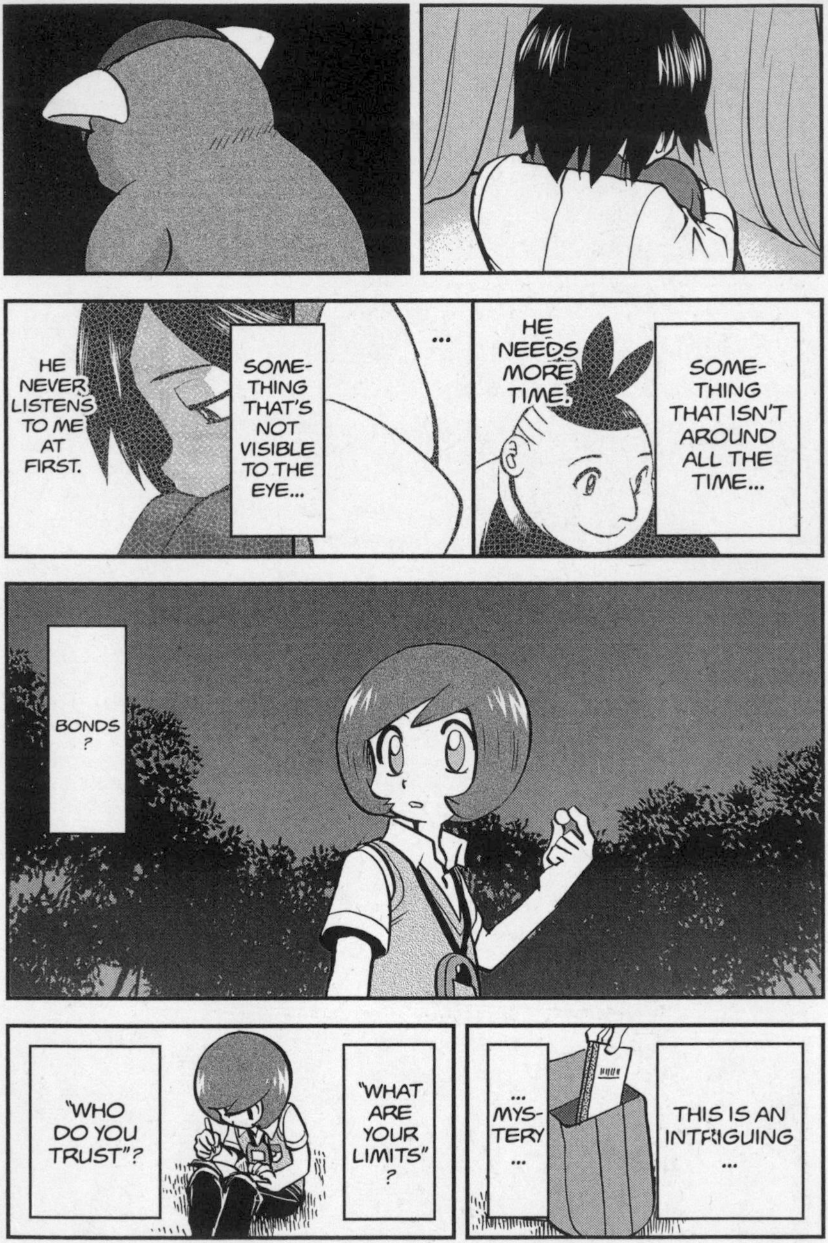
SOMETHING THAT ISN'T AROUND ALL THE TIME...
HE NEEDS MORE TIME.
...
SOMETHING THAT'S NOT VISIBLE TO THE EYE...
HE NEVER LISTENS TO ME AT FIRST.
BONDS ?
THIS IS AN INTRIGUING ...
... MYSTERY ...
"WHAT ARE YOUR LIMITS" ?
"WHO DO YOU TRUST"?

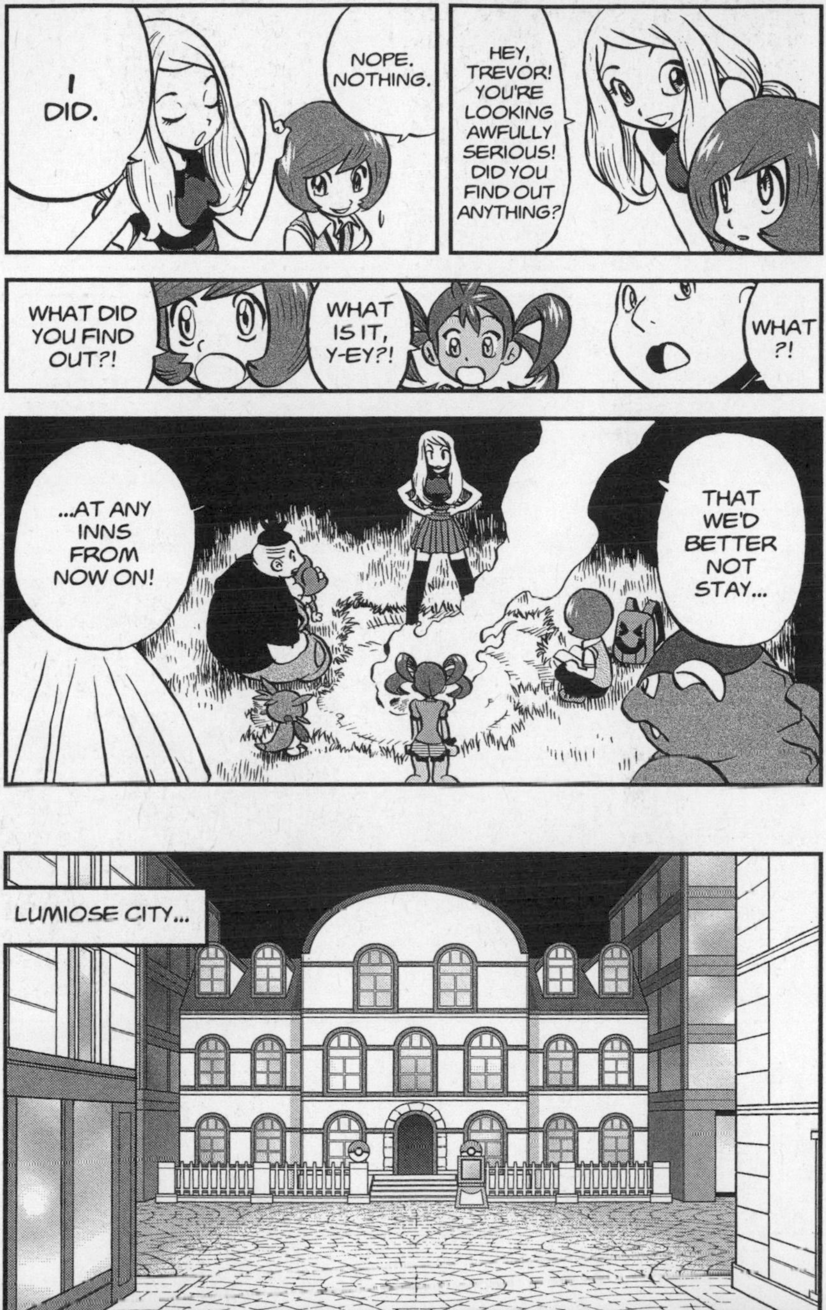
HEY, TREVOR! YOU'RE LOOKING AWFULLY SERIOUS! DID YOU FIND OUT ANYTHING?
NOPE. NOTHING.
I DID.
WHAT?!
WHAT IS IT, Y-EY?!
WHAT DID YOU FIND OUT?!
THAT WE'D BETTER NOT STAY...
...AT ANY INNS FROM NOW ON!
LUMIOSE CITY...

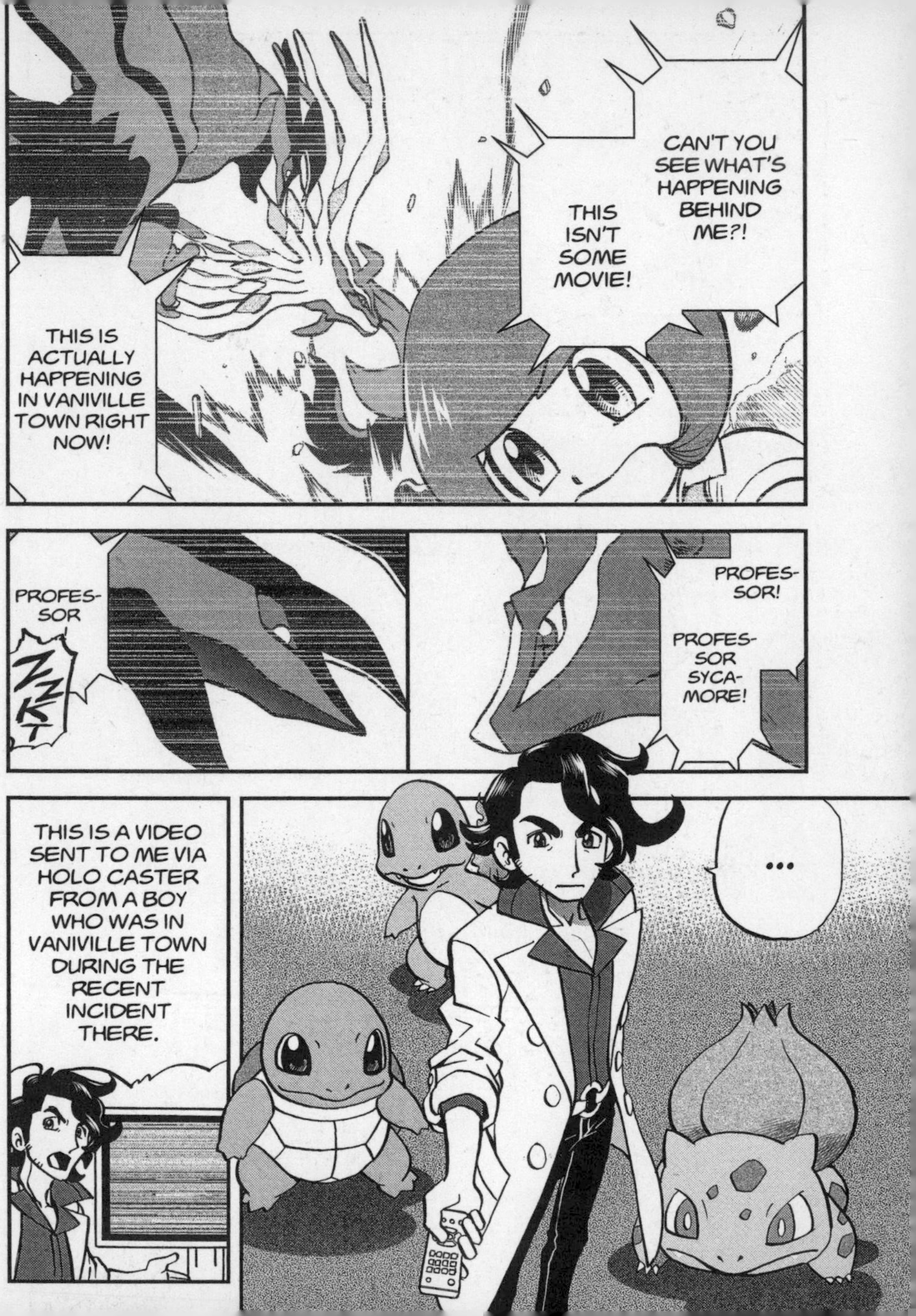
CAN'T YOU SEE WHAT'S HAPPENING BEHIND ME?!
THIS ISN'T SOME MOVIE!
THIS IS ACTUALLY HAPPENING IN VANIVILLE TOWN RIGHT NOW!
PROFES-SOR!
PROFES-SOR SYCA-MORE!
PROFES-SOR
ZZKT
...
THIS IS A VIDEO SENT TO ME VIA HOLO CASTER FROM A BOY WHO WAS IN VANIVILLE TOWN DURING THE RECENT INCIDENT THERE.

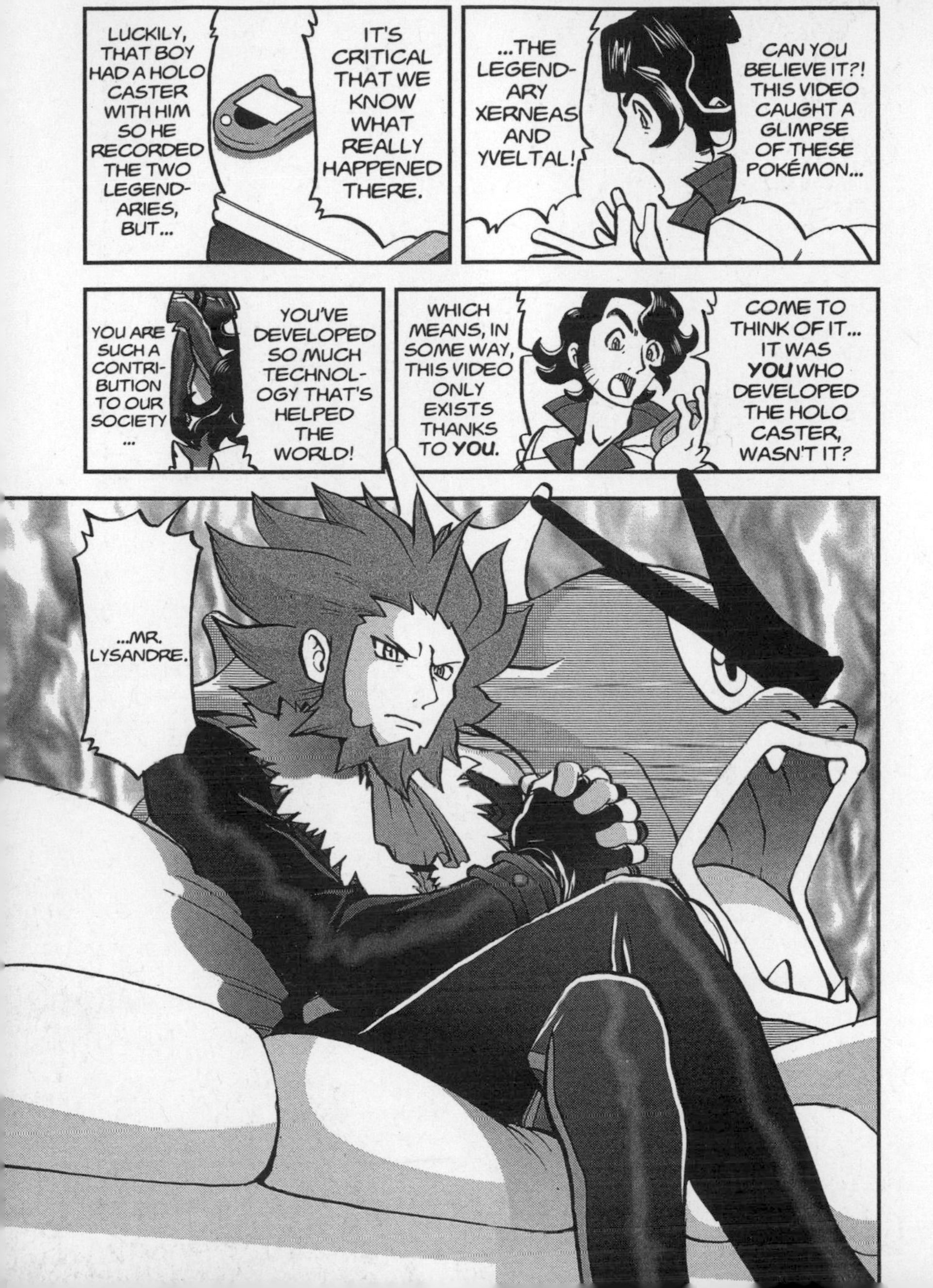
CAN YOU BELIEVE IT?! THIS VIDEO CAUGHT A GLIMPSE OF THESE POKÉMON...
...THE LEGENDARY XERNEAS AND YVELTAL!
IT'S CRITICAL THAT WE KNOW WHAT REALLY HAPPENED THERE.
LUCKILY, THAT BOY HAD A HOLO CASTER WITH HIM SO HE RECORDED THE TWO LEGENDARIES, BUT...
COME TO THINK OF IT... IT WAS **YOU** WHO DEVELOPED THE HOLO CASTER, WASN'T IT?
WHICH MEANS, IN SOME WAY, THIS VIDEO ONLY EXISTS THANKS TO **YOU**.
YOU'VE DEVELOPED SO MUCH TECHNOLOGY THAT'S HELPED THE WORLD!
YOU ARE SUCH A CONTRIBUTION TO OUR SOCIETY...
...MR. LYSANDRE.

Current Location

A town that naturally sprang up as people flocked to this pristine riverside.

Adventure 5 Kangaskhan...Kangascan't

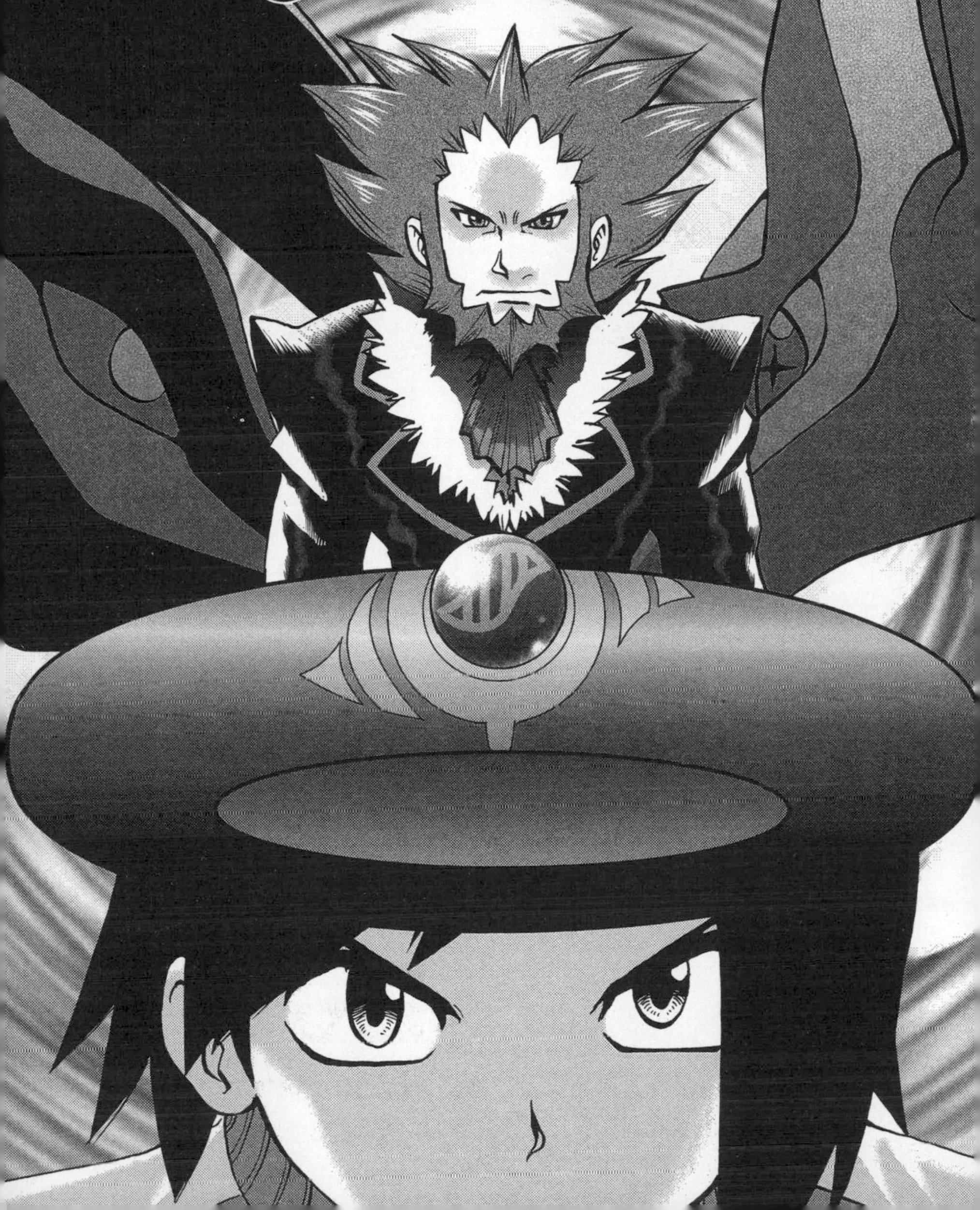

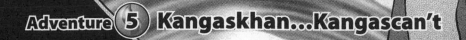

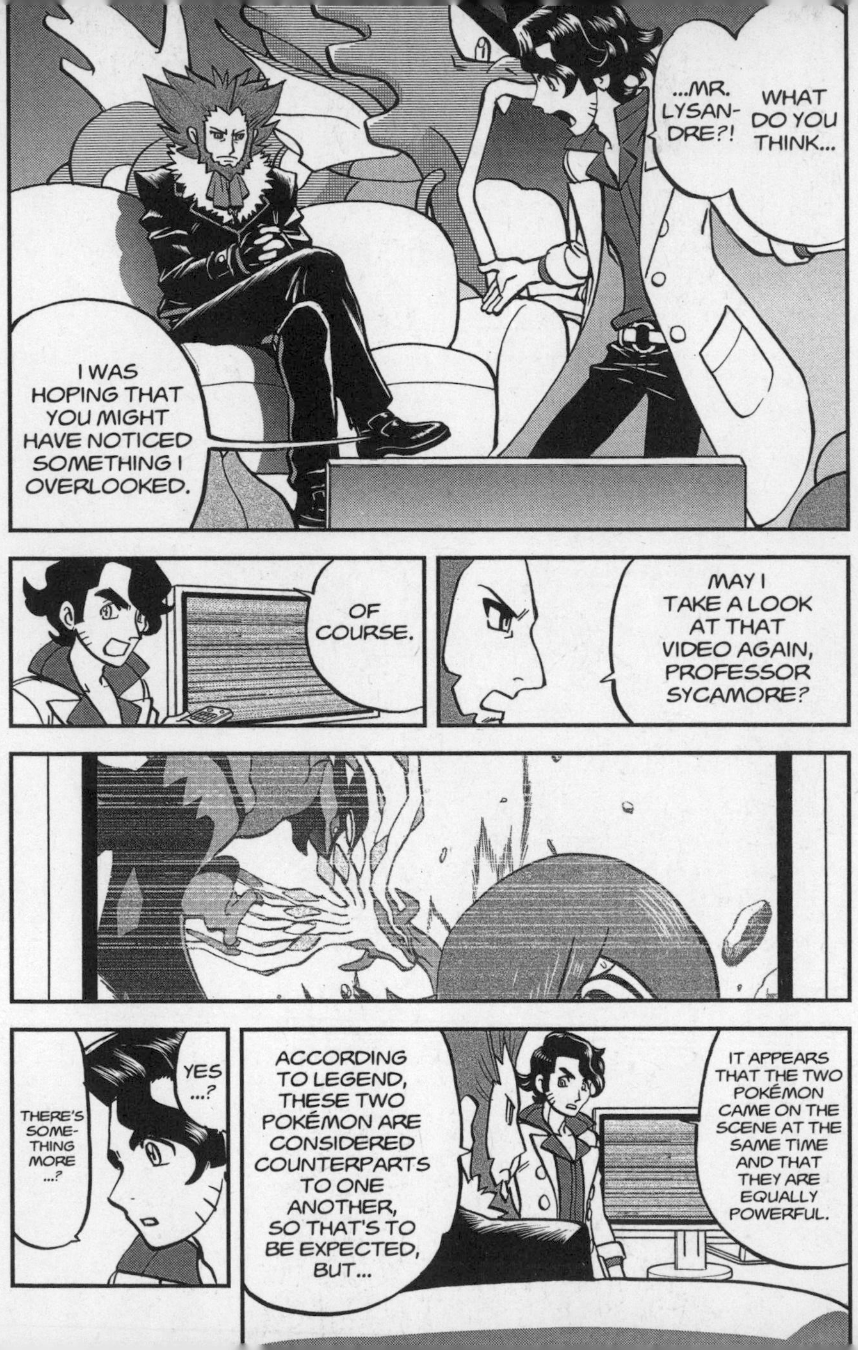
WHAT DO YOU THINK...
...MR. LYSANDRE?!
I WAS HOPING THAT YOU MIGHT HAVE NOTICED SOMETHING I OVERLOOKED.
MAY I TAKE A LOOK AT THAT VIDEO AGAIN, PROFESSOR SYCAMORE?
OF COURSE.
IT APPEARS THAT THE TWO POKÉMON CAME ON THE SCENE AT THE SAME TIME AND THAT THEY ARE EQUALLY POWERFUL.
ACCORDING TO LEGEND, THESE TWO POKÉMON ARE CONSIDERED COUNTERPARTS TO ONE ANOTHER, SO THAT'S TO BE EXPECTED, BUT...
YES ...?
THERE'S SOMETHING MORE ...?

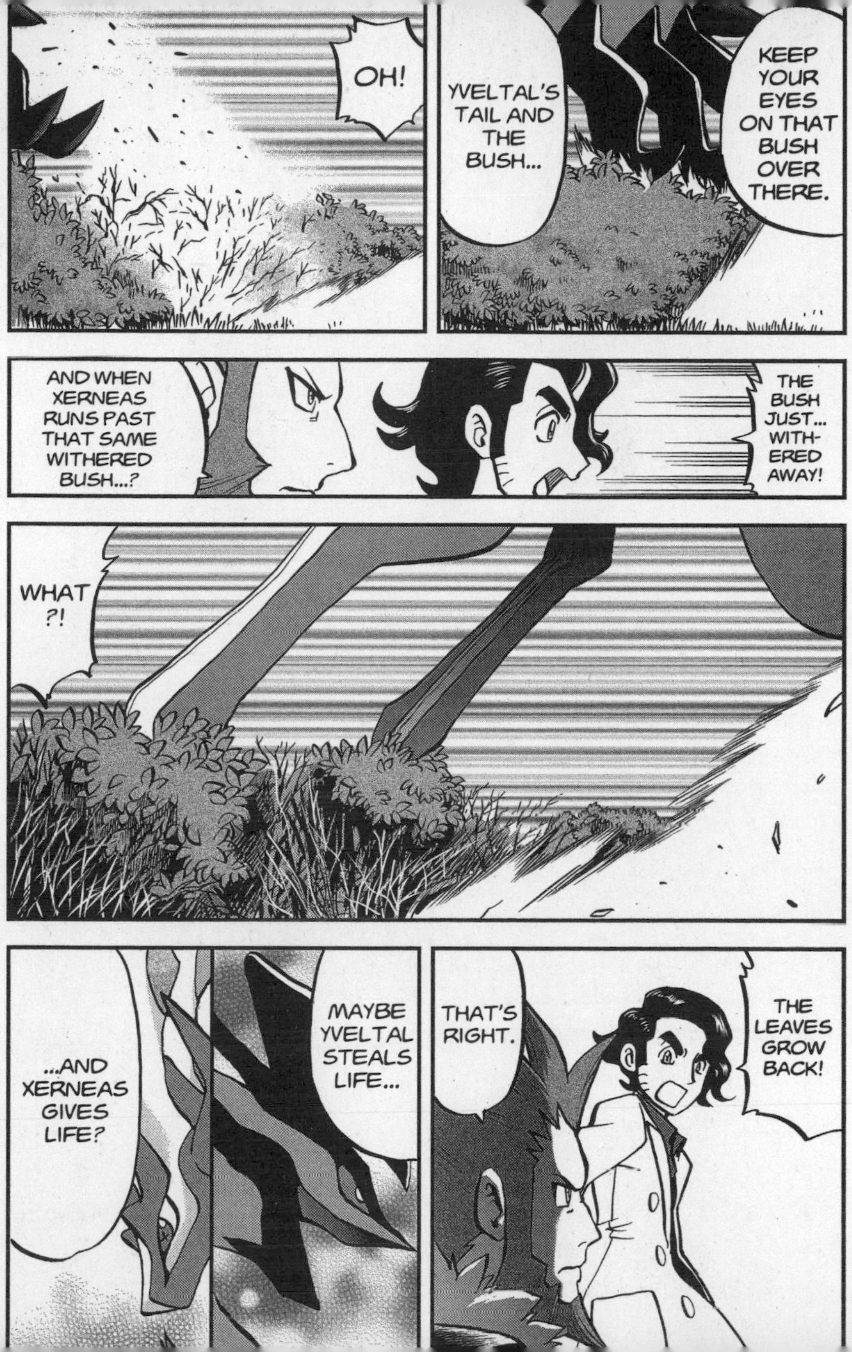
KEEP YOUR EYES ON THAT BUSH OVER THERE.
YVELTAL'S TAIL AND THE BUSH...
OH!
THE BUSH JUST... WITH-ERED AWAY!
AND WHEN XERNEAS RUNS PAST THAT SAME WITHERED BUSH...?
WHAT ?!
THE LEAVES GROW BACK!
THAT'S RIGHT.
MAYBE YVELTAL STEALS LIFE...
...AND XERNEAS GIVES LIFE?

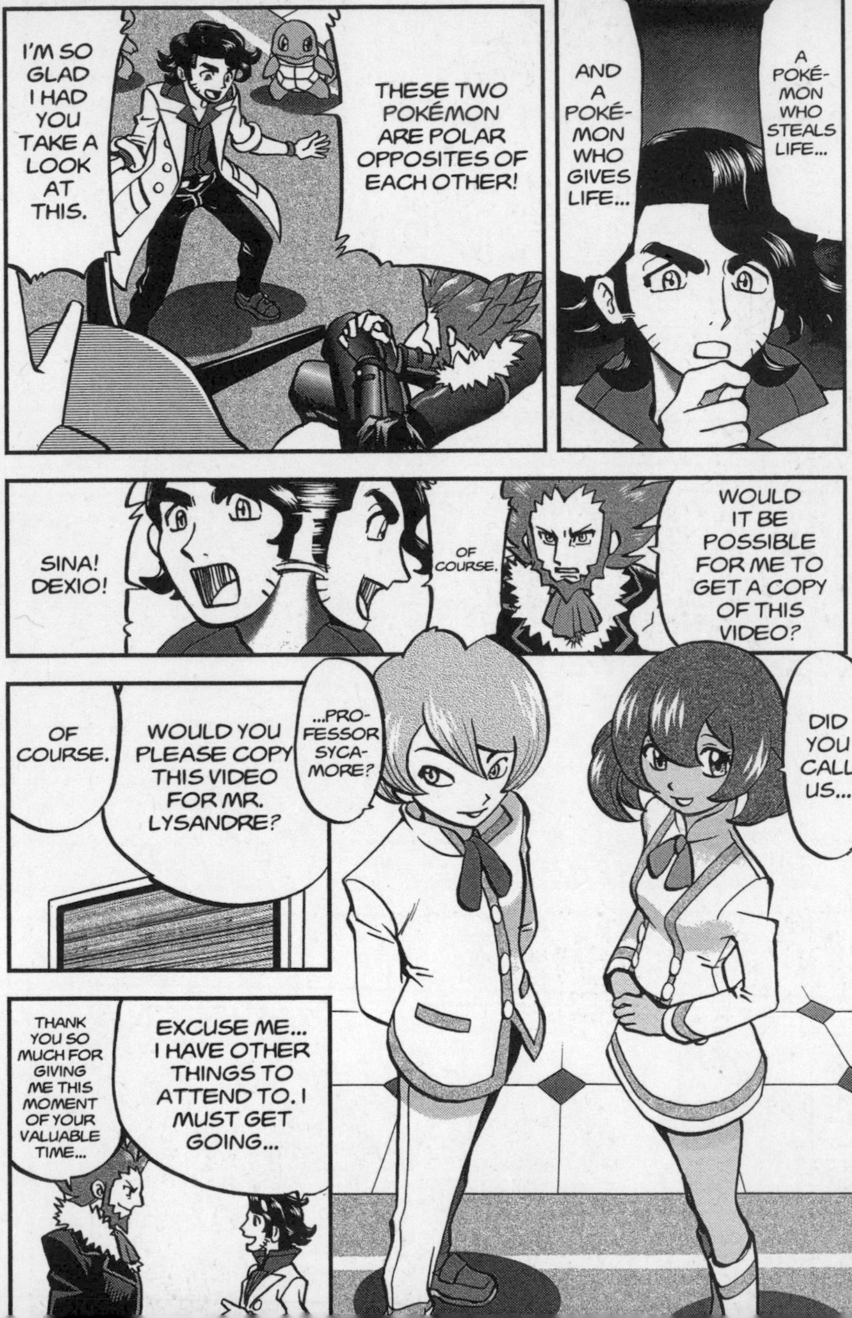
A POKÉ-MON WHO STEALS LIFE...
AND A POKÉ-MON WHO GIVES LIFE...
THESE TWO POKÉMON ARE POLAR OPPOSITES OF EACH OTHER!
I'M SO GLAD I HAD YOU TAKE A LOOK AT THIS.
WOULD IT BE POSSIBLE FOR ME TO GET A COPY OF THIS VIDEO?
OF COURSE.
SINA! DEXIO!
DID YOU CALL US...
...PRO-FESSOR SYCA-MORE?
WOULD YOU PLEASE COPY THIS VIDEO FOR MR. LYSANDRE?
OF COURSE.
EXCUSE ME... I HAVE OTHER THINGS TO ATTEND TO. I MUST GET GOING...
THANK YOU SO MUCH FOR GIVING ME THIS MOMENT OF YOUR VALUABLE TIME...

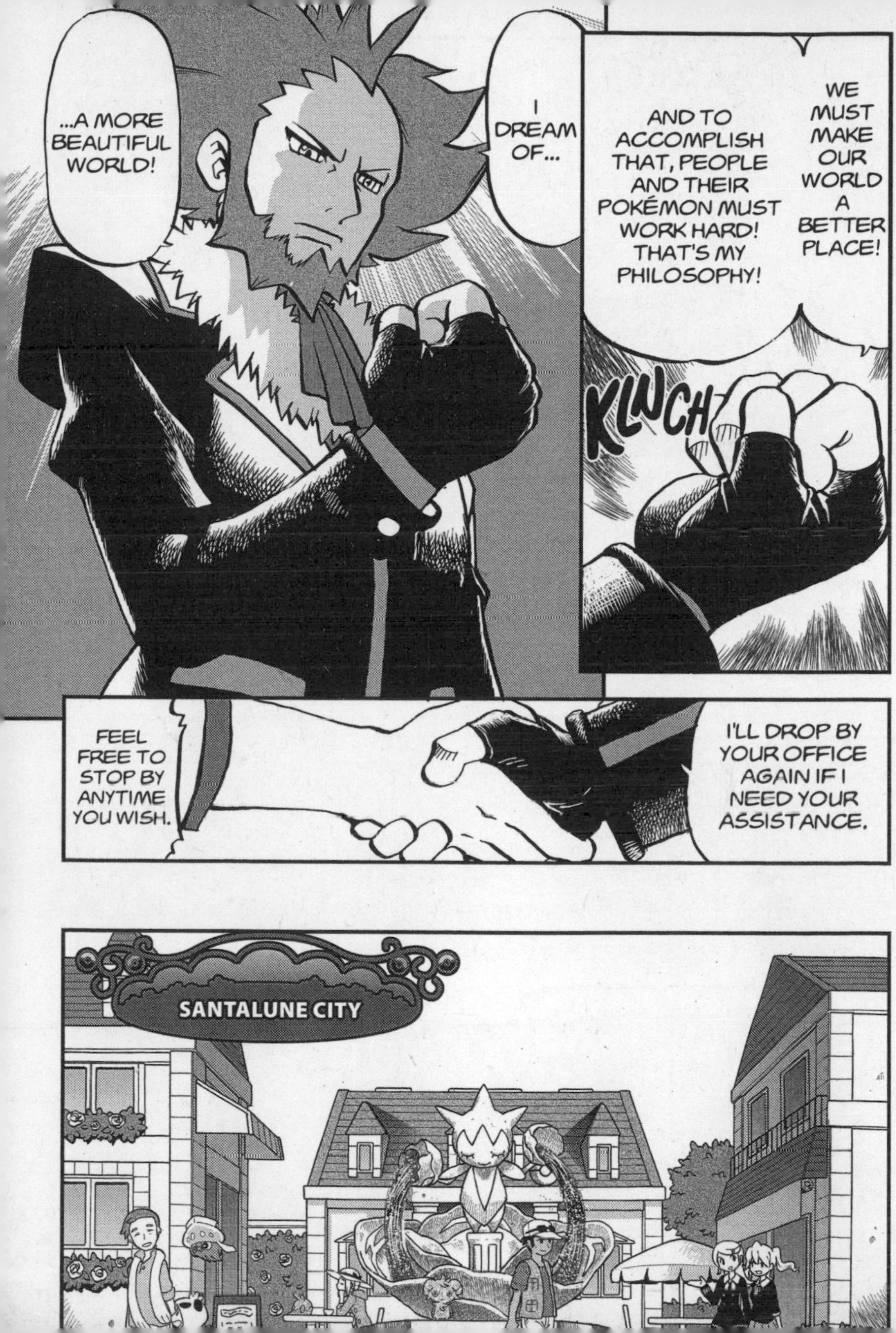
WE MUST MAKE OUR WORLD A BETTER PLACE!
AND TO ACCOMPLISH THAT, PEOPLE AND THEIR POKÉMON MUST WORK HARD! THAT'S MY PHILOSOPHY!
KLUNCH
I DREAM OF...
...A MORE BEAUTIFUL WORLD!
I'LL DROP BY YOUR OFFICE AGAIN IF I NEED YOUR ASSISTANCE.
FEEL FREE TO STOP BY ANYTIME YOU WISH.
SANTALUNE CITY

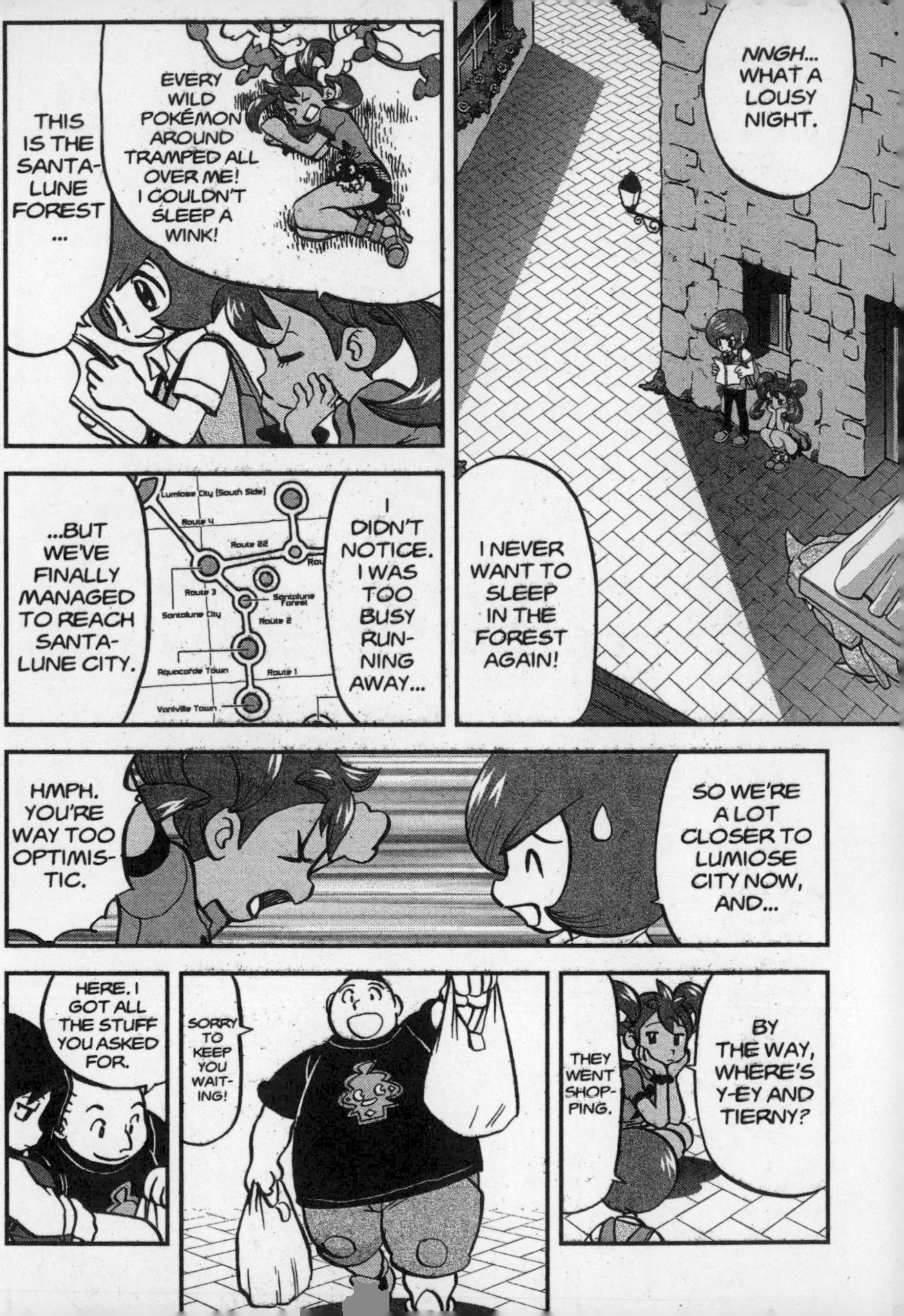

NNGH... WHAT A LOUSY NIGHT.
I NEVER WANT TO SLEEP IN THE FOREST AGAIN!
EVERY WILD POKÉMON AROUND TRAMPED ALL OVER ME! I COULDN'T SLEEP A WINK!
THIS IS THE SANTA-LUNE FOREST ...
I DIDN'T NOTICE. I WAS TOO BUSY RUN-NING AWAY...
Lumiose City (South Side)
Route 4
Route 22
Route 3
Santalune Forest
Santalune City
Route 2
Aquacorde Town
Route 1
Vaniville Town
...BUT WE'VE FINALLY MANAGED TO REACH SANTA-LUNE CITY.
SO WE'RE A LOT CLOSER TO LUMIOSE CITY NOW, AND...
HMPH. YOU'RE WAY TOO OPTIMIS-TIC.
BY THE WAY, WHERE'S Y-EY AND TIERNY?
THEY WENT SHOP-PING.
SORRY TO KEEP YOU WAIT-ING!
HERE. I GOT ALL THE STUFF YOU ASKED FOR.

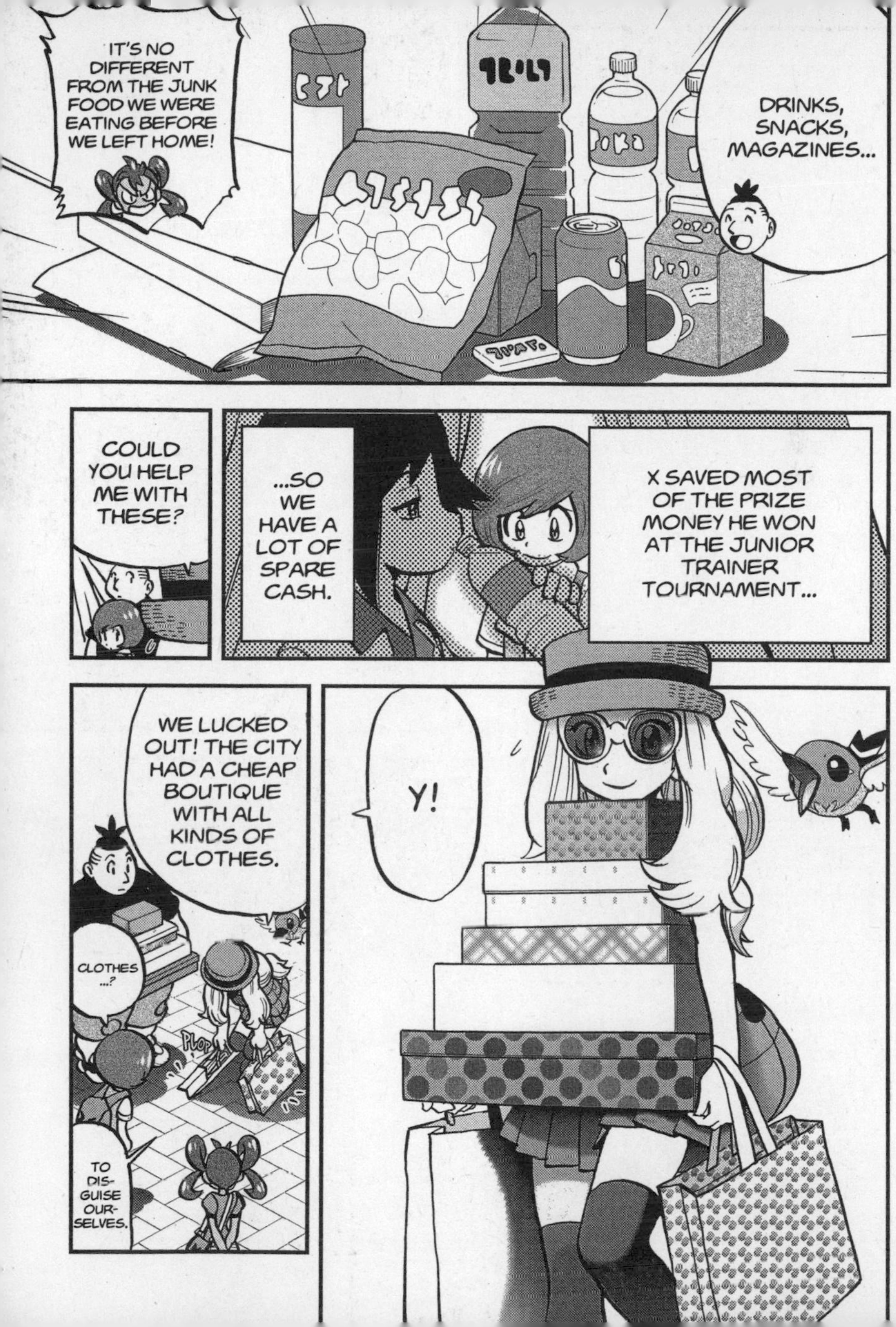
DRINKS, SNACKS, MAGAZINES...
IT'S NO DIFFERENT FROM THE JUNK FOOD WE WERE EATING BEFORE WE LEFT HOME!
X SAVED MOST OF THE PRIZE MONEY HE WON AT THE JUNIOR TRAINER TOURNAMENT...
...SO WE HAVE A LOT OF SPARE CASH.
COULD YOU HELP ME WITH THESE?
Y!
WE LUCKED OUT! THE CITY HAD A CHEAP BOUTIQUE WITH ALL KINDS OF CLOTHES.
CLOTHES ...?
PLOP
TO DIS-GUISE OUR-SELVES.

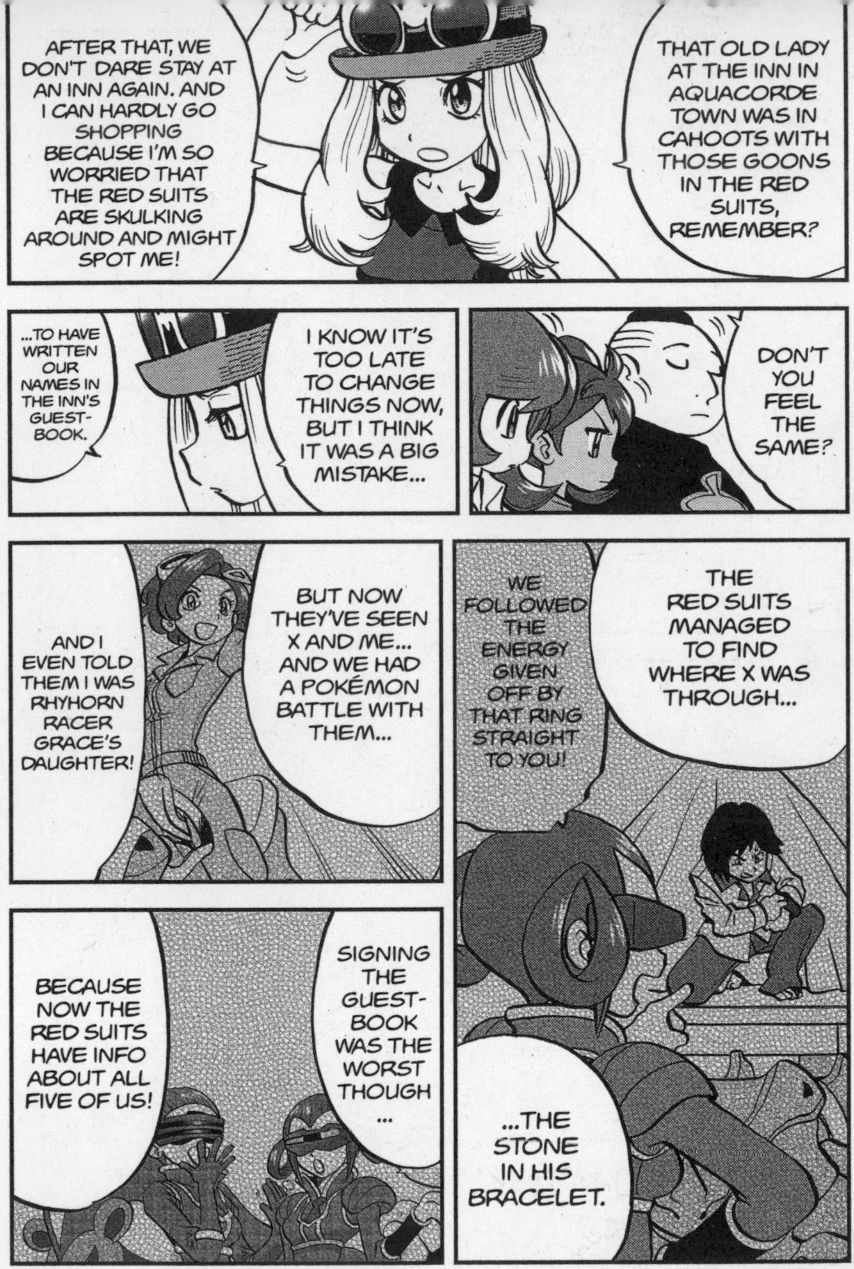
THAT OLD LADY AT THE INN IN AQUACORDE TOWN WAS IN CAHOOTS WITH THOSE GOONS IN THE RED SUITS, REMEMBER?
AFTER THAT, WE DON'T DARE STAY AT AN INN AGAIN. AND I CAN HARDLY GO SHOPPING BECAUSE I'M SO WORRIED THAT THE RED SUITS ARE SKULKING AROUND AND MIGHT SPOT ME!
DON'T YOU FEEL THE SAME?
I KNOW IT'S TOO LATE TO CHANGE THINGS NOW, BUT I THINK IT WAS A BIG MISTAKE...
...TO HAVE WRITTEN OUR NAMES IN THE INN'S GUEST-BOOK.
THE RED SUITS MANAGED TO FIND WHERE X WAS THROUGH...
WE FOLLOWED THE ENERGY GIVEN OFF BY THAT RING STRAIGHT TO YOU!
...THE STONE IN HIS BRACELET.
BUT NOW THEY'VE SEEN X AND ME... AND WE HAD A POKÉMON BATTLE WITH THEM...
AND I EVEN TOLD THEM I WAS RHYHORN RACER GRACE'S DAUGHTER!
SIGNING THE GUEST-BOOK WAS THE WORST THOUGH...
BECAUSE NOW THE RED SUITS HAVE INFO ABOUT ALL FIVE OF US!

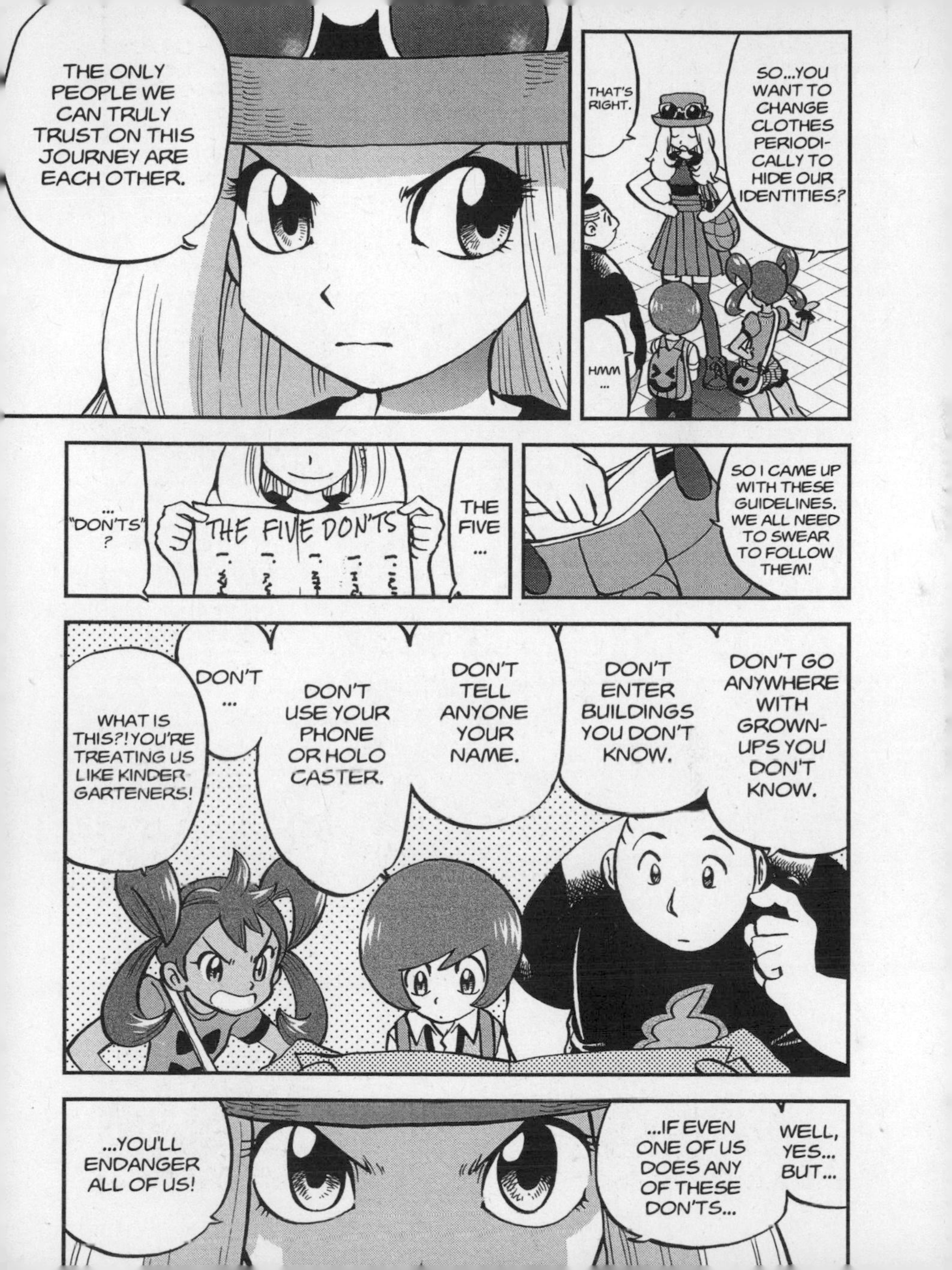
SO...YOU WANT TO CHANGE CLOTHES PERIODICALLY TO HIDE OUR IDENTITIES?
THAT'S RIGHT.
HMM...
THE ONLY PEOPLE WE CAN TRULY TRUST ON THIS JOURNEY ARE EACH OTHER.
SO I CAME UP WITH THESE GUIDELINES. WE ALL NEED TO SWEAR TO FOLLOW THEM!
THE FIVE...
THE FIVE DON'TS
..."DON'TS"?
DON'T GO ANYWHERE WITH GROWN-UPS YOU DON'T KNOW.
DON'T ENTER BUILDINGS YOU DON'T KNOW.
DON'T TELL ANYONE YOUR NAME.
DON'T USE YOUR PHONE OR HOLO CASTER.
DON'T...
WHAT IS THIS?! YOU'RE TREATING US LIKE KINDERGARTENERS!
WELL, YES... BUT...
...IF EVEN ONE OF US DOES ANY OF THESE DON'TS...
...YOU'LL ENDANGER ALL OF US!

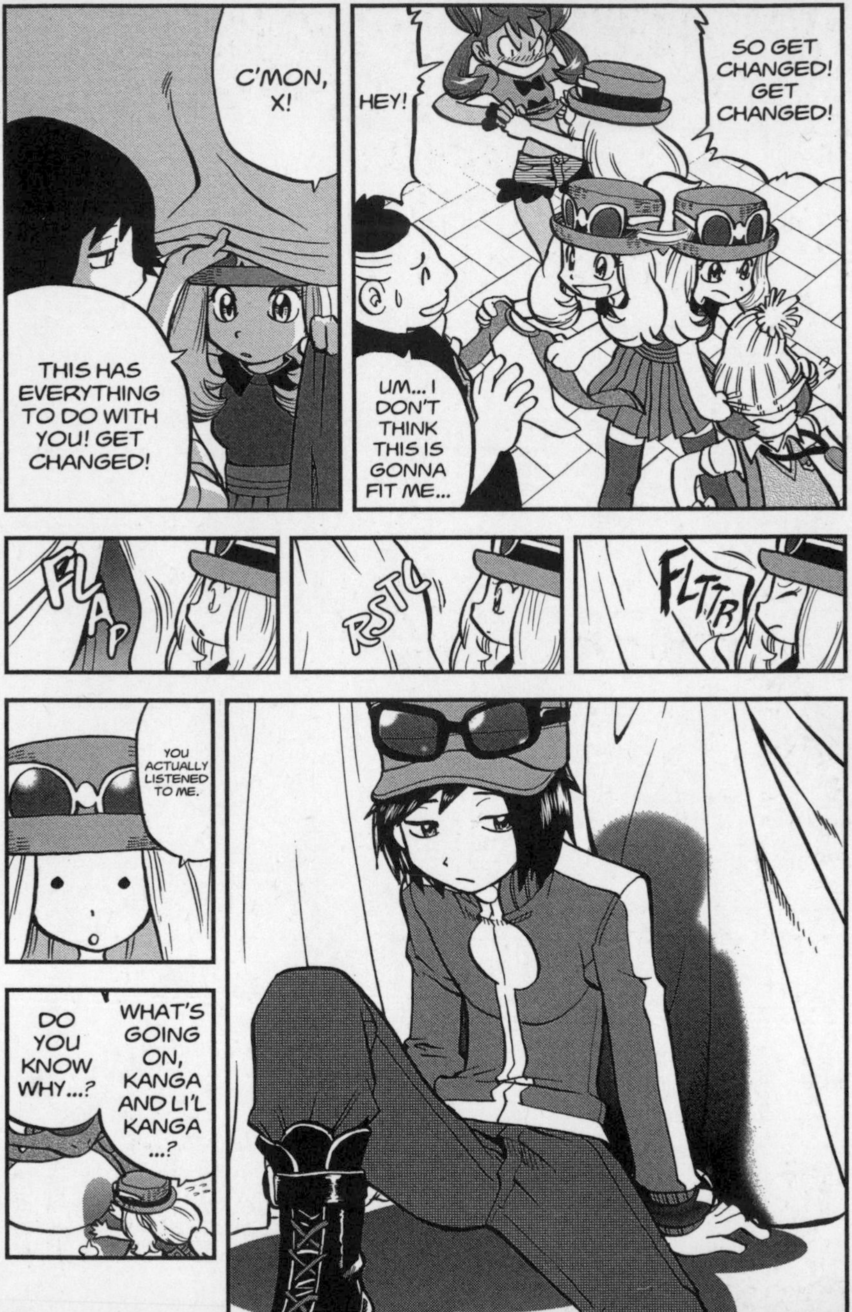
SO GET CHANGED! GET CHANGED!
HEY!
UM... I DON'T THINK THIS IS GONNA FIT ME...
C'MON, X!
THIS HAS EVERYTHING TO DO WITH YOU! GET CHANGED!
FLTTR
RSTL
FLAP
YOU ACTUALLY LISTENED TO ME.
WHAT'S GOING ON, KANGA AND LI'L KANGA...?
DO YOU KNOW WHY...?

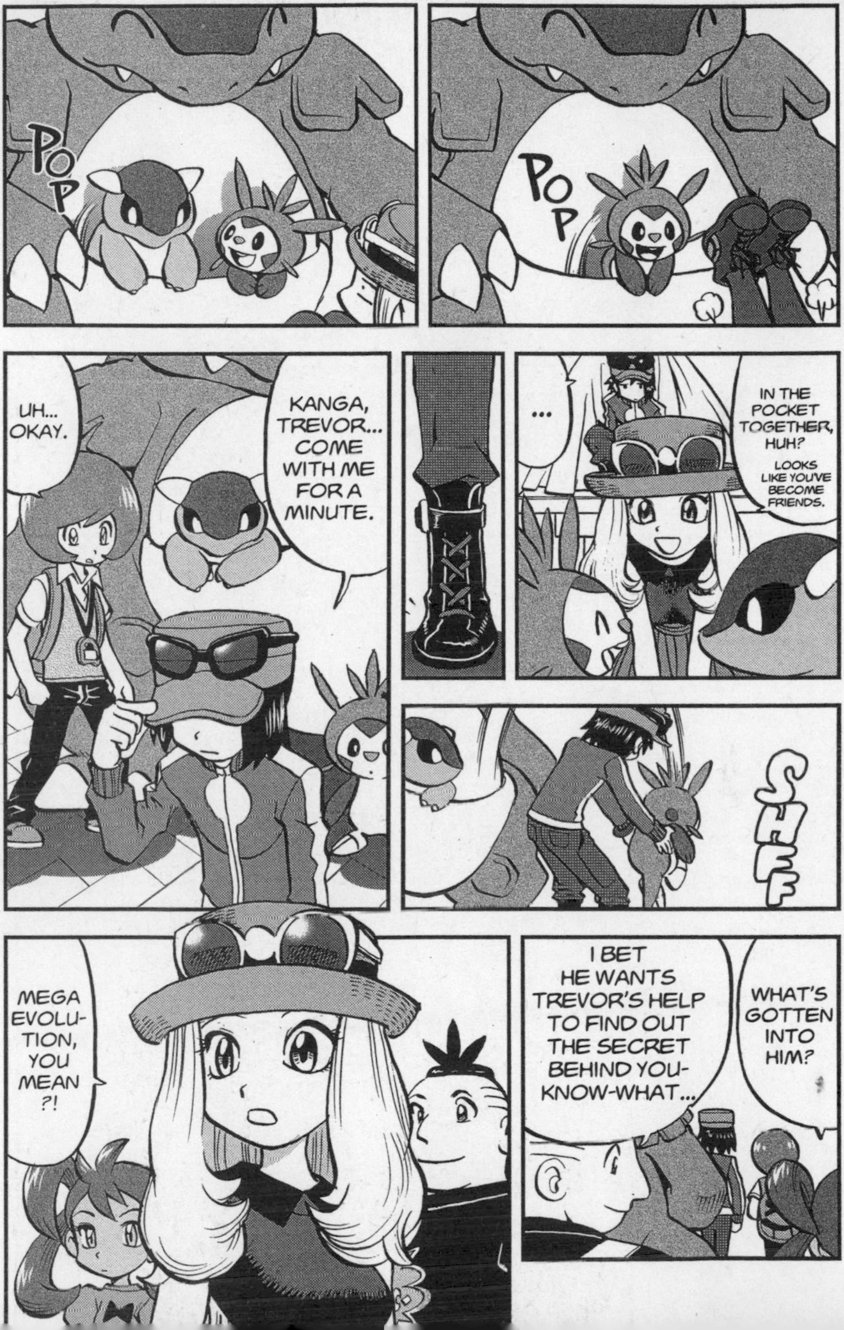
POP
POP
IN THE POCKET TOGETHER, HUH?
LOOKS LIKE YOU'VE BECOME FRIENDS.
...
SHFF
KANGA, TREVOR... COME WITH ME FOR A MINUTE.
UH... OKAY.
WHAT'S GOTTEN INTO HIM?
I BET HE WANTS TREVOR'S HELP TO FIND OUT THE SECRET BEHIND YOU-KNOW-WHAT...
MEGA EVOLU-TION, YOU MEAN?!

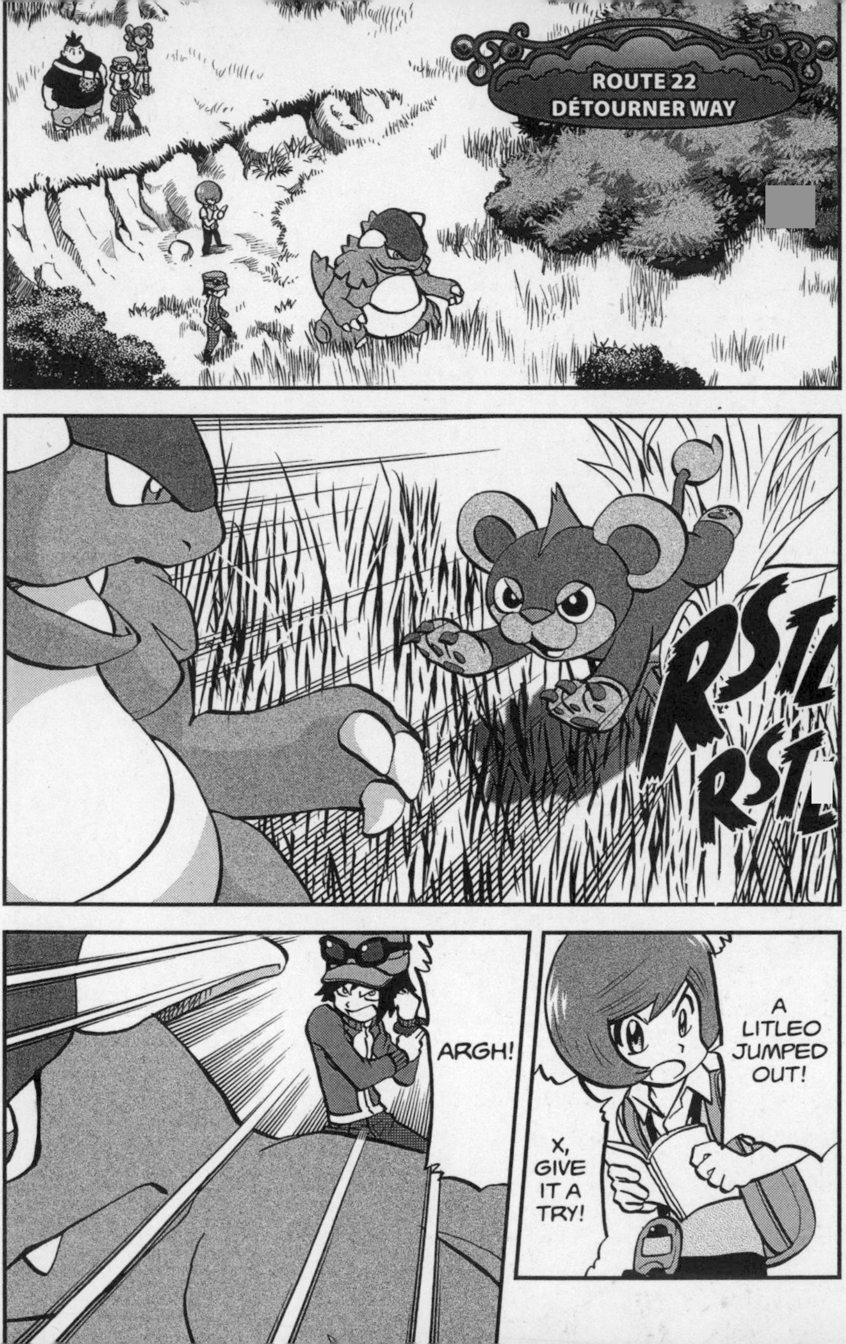
ROUTE 22
DÉTOURNER WAY
RSL
RSL
A LITLEO JUMPED OUT!
X, GIVE IT A TRY!
ARGH!

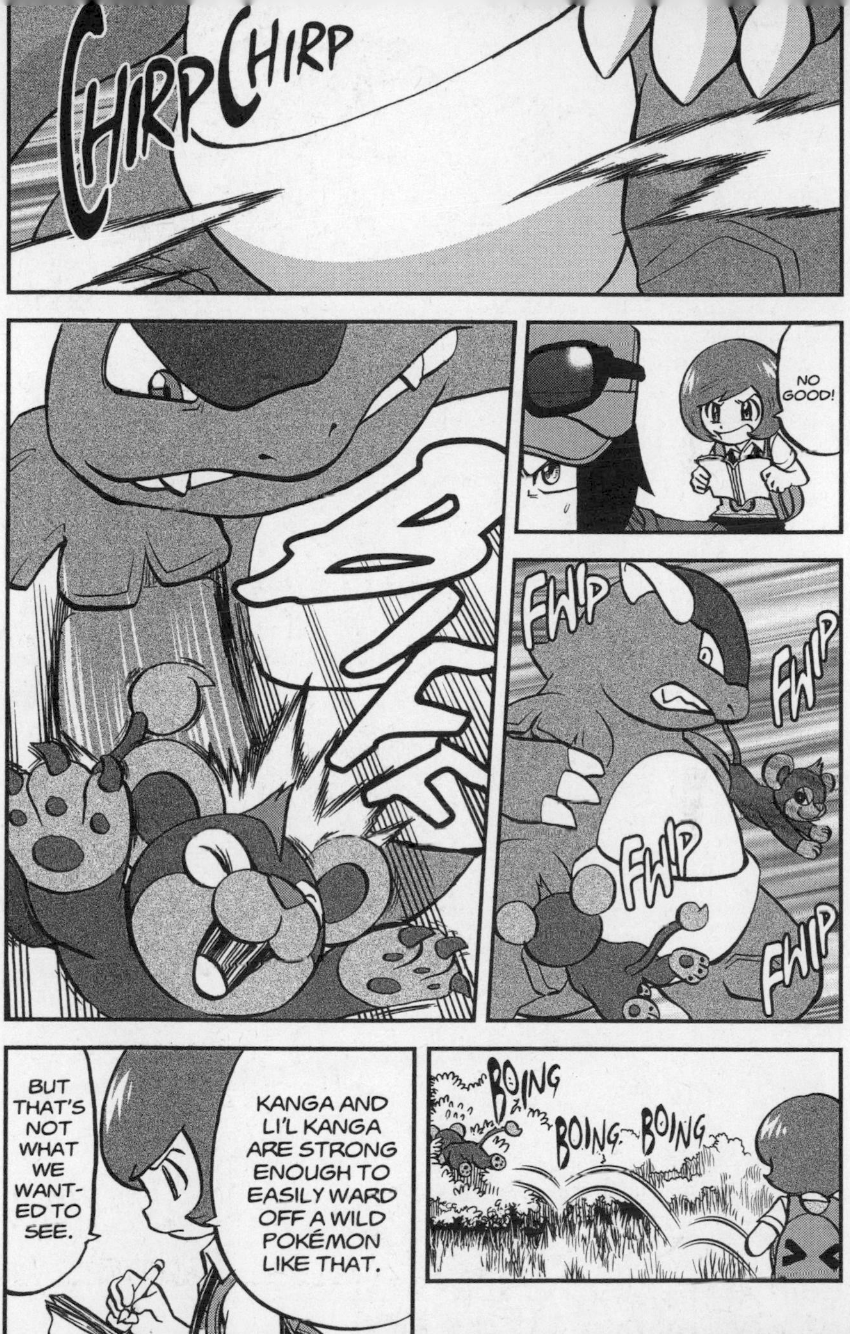
CHIRP CHIRP
NO GOOD!
FWIP
FWIP
FWIP
FWIP
BOING BOING BOING
KANGA AND LI'L KANGA ARE STRONG ENOUGH TO EASILY WARD OFF A WILD POKÉMON LIKE THAT.
BUT THAT'S NOT WHAT WE WANT-ED TO SEE.

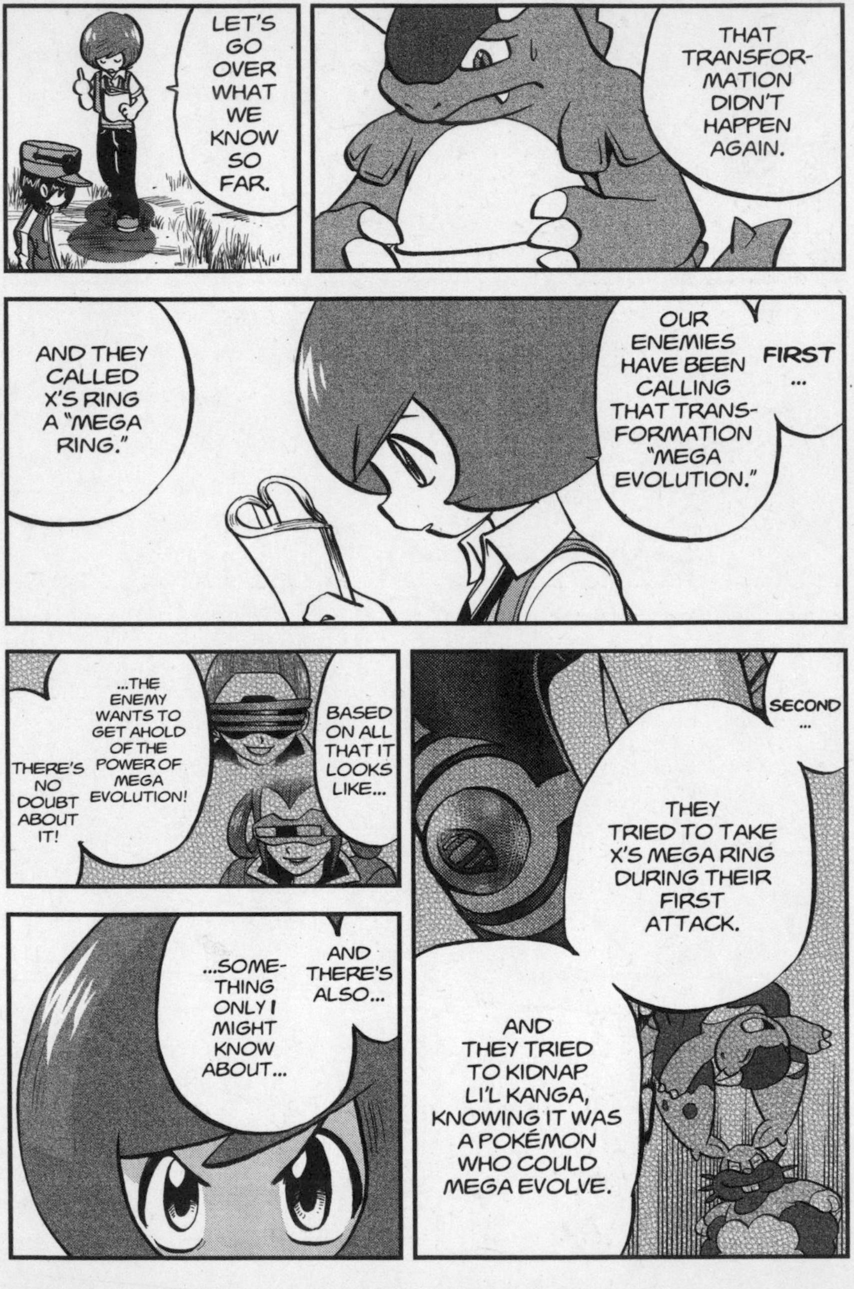
THAT TRANSFORMATION DIDN'T HAPPEN AGAIN.
LET'S GO OVER WHAT WE KNOW SO FAR.
FIRST...
OUR ENEMIES HAVE BEEN CALLING THAT TRANSFORMATION "MEGA EVOLUTION."
AND THEY CALLED X'S RING A "MEGA RING."
SECOND...
THEY TRIED TO TAKE X'S MEGA RING DURING THEIR FIRST ATTACK.
AND THEY TRIED TO KIDNAP LI'L KANGA, KNOWING IT WAS A POKÉMON WHO COULD MEGA EVOLVE.
BASED ON ALL THAT IT LOOKS LIKE...
...THE ENEMY WANTS TO GET AHOLD OF THE POWER OF MEGA EVOLUTION!
THERE'S NO DOUBT ABOUT IT!
AND THERE'S ALSO...
...SOMETHING ONLY I MIGHT KNOW ABOUT...

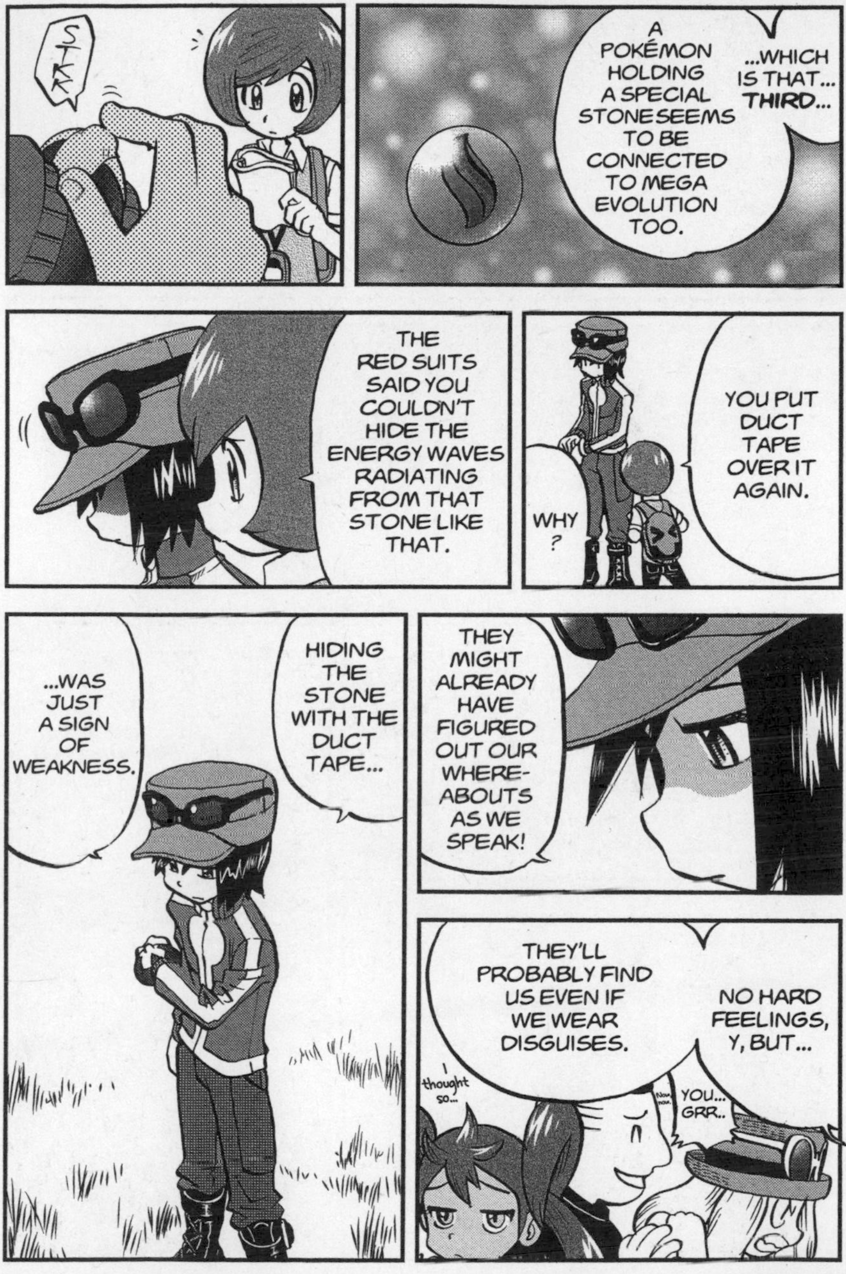
A POKÉMON HOLDING A SPECIAL STONE SEEMS TO BE CONNECTED TO MEGA EVOLUTION TOO.
...WHICH IS THAT... **THIRD**...
STKK
YOU PUT DUCT TAPE OVER IT AGAIN.
WHY?
THE RED SUITS SAID YOU COULDN'T HIDE THE ENERGY WAVES RADIATING FROM THAT STONE LIKE THAT.
THEY MIGHT ALREADY HAVE FIGURED OUT OUR WHERE-ABOUTS AS WE SPEAK!
NO HARD FEELINGS, Y, BUT...
THEY'LL PROBABLY FIND US EVEN IF WE WEAR DISGUISES.
YOU... GRR..
Now now.
I thought so...
HIDING THE STONE WITH THE DUCT TAPE...
...WAS JUST A SIGN OF WEAKNESS.

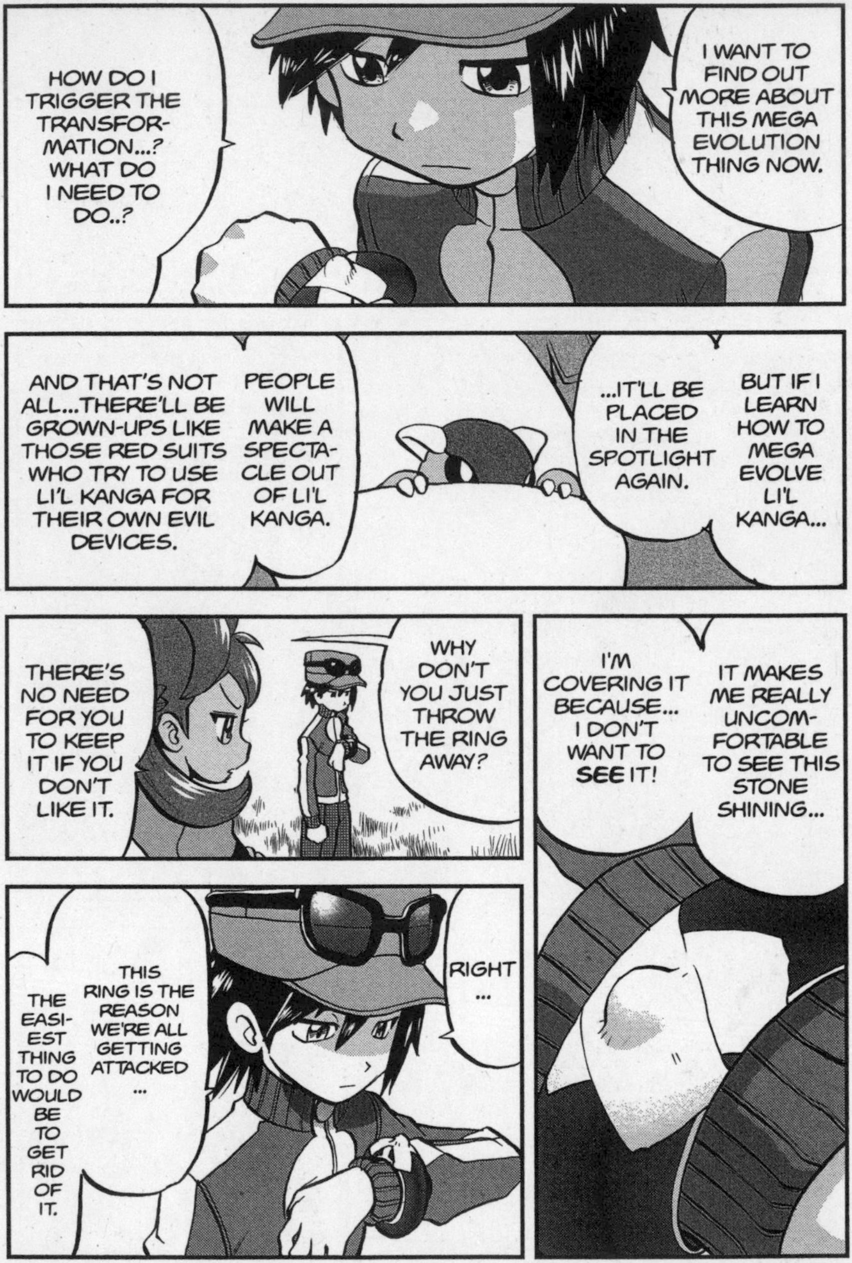
I WANT TO FIND OUT MORE ABOUT THIS MEGA EVOLUTION THING NOW.
HOW DO I TRIGGER THE TRANSFORMATION...? WHAT DO I NEED TO DO..?
BUT IF I LEARN HOW TO MEGA EVOLVE LI'L KANGA...
...IT'LL BE PLACED IN THE SPOTLIGHT AGAIN.
PEOPLE WILL MAKE A SPECTACLE OUT OF LI'L KANGA.
AND THAT'S NOT ALL...THERE'LL BE GROWN-UPS LIKE THOSE RED SUITS WHO TRY TO USE LI'L KANGA FOR THEIR OWN EVIL DEVICES.
IT MAKES ME REALLY UNCOMFORTABLE TO SEE THIS STONE SHINING...
I'M COVERING IT BECAUSE... I DON'T WANT TO **SEE** IT!
WHY DON'T YOU JUST THROW THE RING AWAY?
THERE'S NO NEED FOR YOU TO KEEP IT IF YOU DON'T LIKE IT.
RIGHT...
THIS RING IS THE REASON WE'RE ALL GETTING ATTACKED...
THE EASIEST THING TO DO WOULD BE TO GET RID OF IT.

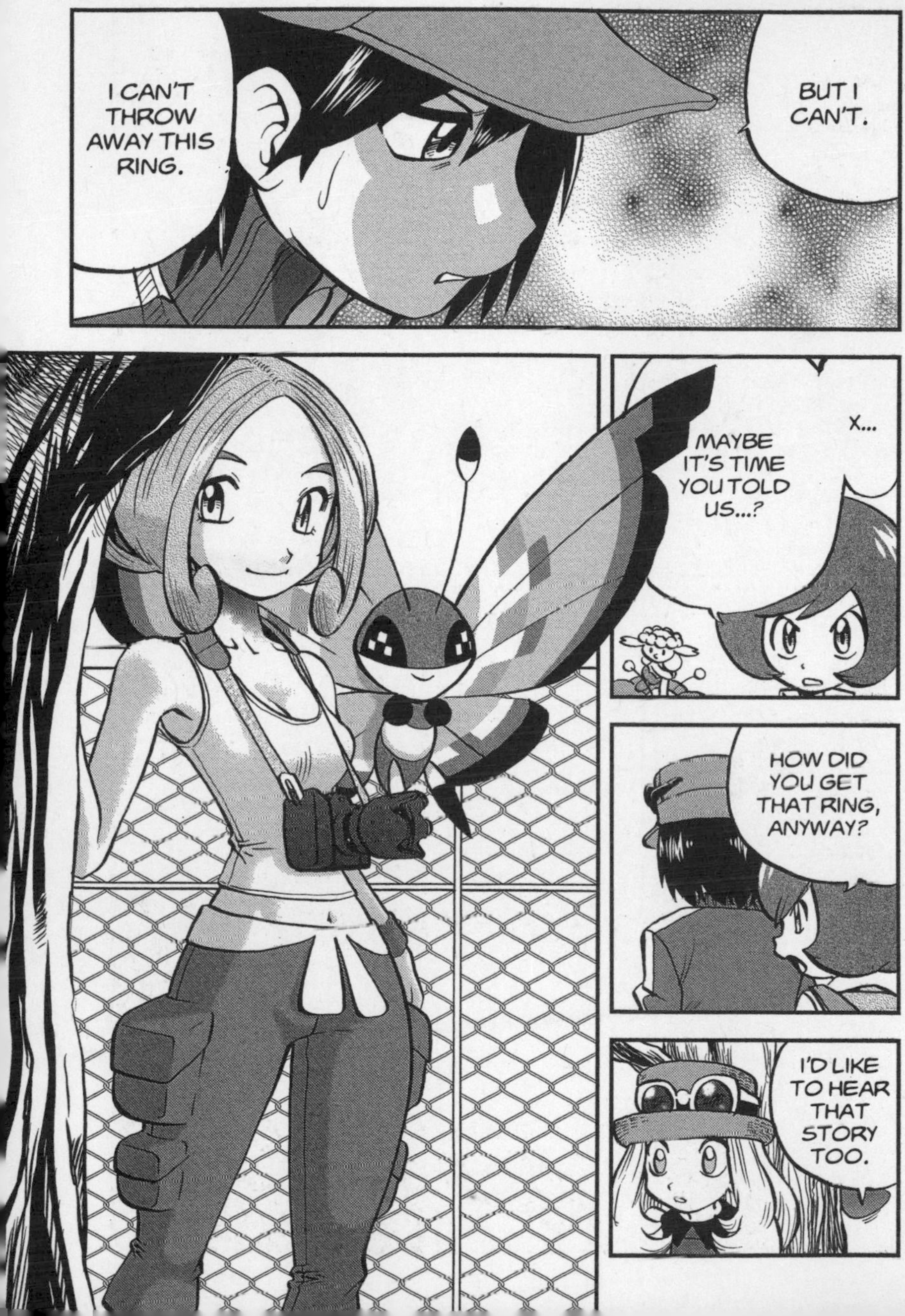
BUT I CAN'T.
I CAN'T THROW AWAY THIS RING.
X...
MAYBE IT'S TIME YOU TOLD US...?
HOW DID YOU GET THAT RING, ANYWAY?
I'D LIKE TO HEAR THAT STORY TOO.

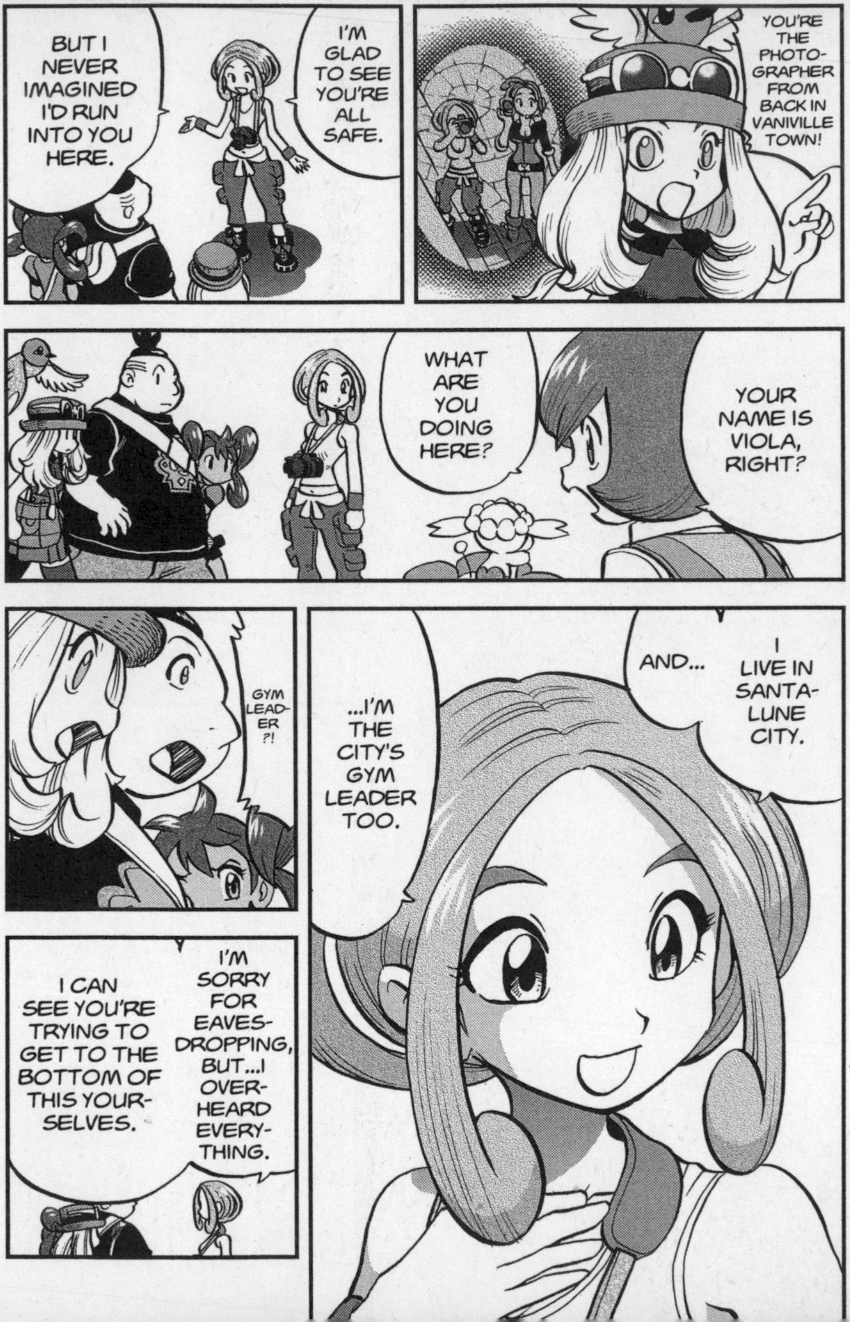

YOU'RE THE PHOTOGRAPHER FROM BACK IN VANIVILLE TOWN!
I'M GLAD TO SEE YOU'RE ALL SAFE.
BUT I NEVER IMAGINED I'D RUN INTO YOU HERE.
YOUR NAME IS VIOLA, RIGHT?
WHAT ARE YOU DOING HERE?
I LIVE IN SANTALUNE CITY.
AND...
...I'M THE CITY'S GYM LEADER TOO.
GYM LEADER?!
I'M SORRY FOR EAVESDROPPING, BUT...I OVERHEARD EVERYTHING.
I CAN SEE YOU'RE TRYING TO GET TO THE BOTTOM OF THIS YOURSELVES.

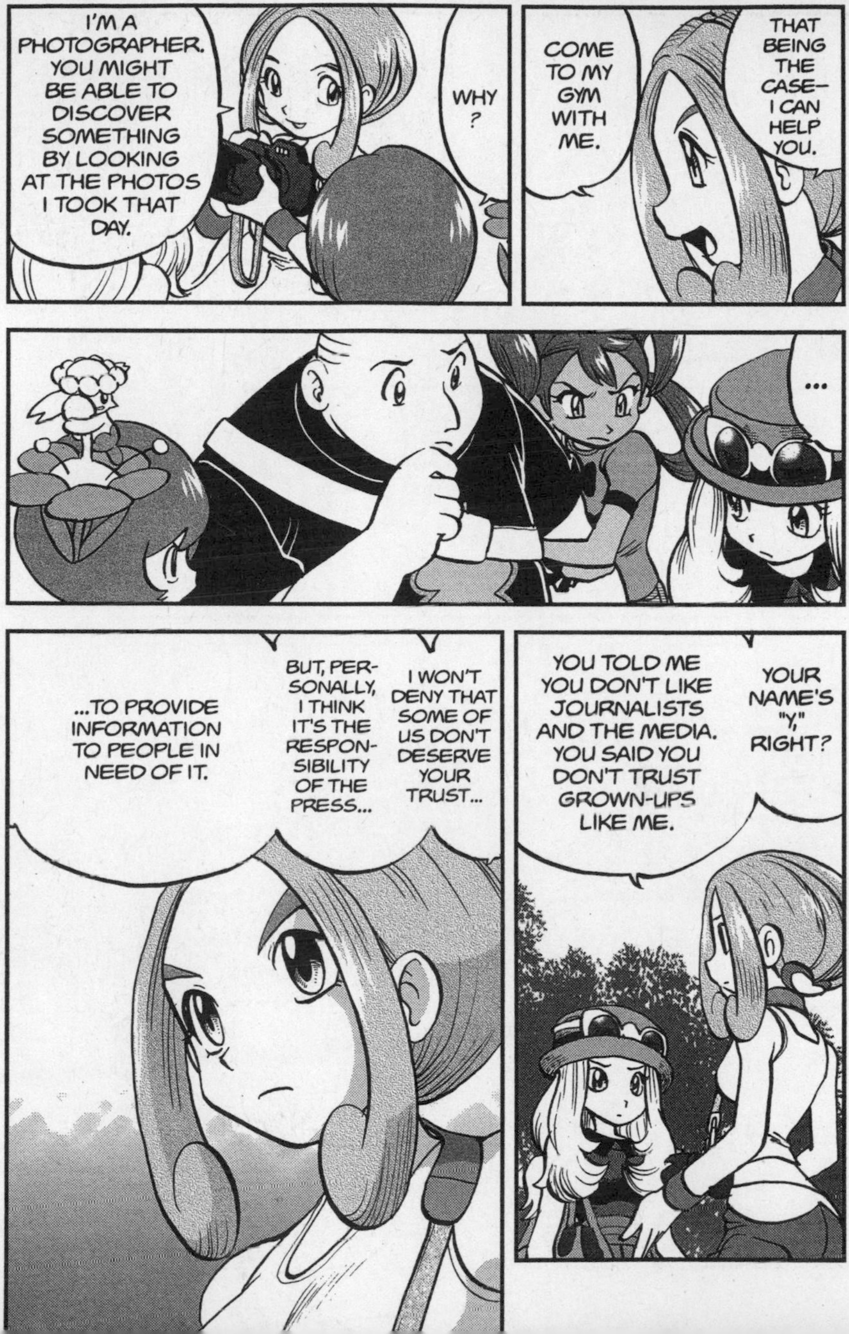
THAT BEING THE CASE— I CAN HELP YOU.
COME TO MY GYM WITH ME.
WHY?
I'M A PHOTOGRAPHER. YOU MIGHT BE ABLE TO DISCOVER SOMETHING BY LOOKING AT THE PHOTOS I TOOK THAT DAY.
...
YOUR NAME'S "Y," RIGHT?
YOU TOLD ME YOU DON'T LIKE JOURNALISTS AND THE MEDIA. YOU SAID YOU DON'T TRUST GROWN-UPS LIKE ME.
I WON'T DENY THAT SOME OF US DON'T DESERVE YOUR TRUST...
BUT, PERSONALLY, I THINK IT'S THE RESPONSIBILITY OF THE PRESS...
...TO PROVIDE INFORMATION TO PEOPLE IN NEED OF IT.

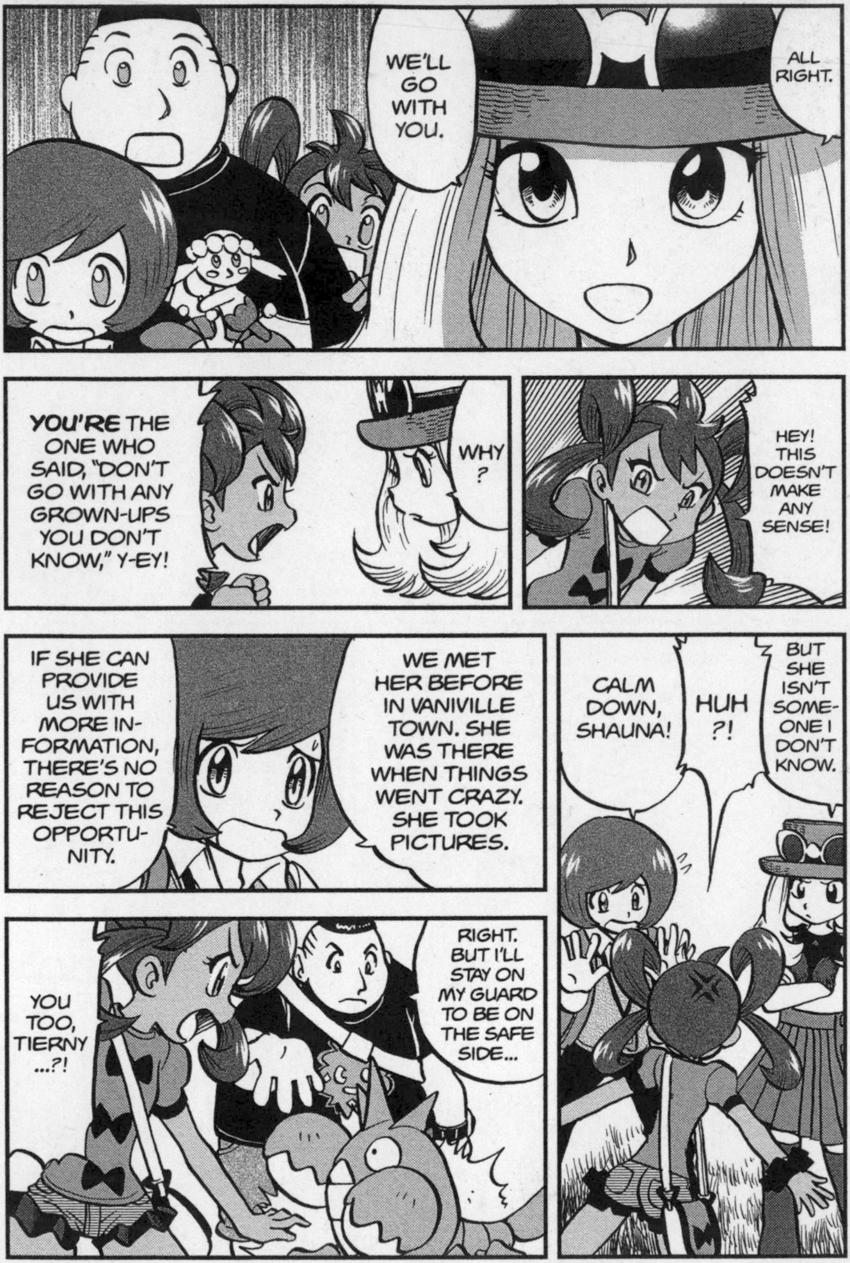
ALL RIGHT.
WE'LL GO WITH YOU.
HEY! THIS DOESN'T MAKE ANY SENSE!
WHY ?
YOU'RE THE ONE WHO SAID, "DON'T GO WITH ANY GROWN-UPS YOU DON'T KNOW," Y-EY!
BUT SHE ISN'T SOME-ONE I DON'T KNOW.
HUH ?!
CALM DOWN, SHAUNA!
WE MET HER BEFORE IN VANIVILLE TOWN. SHE WAS THERE WHEN THINGS WENT CRAZY. SHE TOOK PICTURES.
IF SHE CAN PROVIDE US WITH MORE IN-FORMATION, THERE'S NO REASON TO REJECT THIS OPPORTU-NITY.
RIGHT. BUT I'LL STAY ON MY GUARD TO BE ON THE SAFE SIDE...
YOU TOO, TIERNY ...?!

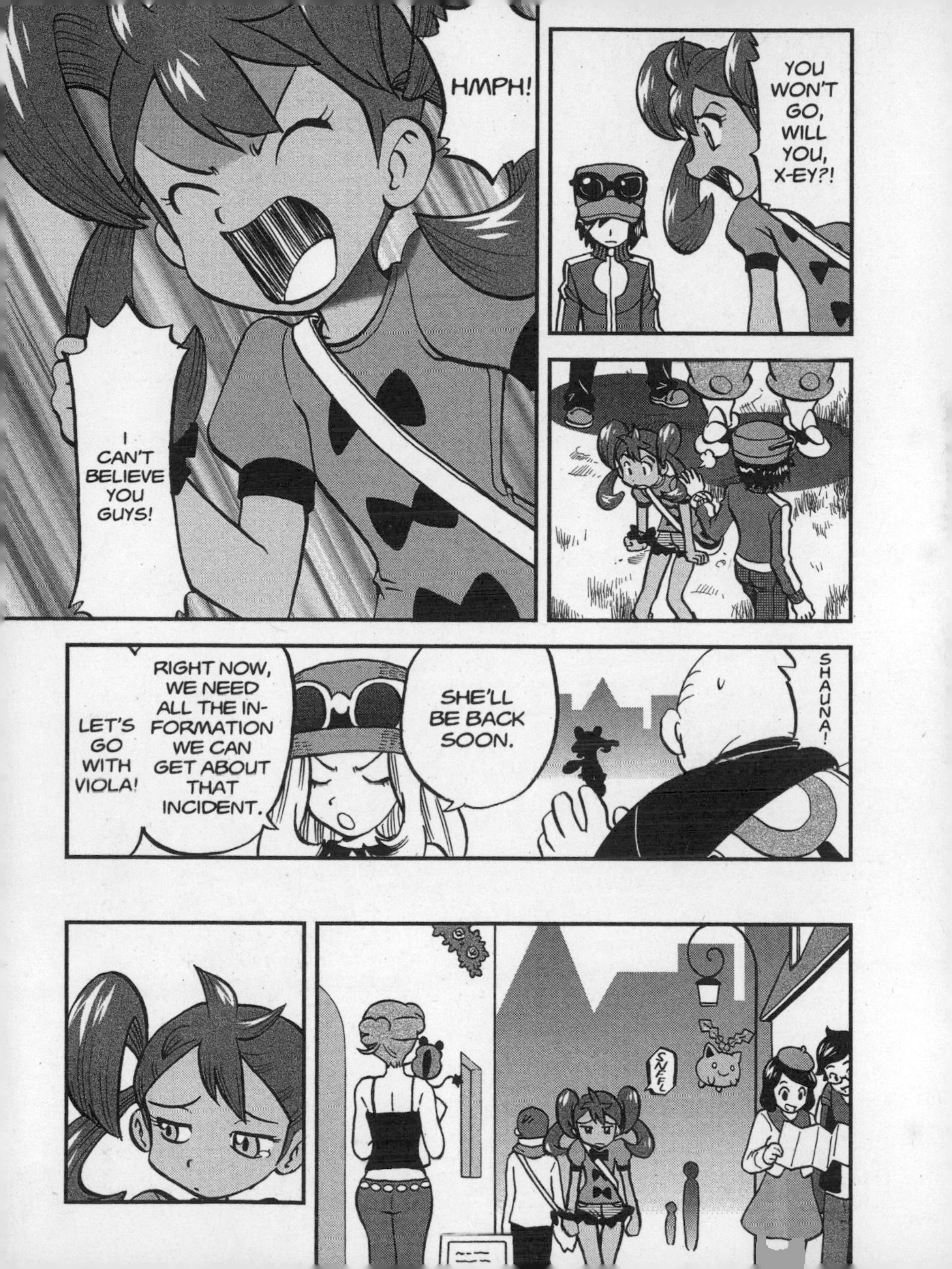
YOU WON'T GO, WILL YOU, X-EY?!
HMPH!
I CAN'T BELIEVE YOU GUYS!
SHAUNA!
SHE'LL BE BACK SOON.
RIGHT NOW, WE NEED ALL THE IN-FORMATION WE CAN GET ABOUT THAT INCIDENT.
LET'S GO WITH VIOLA!
SNFFL

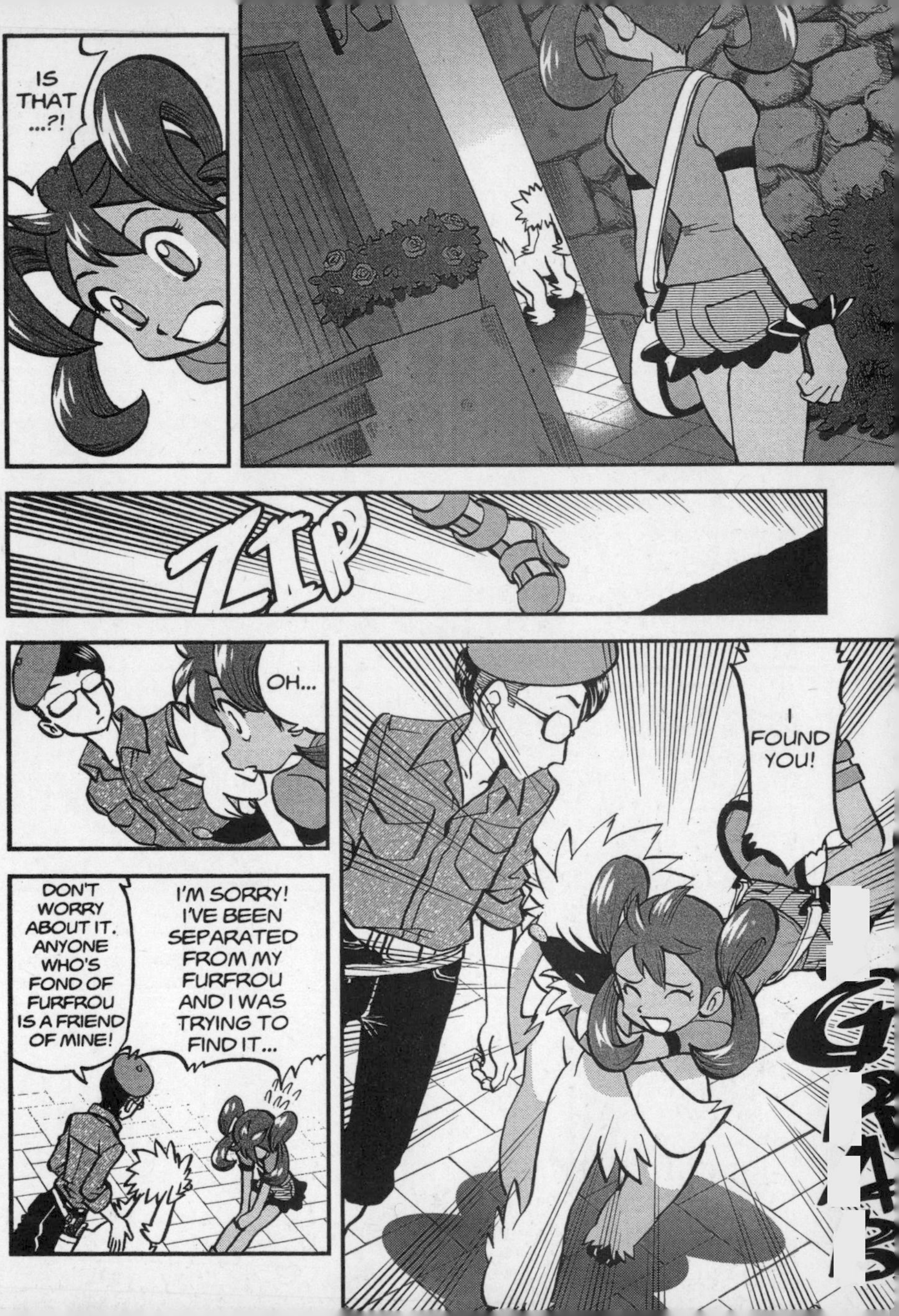
IS THAT ...?!
ZIP
I FOUND YOU!
OH...
I'M SORRY! I'VE BEEN SEPARATED FROM MY FURFROU AND I WAS TRYING TO FIND IT...
DON'T WORRY ABOUT IT. ANYONE WHO'S FOND OF FURFROU IS A FRIEND OF MINE!

⊕ Current Location

**Route 2
(Avance Trail)**

You'll find many Pokémon hiding among
the tall grass that grows in tufts along
this trail.

▼

Santalune Forest

The gentle light filtering through this
sun-dappled forest makes it a popular
spot for nature walks.

▼

**Route 3
(Ouvert Way)**

The little rises and hollows of this lush
forest are a favorite place for many kinds
of Pokémon to play.

▼

Santalune City

Many beginning Trainers gather in this
friendly city to start a Pokémon journey.

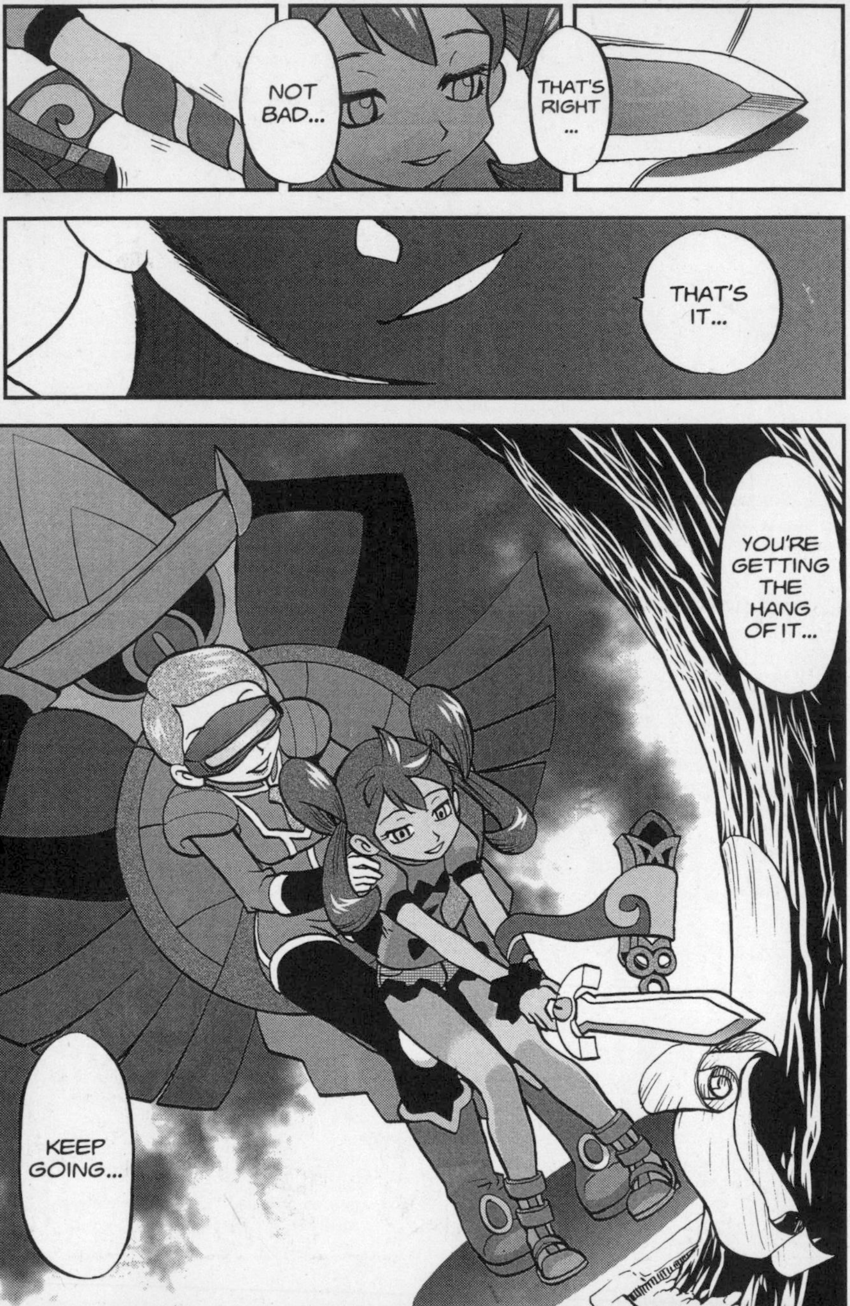
THAT'S RIGHT ...
NOT BAD...
THAT'S IT...
YOU'RE GETTING THE HANG OF IT...
KEEP GOING...

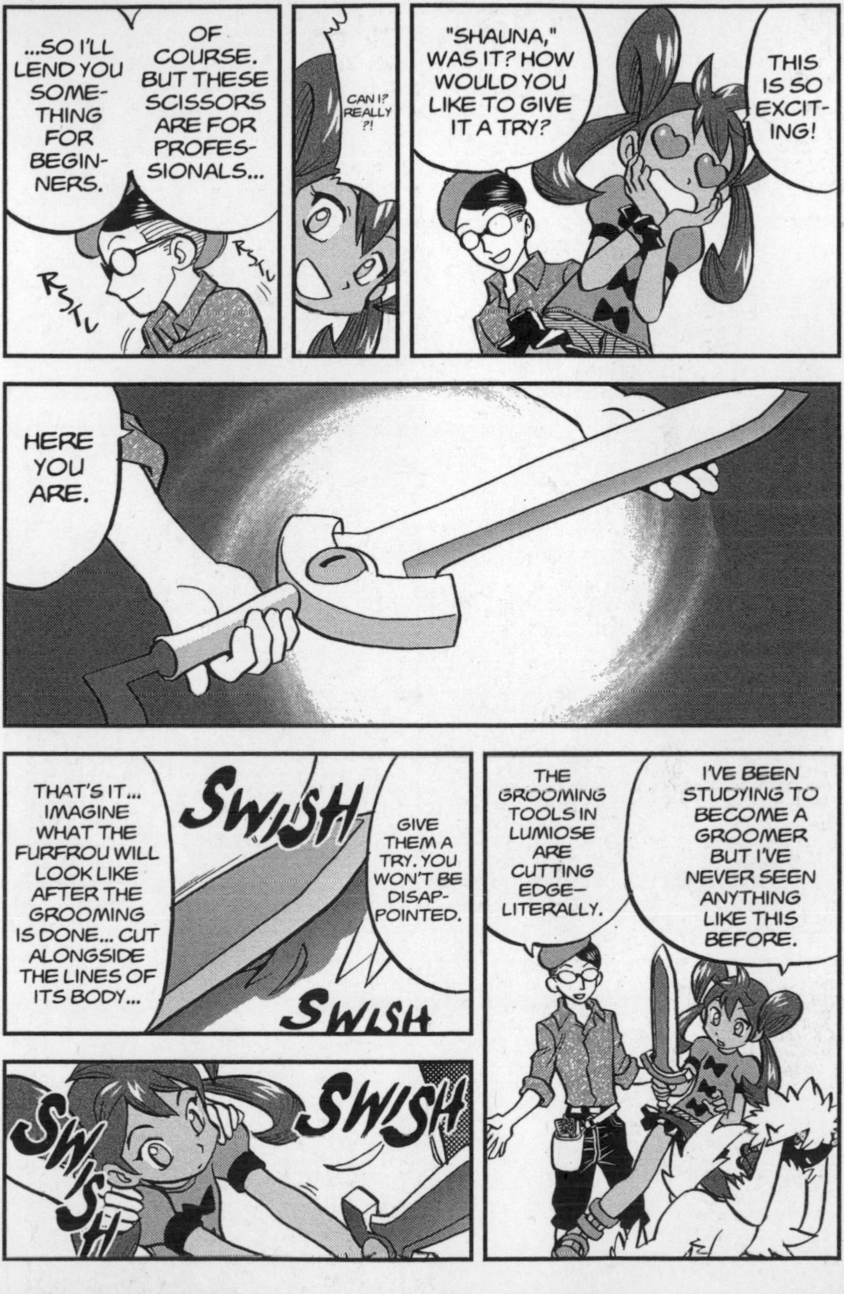
THIS IS SO EXCITING!
"SHAUNA," WAS IT? HOW WOULD YOU LIKE TO GIVE IT A TRY?
CAN I? REALLY ?!
OF COURSE. BUT THESE SCISSORS ARE FOR PROFESSIONALS...
...SO I'LL LEND YOU SOMETHING FOR BEGINNERS.
HERE YOU ARE.
I'VE BEEN STUDYING TO BECOME A GROOMER BUT I'VE NEVER SEEN ANYTHING LIKE THIS BEFORE.
THE GROOMING TOOLS IN LUMIOSE ARE CUTTING EDGE—LITERALLY.
GIVE THEM A TRY. YOU WON'T BE DISAPPOINTED.
SWISH
THAT'S IT... IMAGINE WHAT THE FURFROU WILL LOOK LIKE AFTER THE GROOMING IS DONE... CUT ALONGSIDE THE LINES OF ITS BODY...
SWISH
SWISH
SWISH

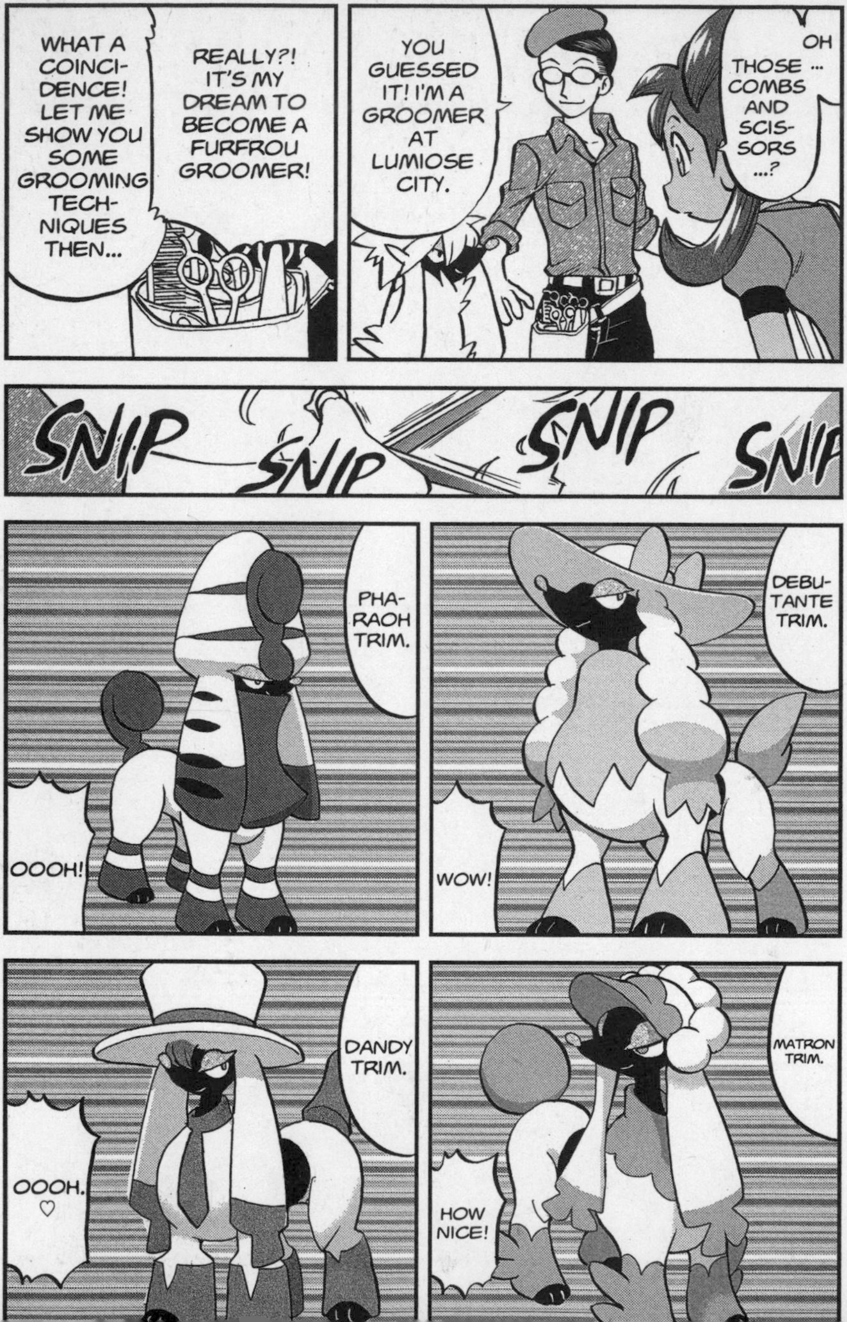
OH THOSE ... COMBS AND SCISSORS ...?
YOU GUESSED IT! I'M A GROOMER AT LUMIOSE CITY.
REALLY?! IT'S MY DREAM TO BECOME A FURFROU GROOMER!
WHAT A COINCIDENCE! LET ME SHOW YOU SOME GROOMING TECHNIQUES THEN...
SNIP
SNIP
SNIP
SNIP
DEBUTANTE TRIM.
WOW!
PHARAOH TRIM.
OOOH!
MATRON TRIM.
HOW NICE!
DANDY TRIM.
OOOH. ♡

Adventure 6 The Aegislash Agenda

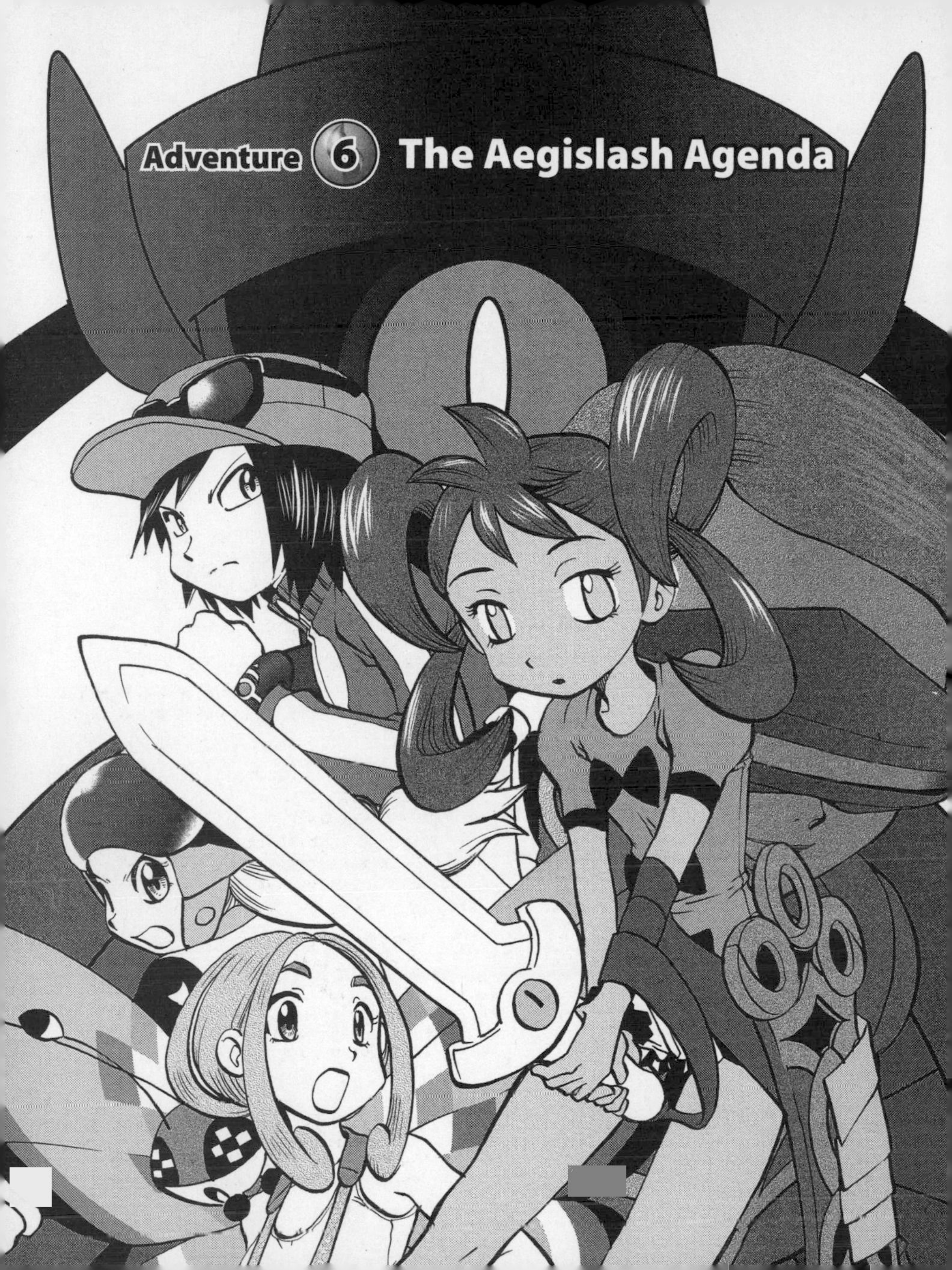

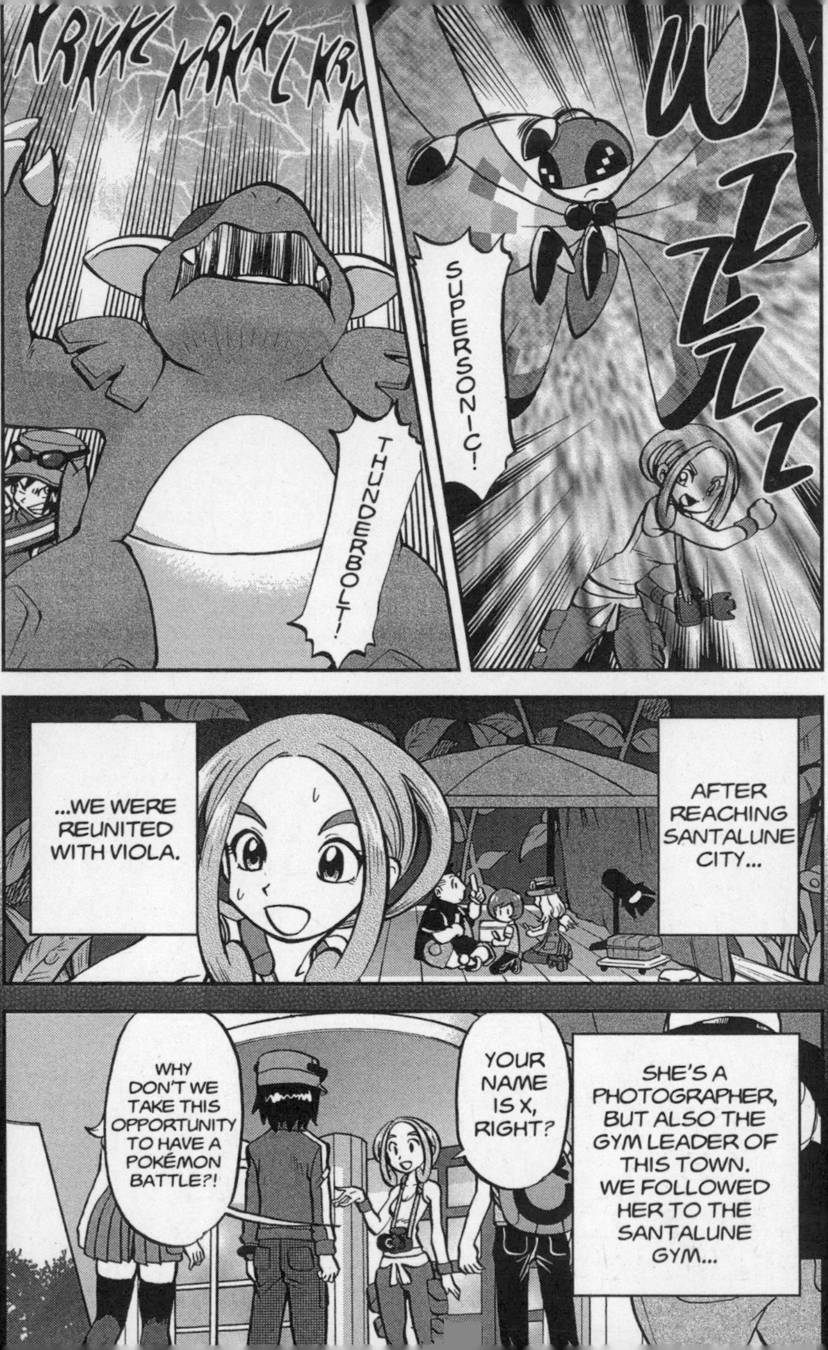

SUPERSONIC!
THUNDERBOLT!
AFTER REACHING SANTALUNE CITY...
...WE WERE REUNITED WITH VIOLA.
SHE'S A PHOTOGRAPHER, BUT ALSO THE GYM LEADER OF THIS TOWN. WE FOLLOWED HER TO THE SANTALUNE GYM...
YOUR NAME IS X, RIGHT?
WHY DON'T WE TAKE THIS OPPORTUNITY TO HAVE A POKÉMON BATTLE?!

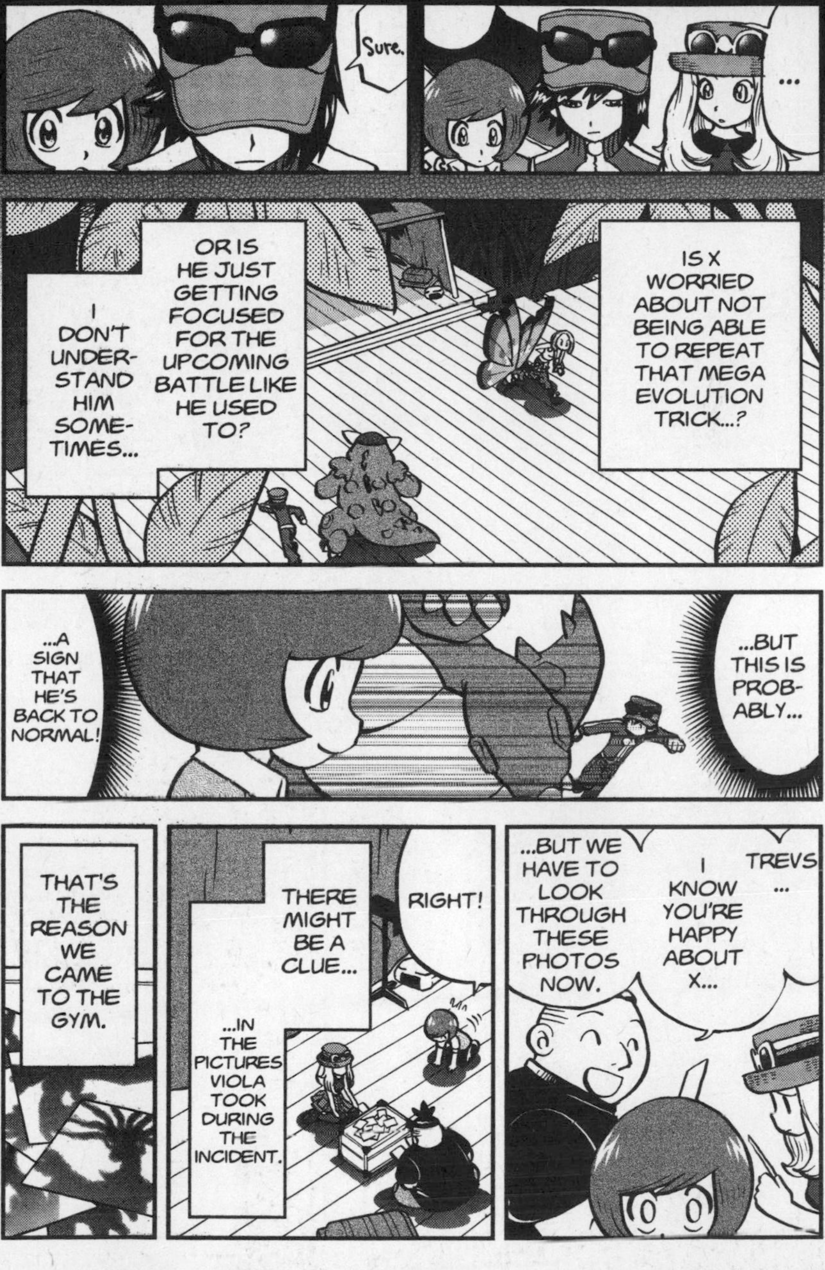
...
Sure.
IS X WORRIED ABOUT NOT BEING ABLE TO REPEAT THAT MEGA EVOLUTION TRICK...?
OR IS HE JUST GETTING FOCUSED FOR THE UPCOMING BATTLE LIKE HE USED TO?
I DON'T UNDERSTAND HIM SOMETIMES...
...BUT THIS IS PROBABLY...
...A SIGN THAT HE'S BACK TO NORMAL!
TREVS...
I KNOW YOU'RE HAPPY ABOUT X...
...BUT WE HAVE TO LOOK THROUGH THESE PHOTOS NOW.
RIGHT!
THERE MIGHT BE A CLUE...
...IN THE PICTURES VIOLA TOOK DURING THE INCIDENT.
THAT'S THE REASON WE CAME TO THE GYM.

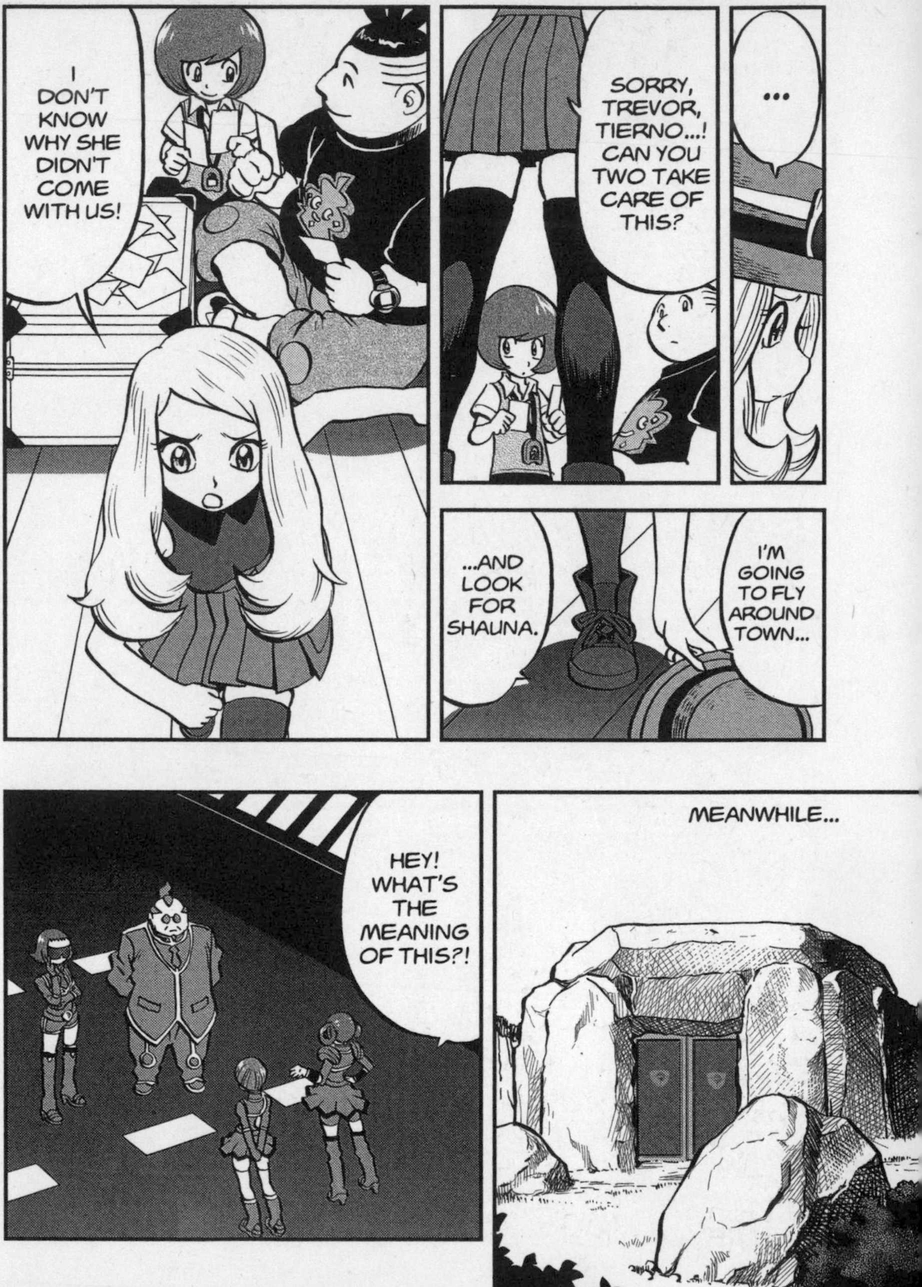
...
SORRY, TREVOR, TIERNO...! CAN YOU TWO TAKE CARE OF THIS?
I'M GOING TO FLY AROUND TOWN...
...AND LOOK FOR SHAUNA.
I DON'T KNOW WHY SHE DIDN'T COME WITH US!
MEANWHILE...
HEY! WHAT'S THE MEANING OF THIS?!

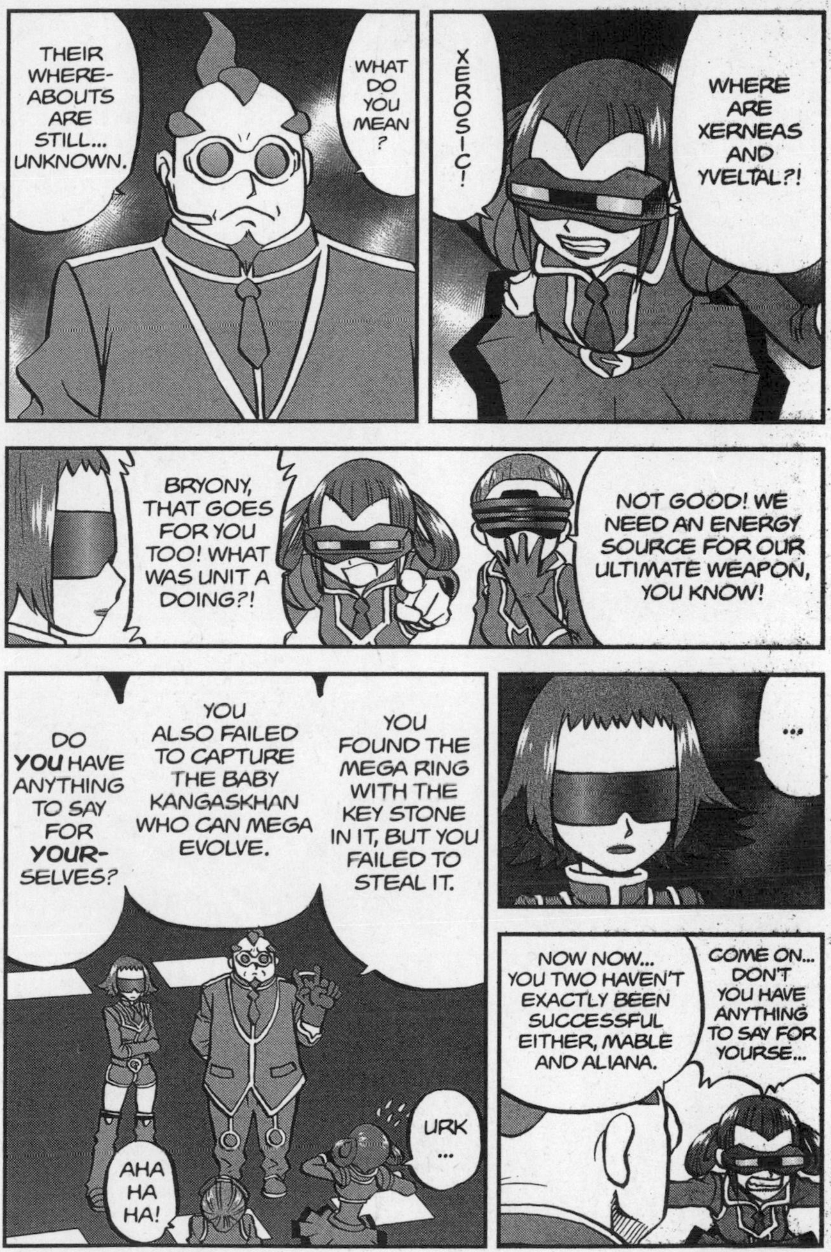
WHERE ARE XERNEAS AND YVELTAL?!
XEROSIC!
WHAT DO YOU MEAN?
THEIR WHERE-ABOUTS ARE STILL... UNKNOWN.
NOT GOOD! WE NEED AN ENERGY SOURCE FOR OUR ULTIMATE WEAPON, YOU KNOW!
BRYONY, THAT GOES FOR YOU TOO! WHAT WAS UNIT A DOING?!
...
COME ON... DON'T YOU HAVE ANYTHING TO SAY FOR YOURSE...
NOW NOW... YOU TWO HAVEN'T EXACTLY BEEN SUCCESSFUL EITHER, MABLE AND ALIANA.
YOU FOUND THE MEGA RING WITH THE KEY STONE IN IT, BUT YOU FAILED TO STEAL IT.
YOU ALSO FAILED TO CAPTURE THE BABY KANGASKHAN WHO CAN MEGA EVOLVE.
DO **YOU** HAVE ANYTHING TO SAY FOR **YOUR-**SELVES?
URK...
AHA HA HA!

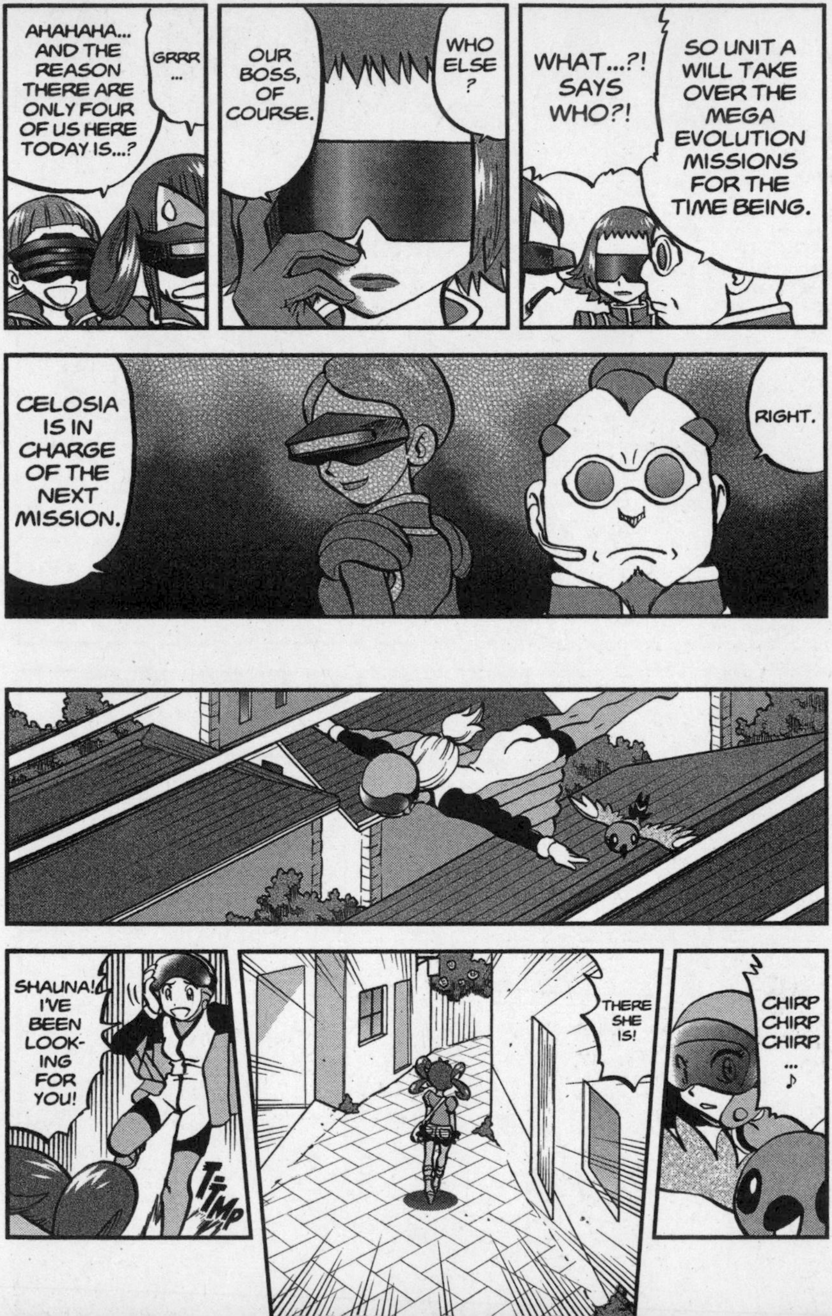
SO UNIT A WILL TAKE OVER THE MEGA EVOLUTION MISSIONS FOR THE TIME BEING.
WHAT...?! SAYS WHO?!
WHO ELSE?
OUR BOSS, OF COURSE.
AHAHAHA... AND THE REASON THERE ARE ONLY FOUR OF US HERE TODAY IS...?
GRRR...
RIGHT.
CELOSIA IS IN CHARGE OF THE NEXT MISSION.
CHIRP CHIRP CHIRP... ♪
THERE SHE IS!
SHAUNA! I'VE BEEN LOOKING FOR YOU!
TTMP

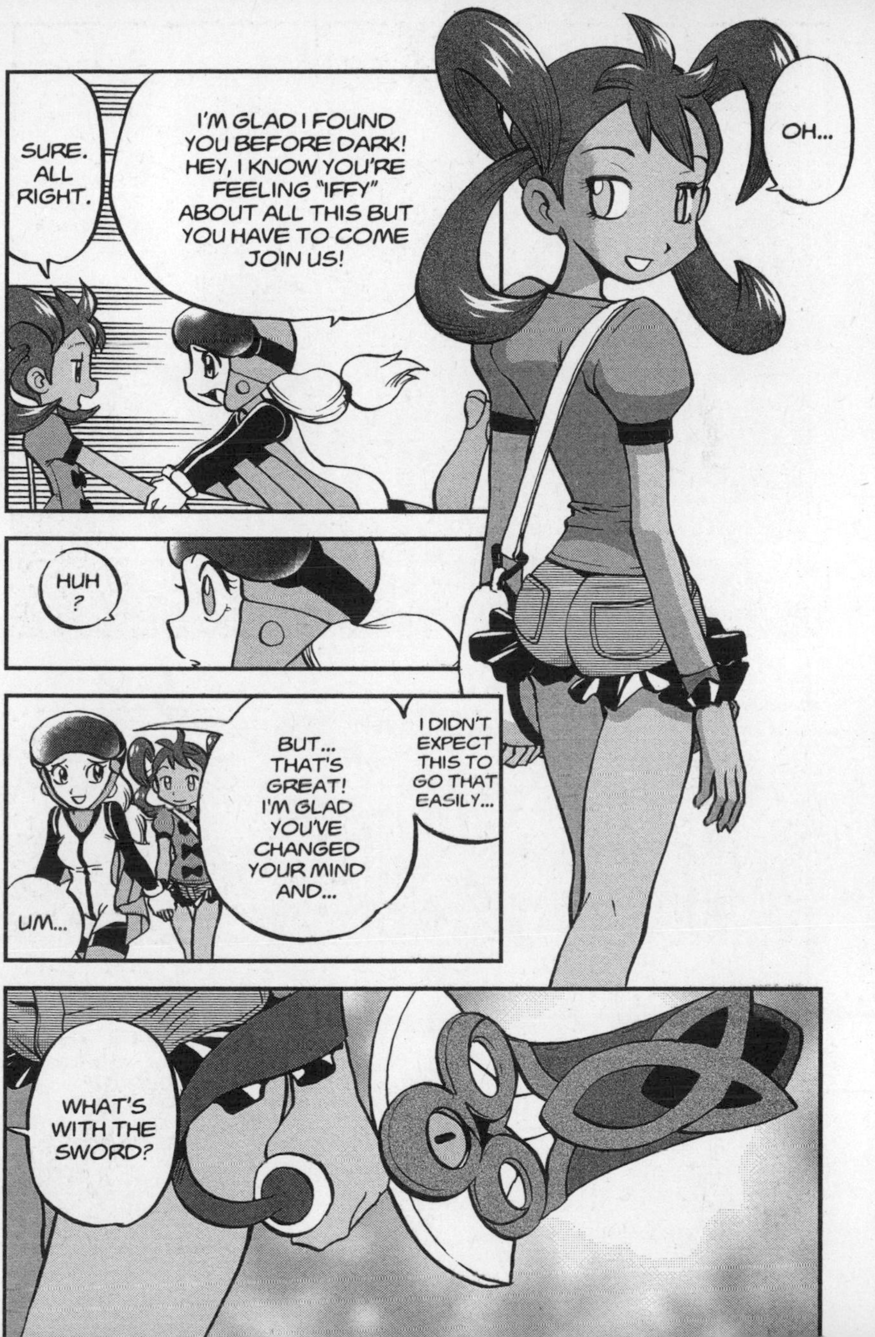
OH...
I DIDN'T EXPECT THIS TO GO THAT EASILY...
I'M GLAD I FOUND YOU BEFORE DARK! HEY, I KNOW YOU'RE FEELING "IFFY" ABOUT ALL THIS BUT YOU HAVE TO COME JOIN US!
SURE. ALL RIGHT.
HUH?
BUT... THAT'S GREAT! I'M GLAD YOU'VE CHANGED YOUR MIND AND...
UM...
WHAT'S WITH THE SWORD?

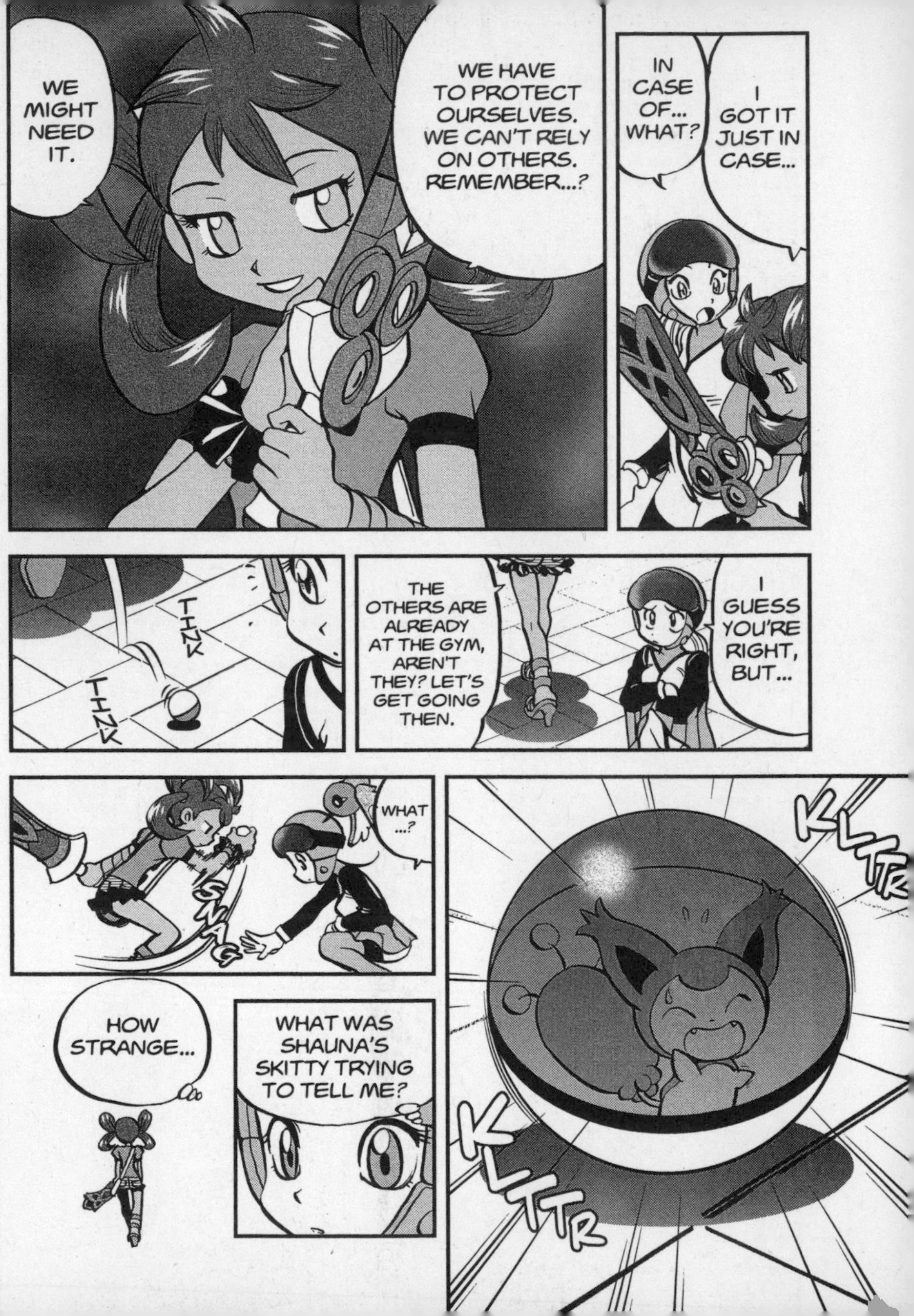

I GOT IT JUST IN CASE...
IN CASE OF... WHAT?
WE HAVE TO PROTECT OURSELVES. WE CAN'T RELY ON OTHERS. REMEMBER...?
WE MIGHT NEED IT.
I GUESS YOU'RE RIGHT, BUT...
THE OTHERS ARE ALREADY AT THE GYM, AREN'T THEY? LET'S GET GOING THEN.
TINK
TINK
KLTTR
KLTTR
WHAT ...?
SNAG
WHAT WAS SHAUNA'S SKITTY TRYING TO TELL ME?
HOW STRANGE...

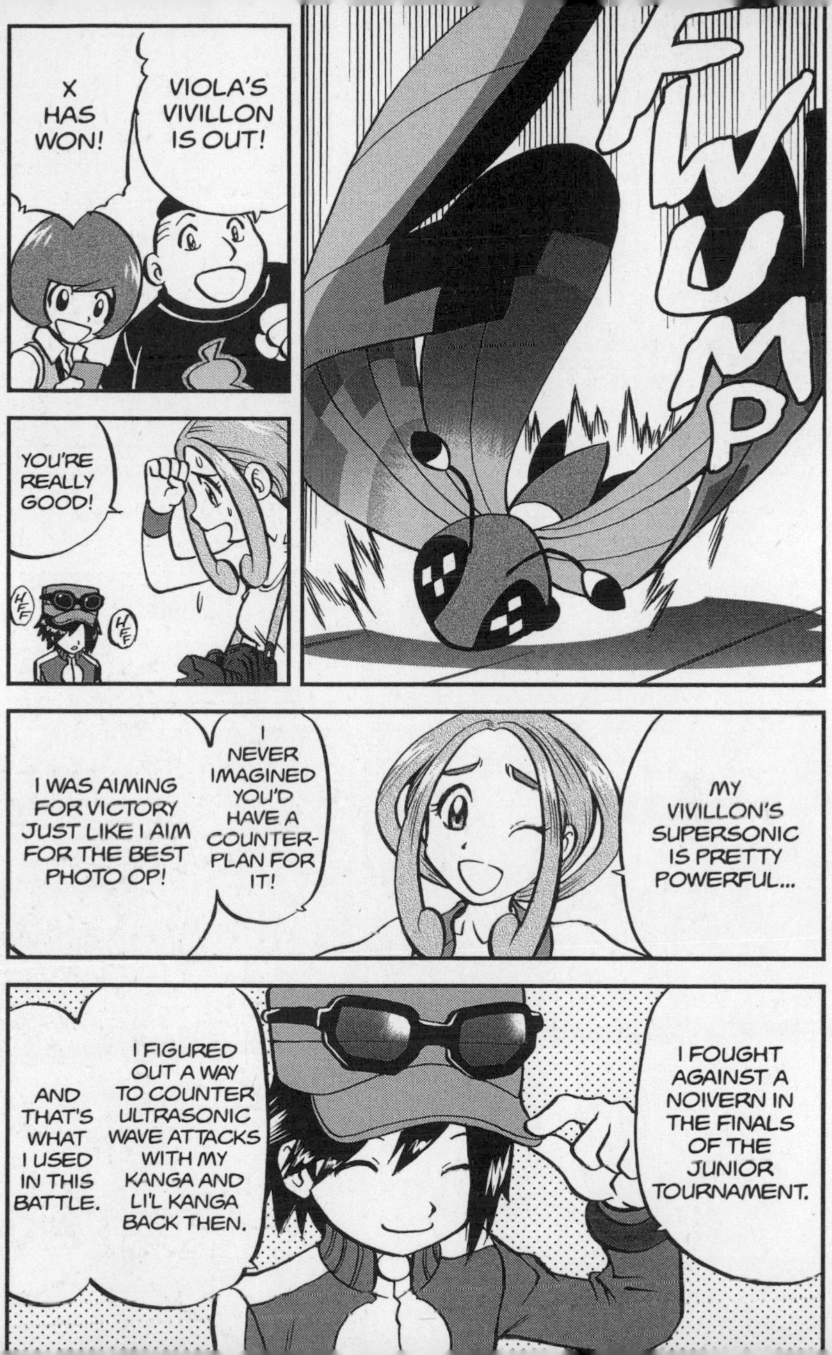
FWUMP
VIOLA'S VIVILLON IS OUT!
X HAS WON!
YOU'RE REALLY GOOD!
HFF
HFF
MY VIVILLON'S SUPERSONIC IS PRETTY POWERFUL...
I NEVER IMAGINED YOU'D HAVE A COUNTER-PLAN FOR IT!
I WAS AIMING FOR VICTORY JUST LIKE I AIM FOR THE BEST PHOTO OP!
I FOUGHT AGAINST A NOIVERN IN THE FINALS OF THE JUNIOR TOURNAMENT.
I FIGURED OUT A WAY TO COUNTER ULTRASONIC WAVE ATTACKS WITH MY KANGA AND LI'L KANGA BACK THEN.
AND THAT'S WHAT I USED IN THIS BATTLE.

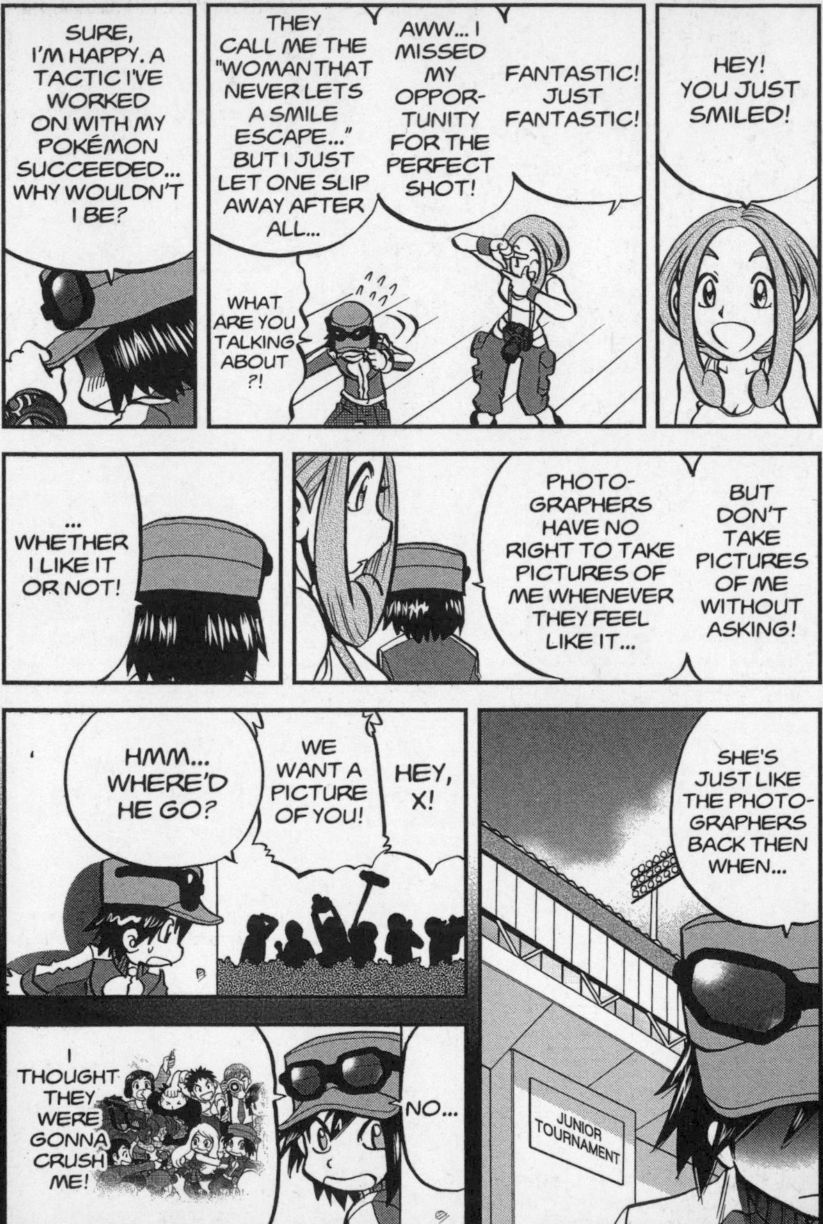
HEY! YOU JUST SMILED!
FANTASTIC! JUST FANTASTIC!
AWW... I MISSED MY OPPOR-TUNITY FOR THE PERFECT SHOT!
THEY CALL ME THE "WOMAN THAT NEVER LETS A SMILE ESCAPE..." BUT I JUST LET ONE SLIP AWAY AFTER ALL...
WHAT ARE YOU TALKING ABOUT ?!
SURE, I'M HAPPY. A TACTIC I'VE WORKED ON WITH MY POKÉMON SUCCEEDED... WHY WOULDN'T I BE?
PHOTO-GRAPHERS HAVE NO RIGHT TO TAKE PICTURES OF ME WHENEVER THEY FEEL LIKE IT...
BUT DON'T TAKE PICTURES OF ME WITHOUT ASKING!
... WHETHER I LIKE IT OR NOT!
SHE'S JUST LIKE THE PHOTO-GRAPHERS BACK THEN WHEN...
JUNIOR TOURNAMENT
HEY, X!
WE WANT A PICTURE OF YOU!
HMM... WHERE'D HE GO?
NO...
I THOUGHT THEY WERE GONNA CRUSH ME!

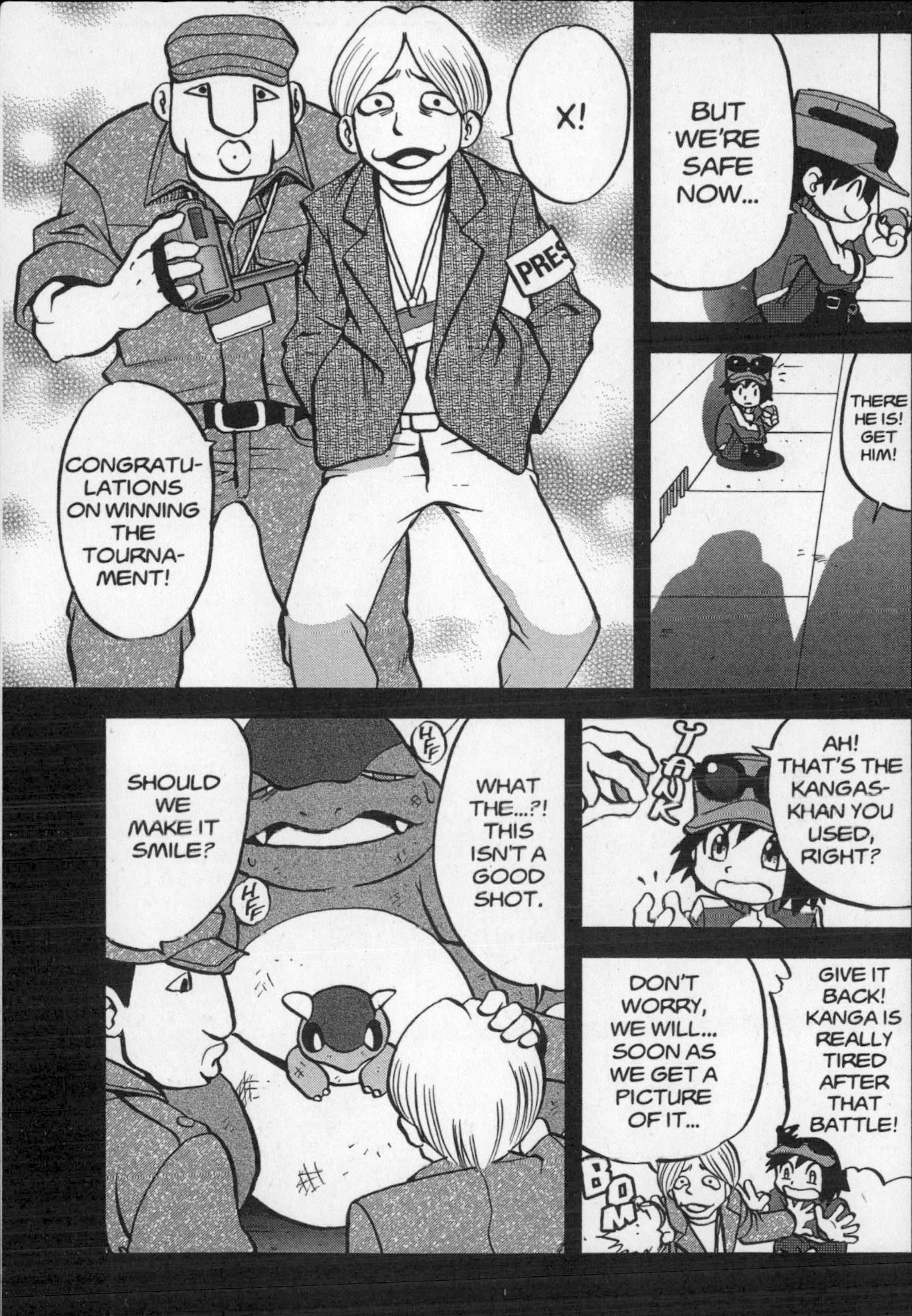
BUT WE'RE SAFE NOW...
THERE HE IS! GET HIM!
X!
CONGRATULATIONS ON WINNING THE TOURNAMENT!
PRES
AH! THAT'S THE KANGASKHAN YOU USED, RIGHT?
GIVE IT BACK! KANGA IS REALLY TIRED AFTER THAT BATTLE!
DON'T WORRY, WE WILL... SOON AS WE GET A PICTURE OF IT...
HFF
WHAT THE...?! THIS ISN'T A GOOD SHOT.
SHOULD WE MAKE IT SMILE?
HFF

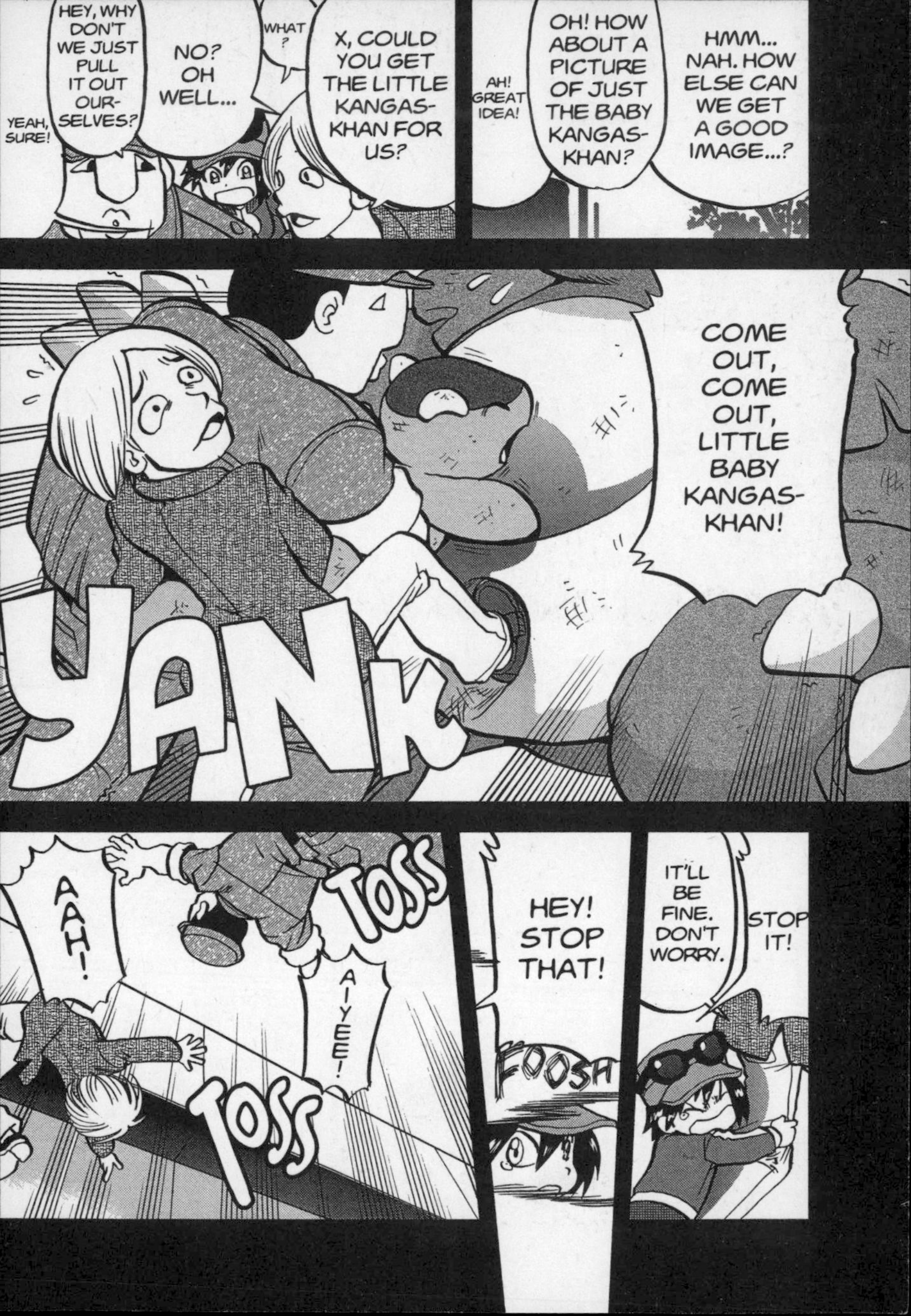
HMM... NAH. HOW ELSE CAN WE GET A GOOD IMAGE...?
OH! HOW ABOUT A PICTURE OF JUST THE BABY KANGASKHAN?
AH! GREAT IDEA!
X, COULD YOU GET THE LITTLE KANGASKHAN FOR US?
WHAT?
NO? OH WELL...
HEY, WHY DON'T WE JUST PULL IT OUT OURSELVES?
YEAH, SURE!
COME OUT, COME OUT, LITTLE BABY KANGASKHAN!
YANK
STOP IT!
IT'LL BE FINE. DON'T WORRY.
HEY! STOP THAT!
FOOSH
TOSS
AIYEE!
AAH!
TOSS

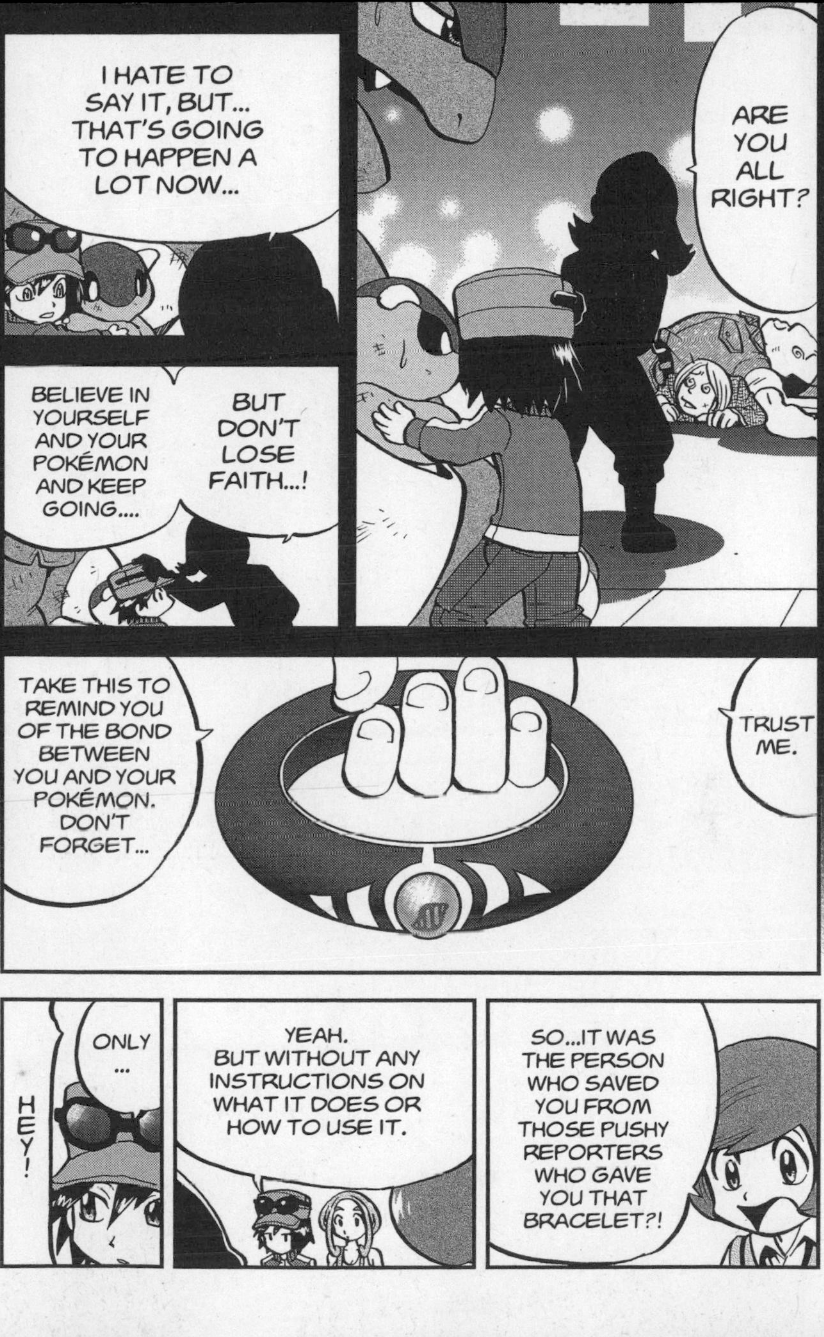
ARE YOU ALL RIGHT?
I HATE TO SAY IT, BUT... THAT'S GOING TO HAPPEN A LOT NOW...
BUT DON'T LOSE FAITH...!
BELIEVE IN YOURSELF AND YOUR POKÉMON AND KEEP GOING....
TRUST ME.
TAKE THIS TO REMIND YOU OF THE BOND BETWEEN YOU AND YOUR POKÉMON. DON'T FORGET...
SO...IT WAS THE PERSON WHO SAVED YOU FROM THOSE PUSHY REPORTERS WHO GAVE YOU THAT BRACELET?!
YEAH. BUT WITHOUT ANY INSTRUCTIONS ON WHAT IT DOES OR HOW TO USE IT.
ONLY ...
HEY!

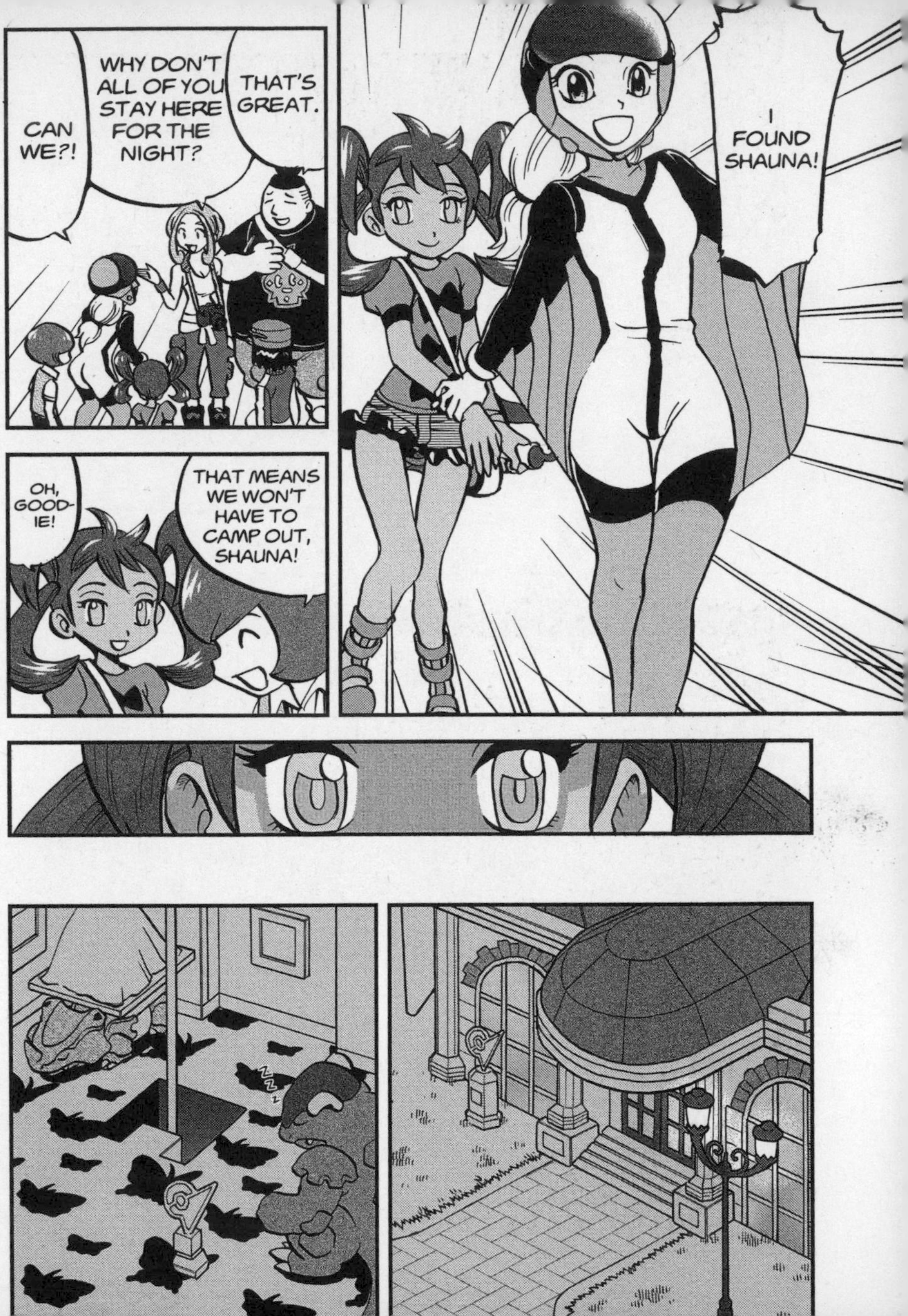
I FOUND SHAUNA!
THAT'S GREAT.
WHY DON'T ALL OF YOU STAY HERE FOR THE NIGHT?
CAN WE?!
THAT MEANS WE WON'T HAVE TO CAMP OUT, SHAUNA!
OH, GOODIE!

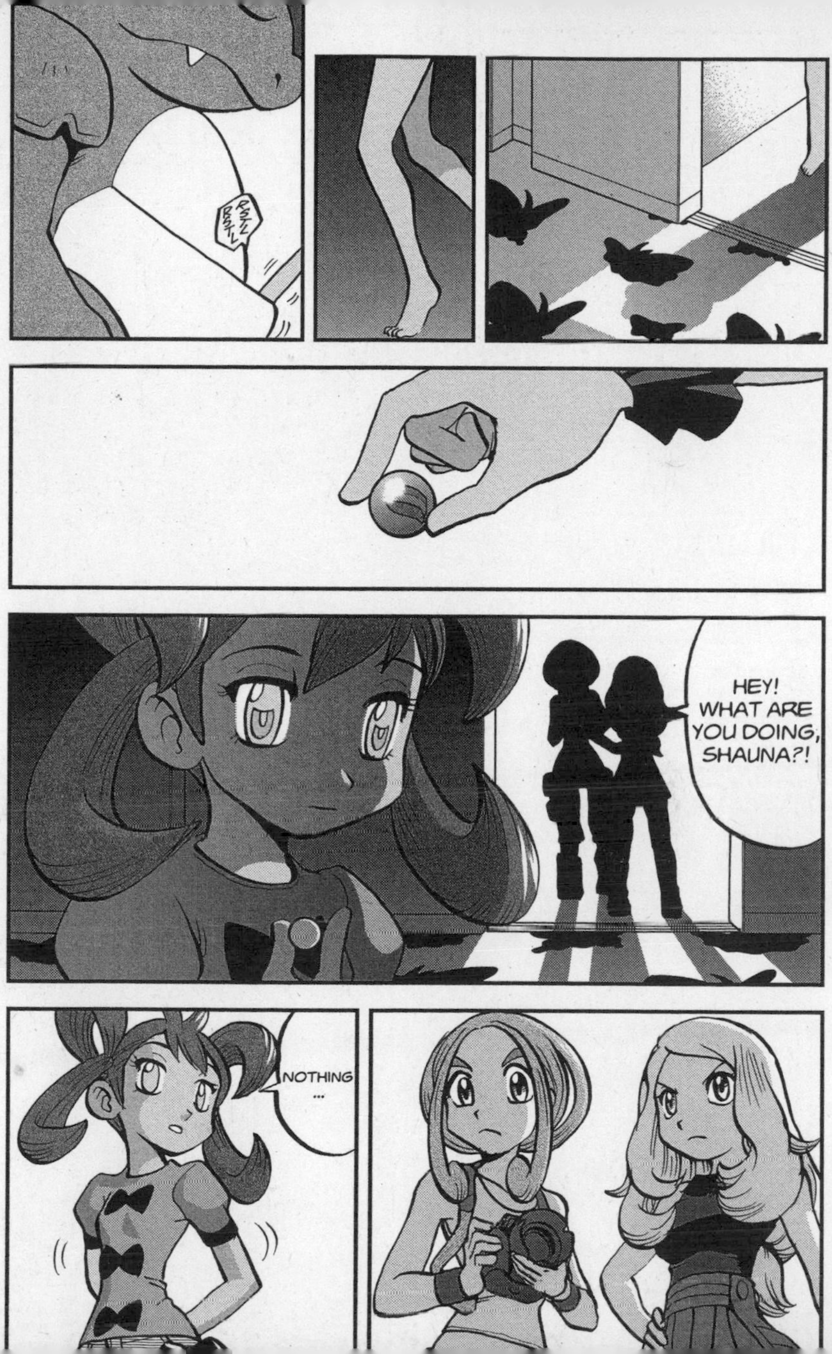
HEY! WHAT ARE YOU DOING, SHAUNA?!
NOTHING ...

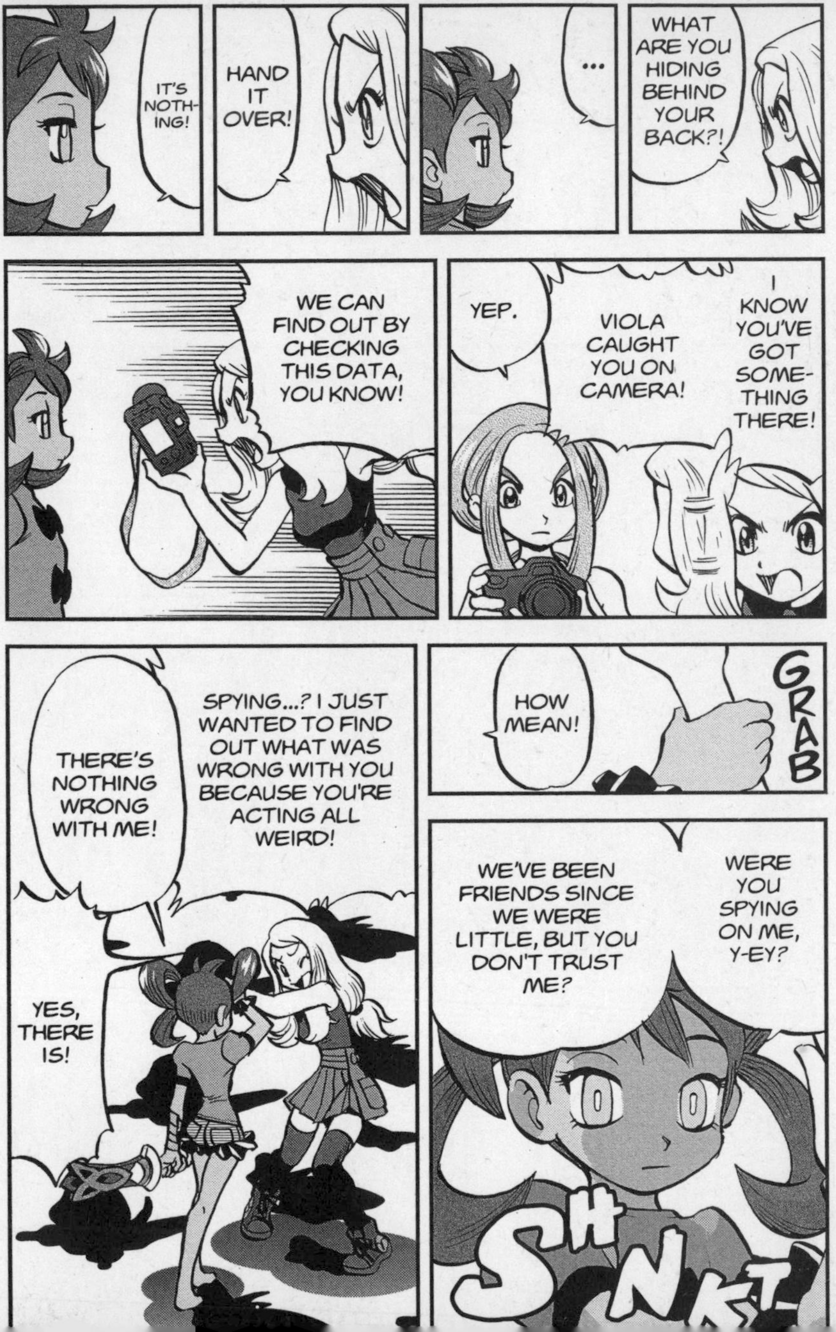
WHAT ARE YOU HIDING BEHIND YOUR BACK?!
...
HAND IT OVER!
IT'S NOTHING!
I KNOW YOU'VE GOT SOMETHING THERE!
VIOLA CAUGHT YOU ON CAMERA!
YEP.
WE CAN FIND OUT BY CHECKING THIS DATA, YOU KNOW!
GRAB
HOW MEAN!
WERE YOU SPYING ON ME, Y-EY?
WE'VE BEEN FRIENDS SINCE WE WERE LITTLE, BUT YOU DON'T TRUST ME?
SHNKT
SPYING...? I JUST WANTED TO FIND OUT WHAT WAS WRONG WITH YOU BECAUSE YOU'RE ACTING ALL WEIRD!
THERE'S NOTHING WRONG WITH ME!
YES, THERE IS!

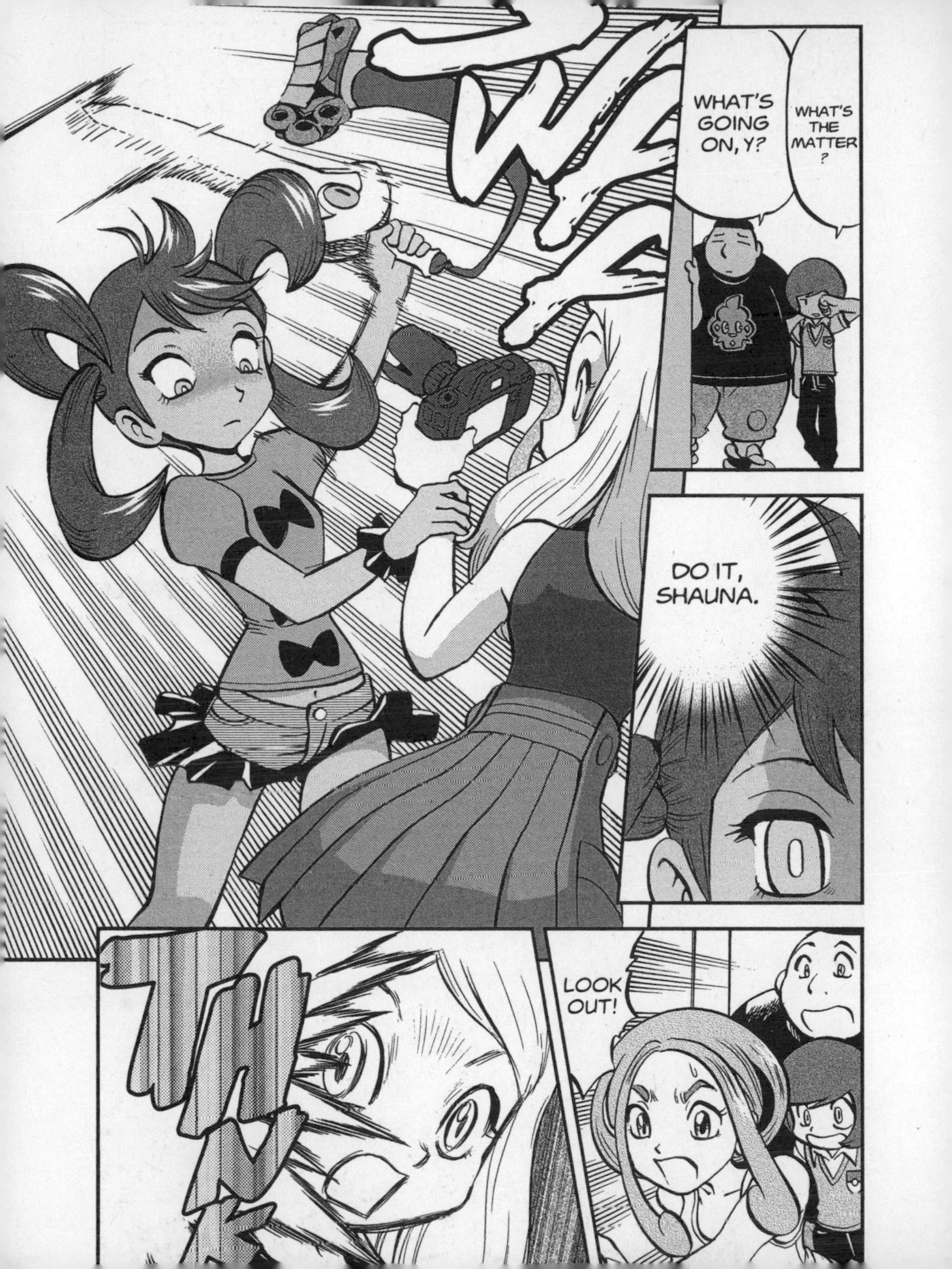
WHAT'S THE MATTER?
WHAT'S GOING ON, Y?
DO IT, SHAUNA.
LOOK OUT!

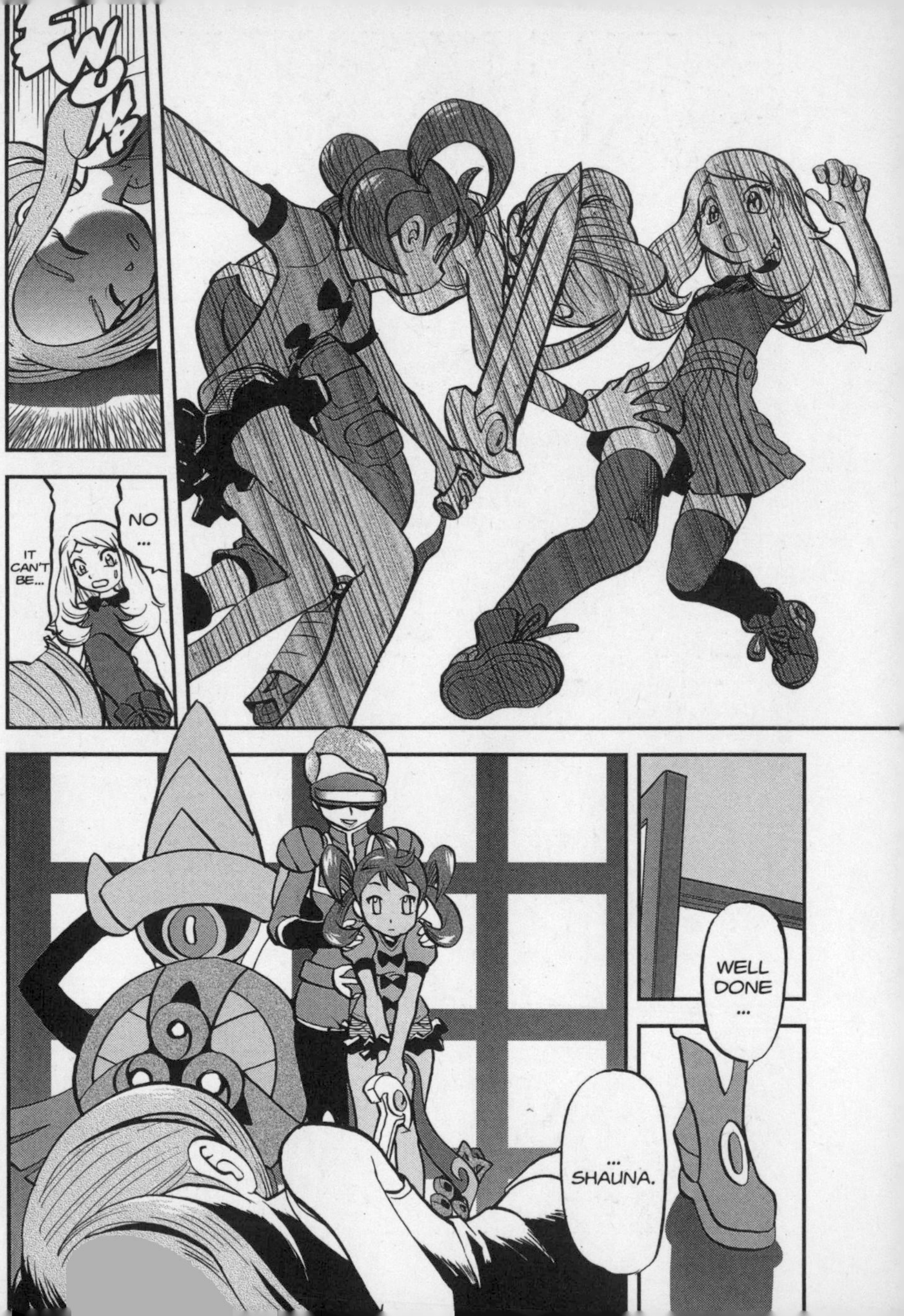
WOMP
NO ...
IT CAN'T BE...
WELL DONE ...
... SHAUNA.

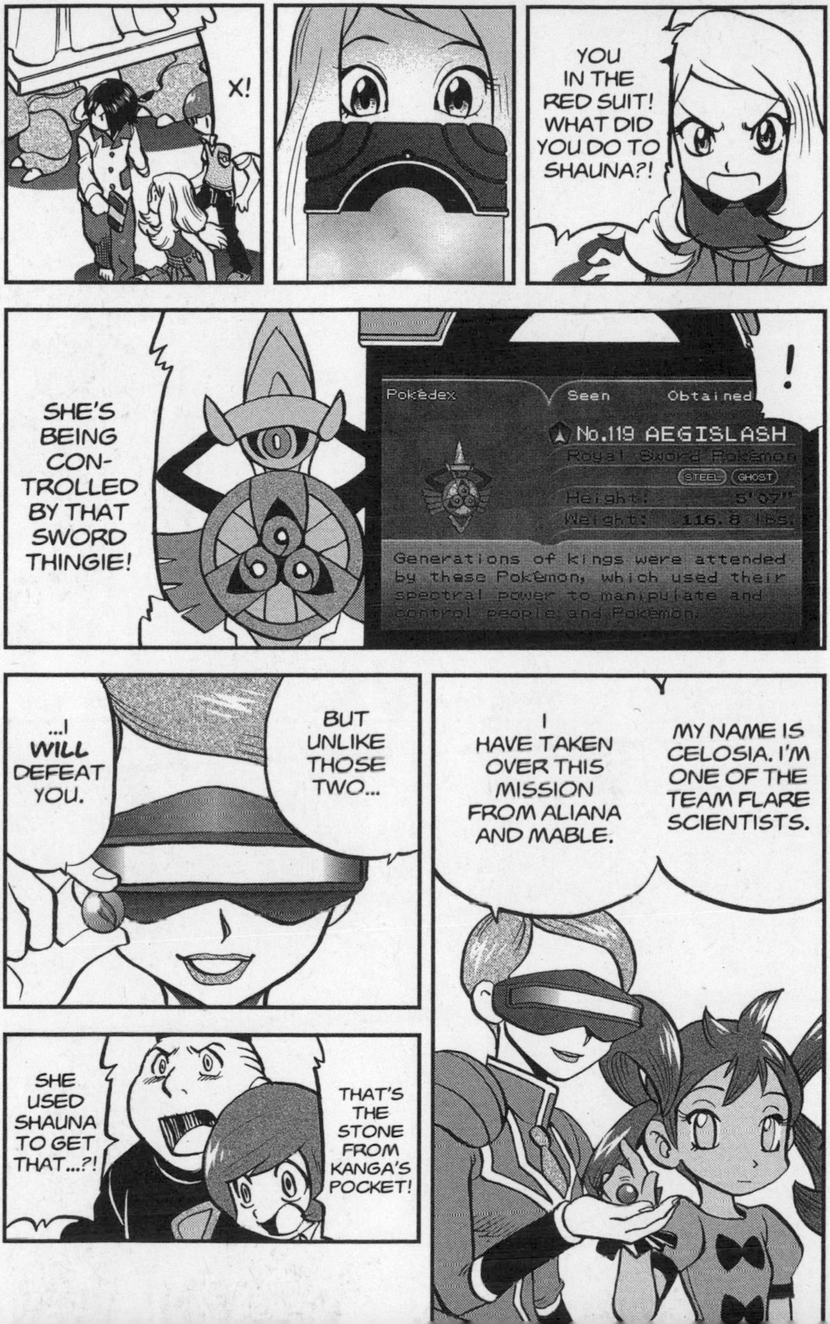

YOU IN THE RED SUIT! WHAT DID YOU DO TO SHAUNA?!
X!
!
SHE'S BEING CON-TROLLED BY THAT SWORD THINGIE!
Pokédex
Seen
Obtained
No.119 AEGISLASH
Royal Sword Pokémon
STEEL
GHOST
Height: 5'07"
Weight: 116.8 lbs.
Generations of kings were attended by these Pokémon, which used their spectral power to manipulate and control people and Pokémon.
MY NAME IS CELOSIA. I'M ONE OF THE TEAM FLARE SCIENTISTS.
I HAVE TAKEN OVER THIS MISSION FROM ALIANA AND MABLE.
BUT UNLIKE THOSE TWO...
...I **WILL** DEFEAT YOU.
THAT'S THE STONE FROM KANGA'S POCKET!
SHE USED SHAUNA TO GET THAT...?!

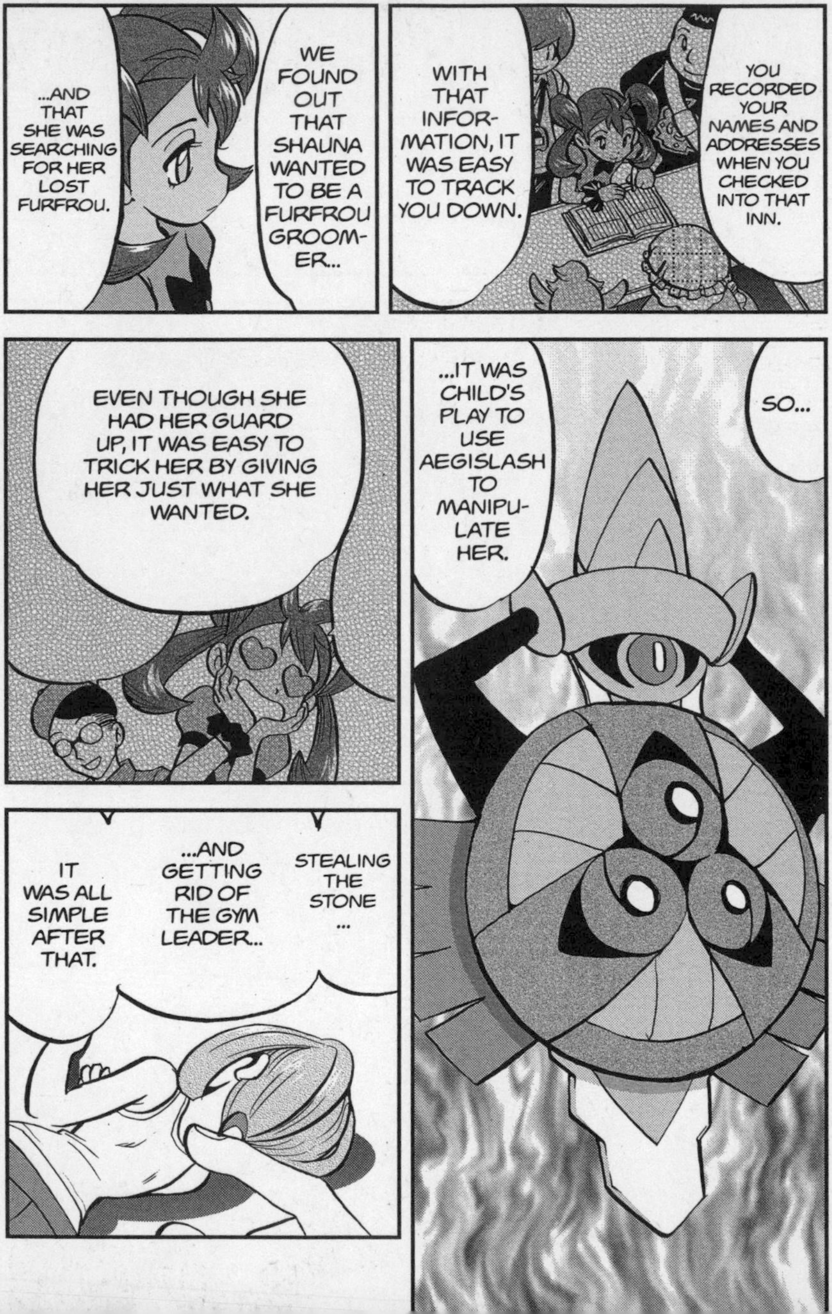
YOU RECORDED YOUR NAMES AND ADDRESSES WHEN YOU CHECKED INTO THAT INN.
WITH THAT INFOR-MATION, IT WAS EASY TO TRACK YOU DOWN.
WE FOUND OUT THAT SHAUNA WANTED TO BE A FURFROU GROOM-ER...
...AND THAT SHE WAS SEARCHING FOR HER LOST FURFROU.
SO...
...IT WAS CHILD'S PLAY TO USE AEGISLASH TO MANIPU-LATE HER.
EVEN THOUGH SHE HAD HER GUARD UP, IT WAS EASY TO TRICK HER BY GIVING HER JUST WHAT SHE WANTED.
STEALING THE STONE ...
...AND GETTING RID OF THE GYM LEADER...
IT WAS ALL SIMPLE AFTER THAT.

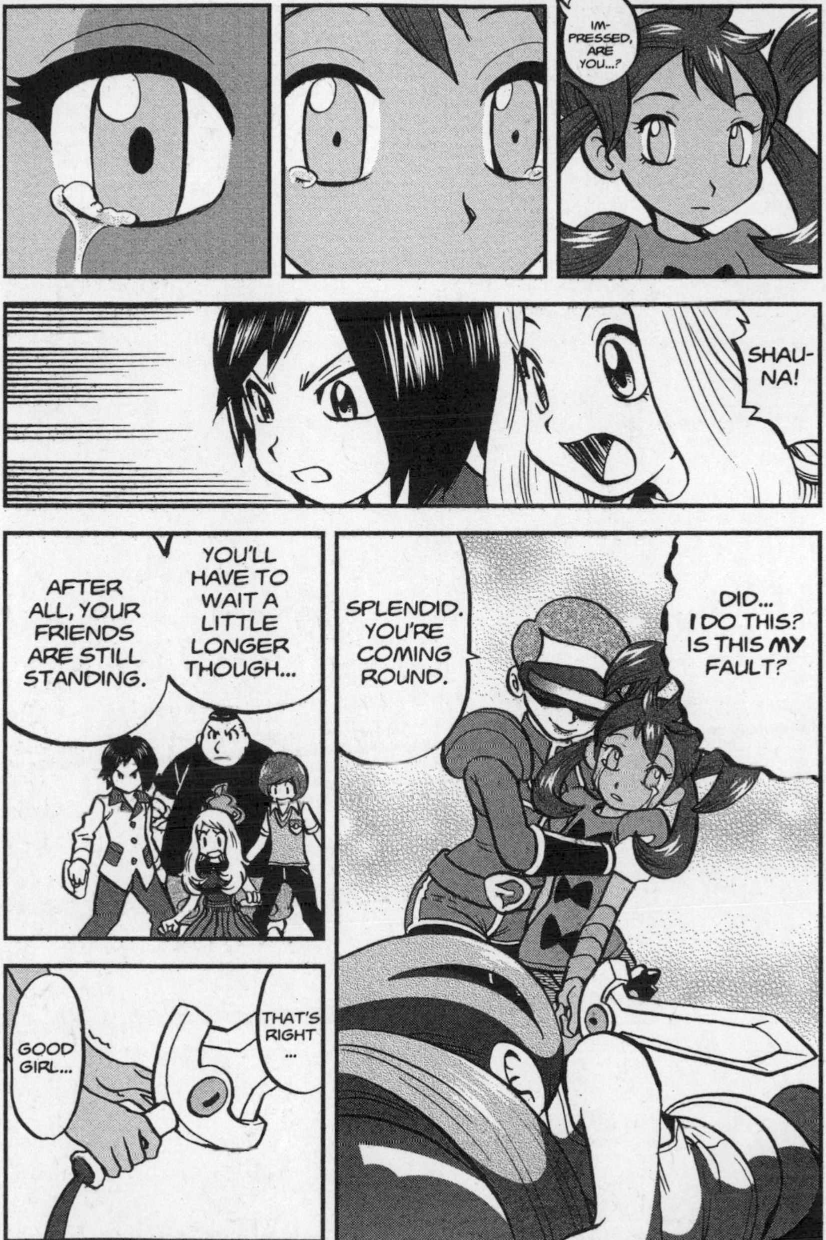
IM-PRESSED, ARE YOU...?
SHAU-NA!
DID... I DO THIS? IS THIS **MY** FAULT?
SPLENDID. YOU'RE COMING ROUND.
YOU'LL HAVE TO WAIT A LITTLE LONGER THOUGH...
AFTER ALL, YOUR FRIENDS ARE STILL STANDING.
THAT'S RIGHT ...
GOOD GIRL...

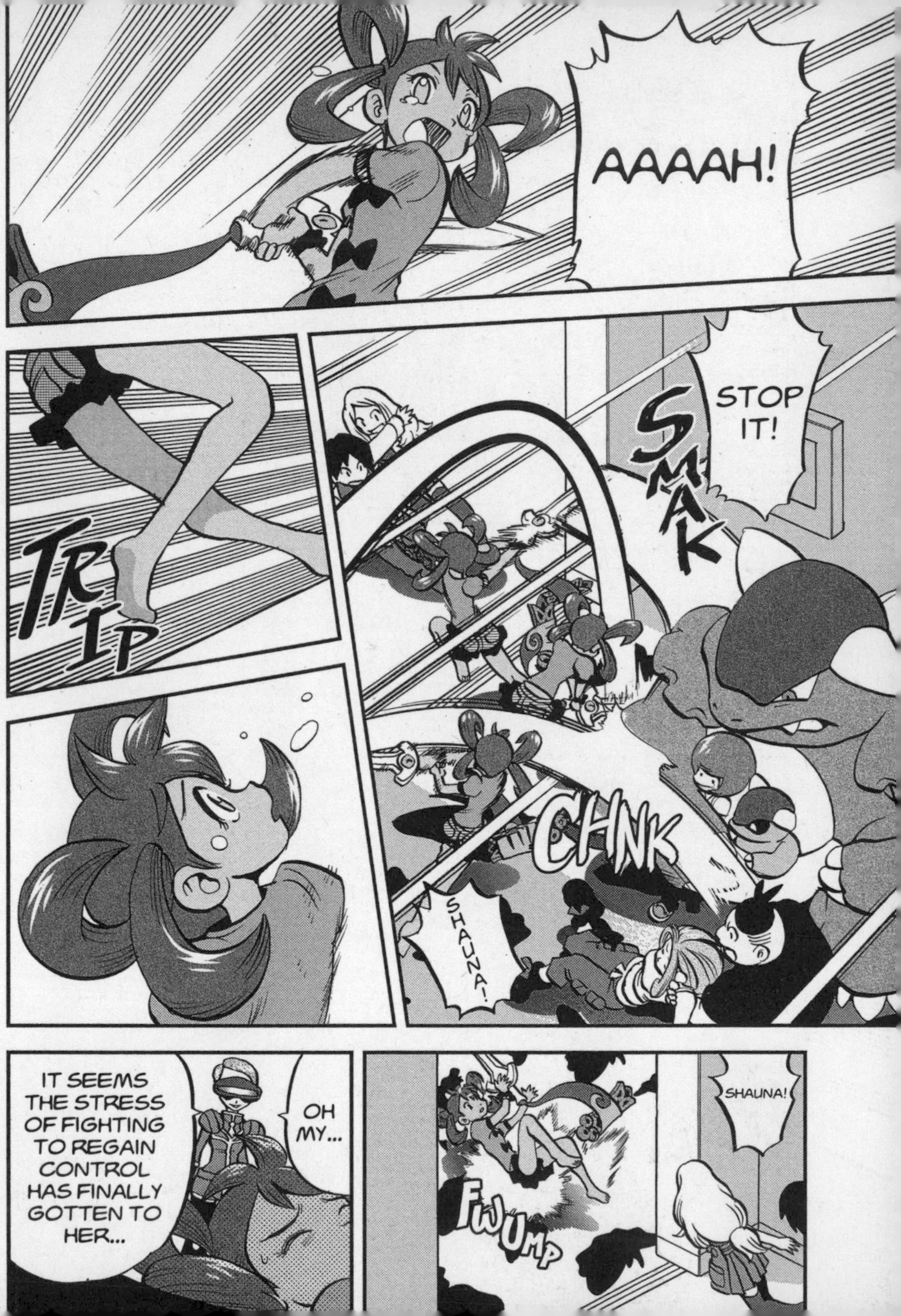
AAAAH!
STOP IT!
SMAK
CHNK
SHAUNA!
TRIP
SHAUNA!
FWUMP
OH MY...
IT SEEMS THE STRESS OF FIGHTING TO REGAIN CONTROL HAS FINALLY GOTTEN TO HER...

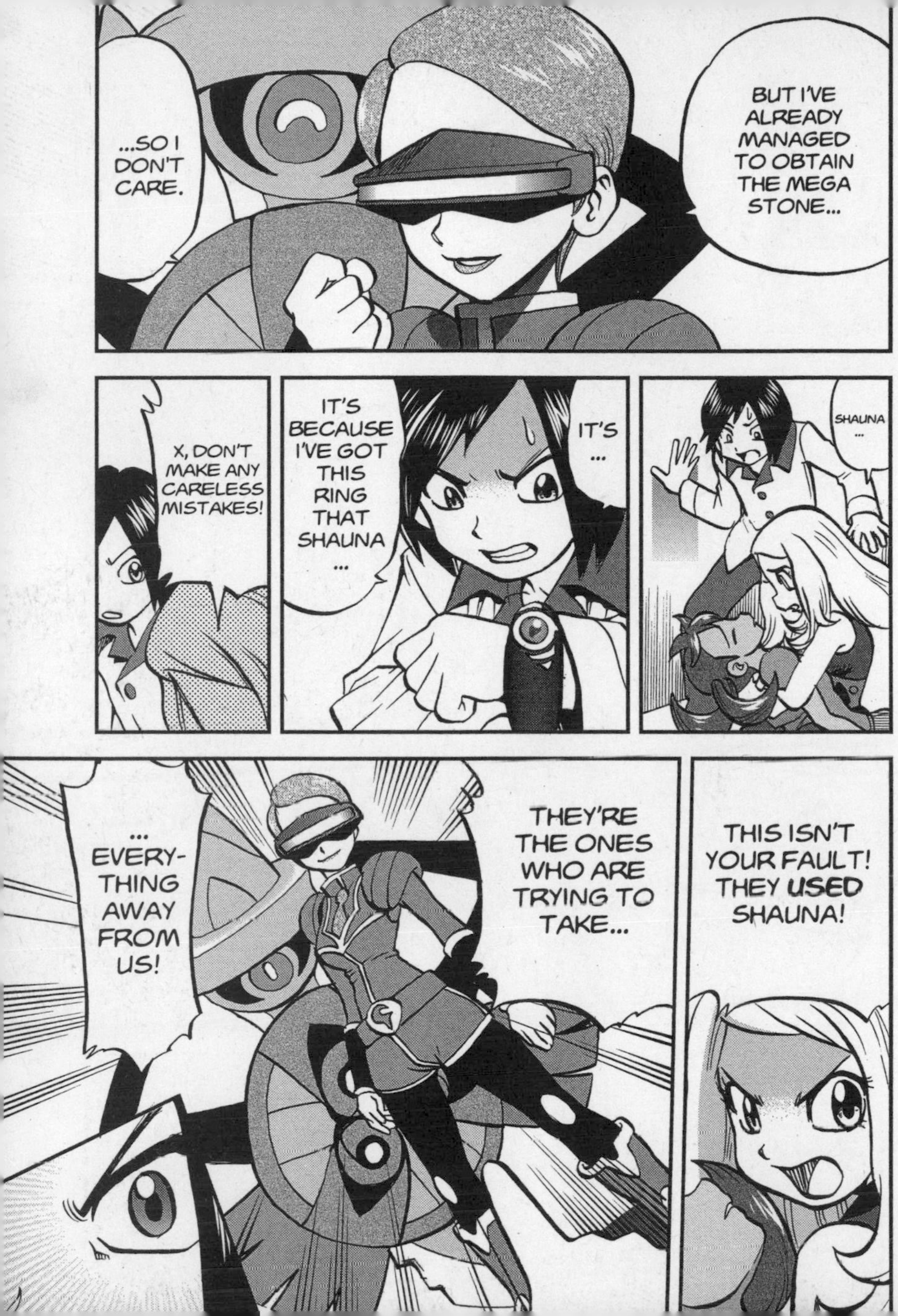
BUT I'VE ALREADY MANAGED TO OBTAIN THE MEGA STONE...
...SO I DON'T CARE.
SHAUNA ...
IT'S ...
IT'S BECAUSE I'VE GOT THIS RING THAT SHAUNA ...
X, DON'T MAKE ANY CARELESS MISTAKES!
THIS ISN'T YOUR FAULT! THEY **USED** SHAUNA!
THEY'RE THE ONES WHO ARE TRYING TO TAKE...
... EVERYTHING AWAY FROM US!

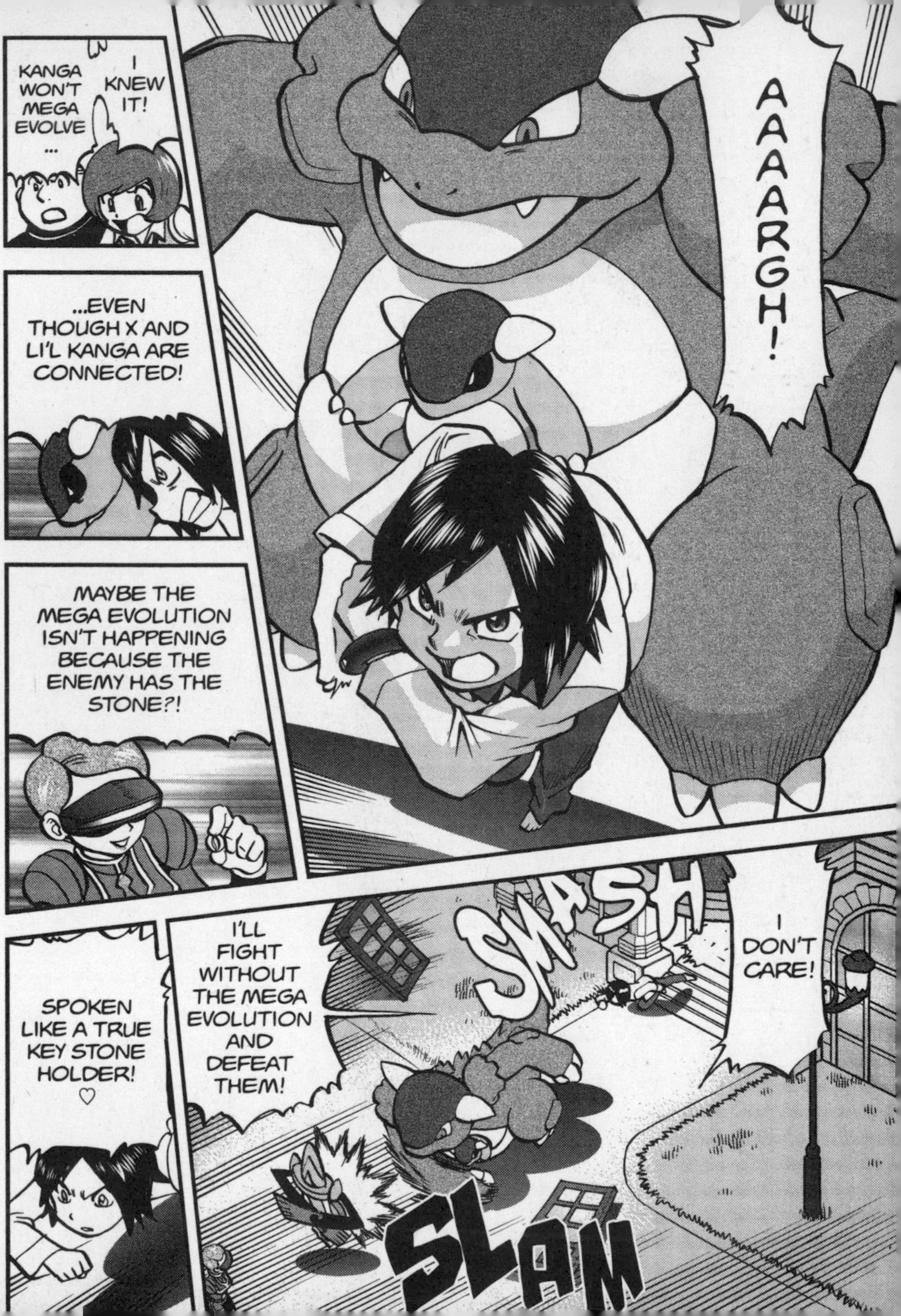
AAAAARGH!
I KNEW IT!
KANGA WON'T MEGA EVOLVE ...
...EVEN THOUGH X AND LI'L KANGA ARE CONNECTED!
MAYBE THE MEGA EVOLUTION ISN'T HAPPENING BECAUSE THE ENEMY HAS THE STONE?!
I DON'T CARE!
SMASH
I'LL FIGHT WITHOUT THE MEGA EVOLUTION AND DEFEAT THEM!
SLAM
SPOKEN LIKE A TRUE KEY STONE HOLDER! ♡

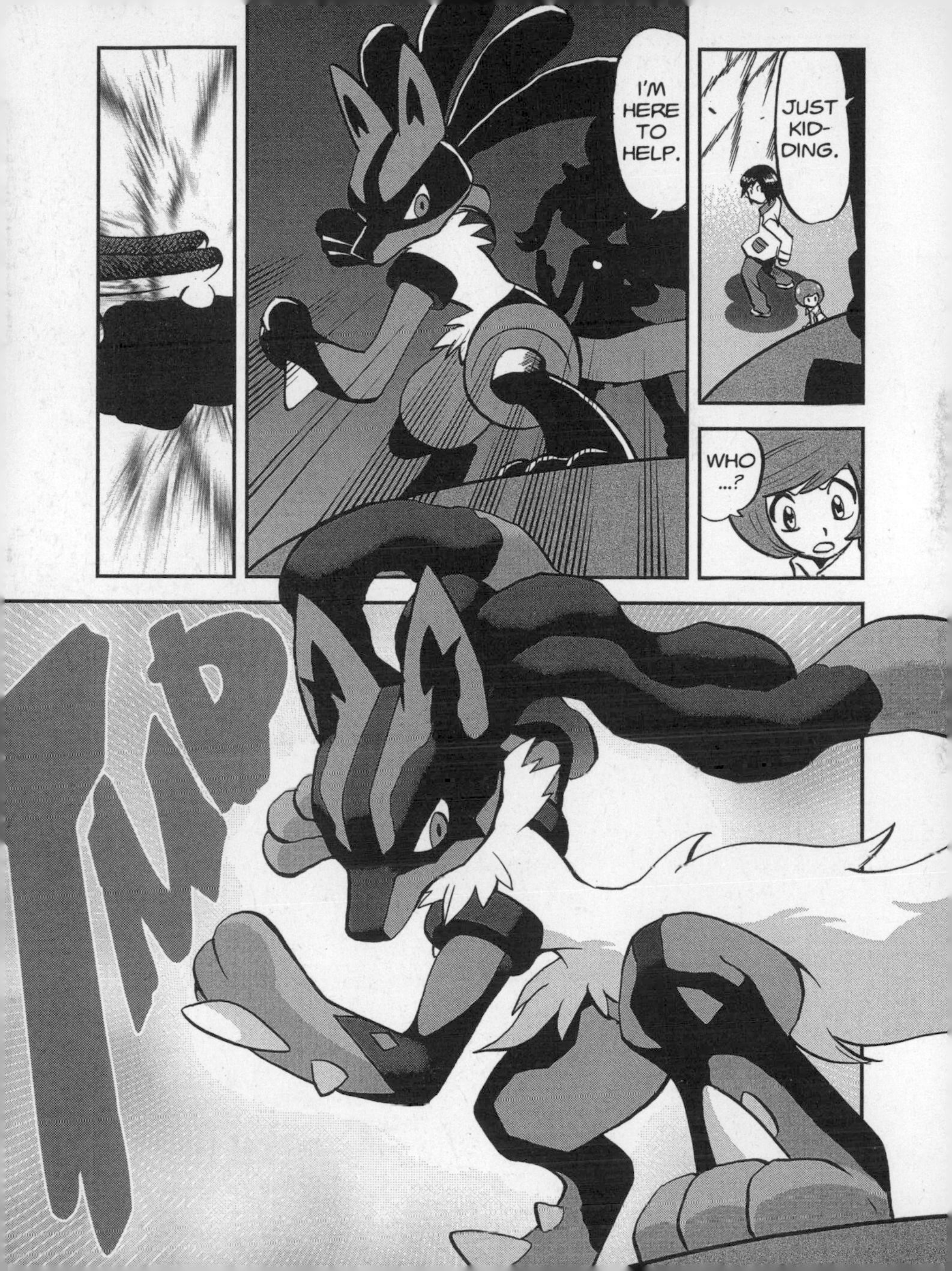
JUST KID-DING.
WHO ...?
I'M HERE TO HELP.

Current Location

Santalune City

Many beginning Trainers gather in this friendly city to start a Pokémon journey.

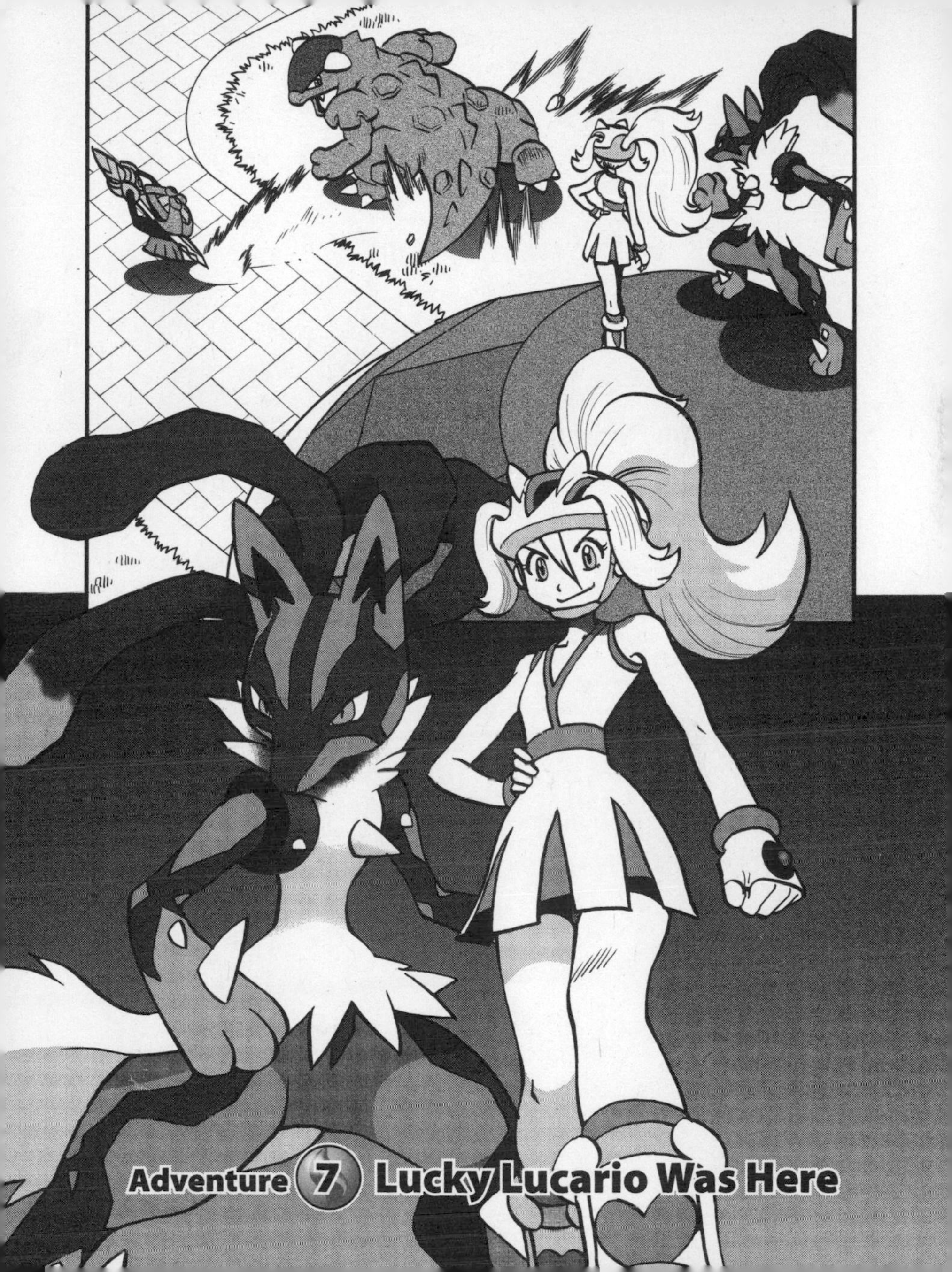
Adventure 7 Lucky Lucario Was Here

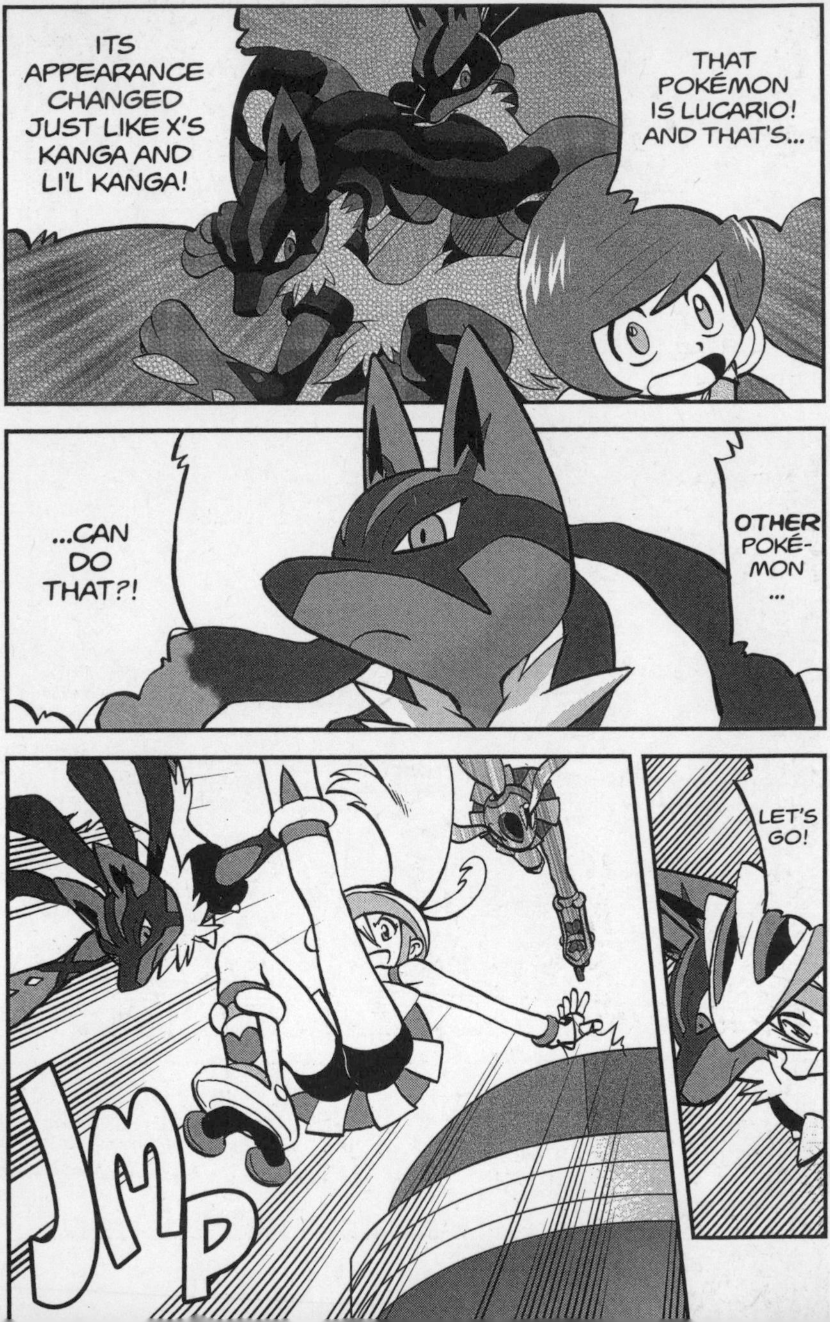
THAT POKÉMON IS LUCARIO! AND THAT'S...
ITS APPEARANCE CHANGED JUST LIKE X'S KANGA AND LI'L KANGA!
OTHER POKÉ-MON ...
...CAN DO THAT?!
LET'S GO!
JMP

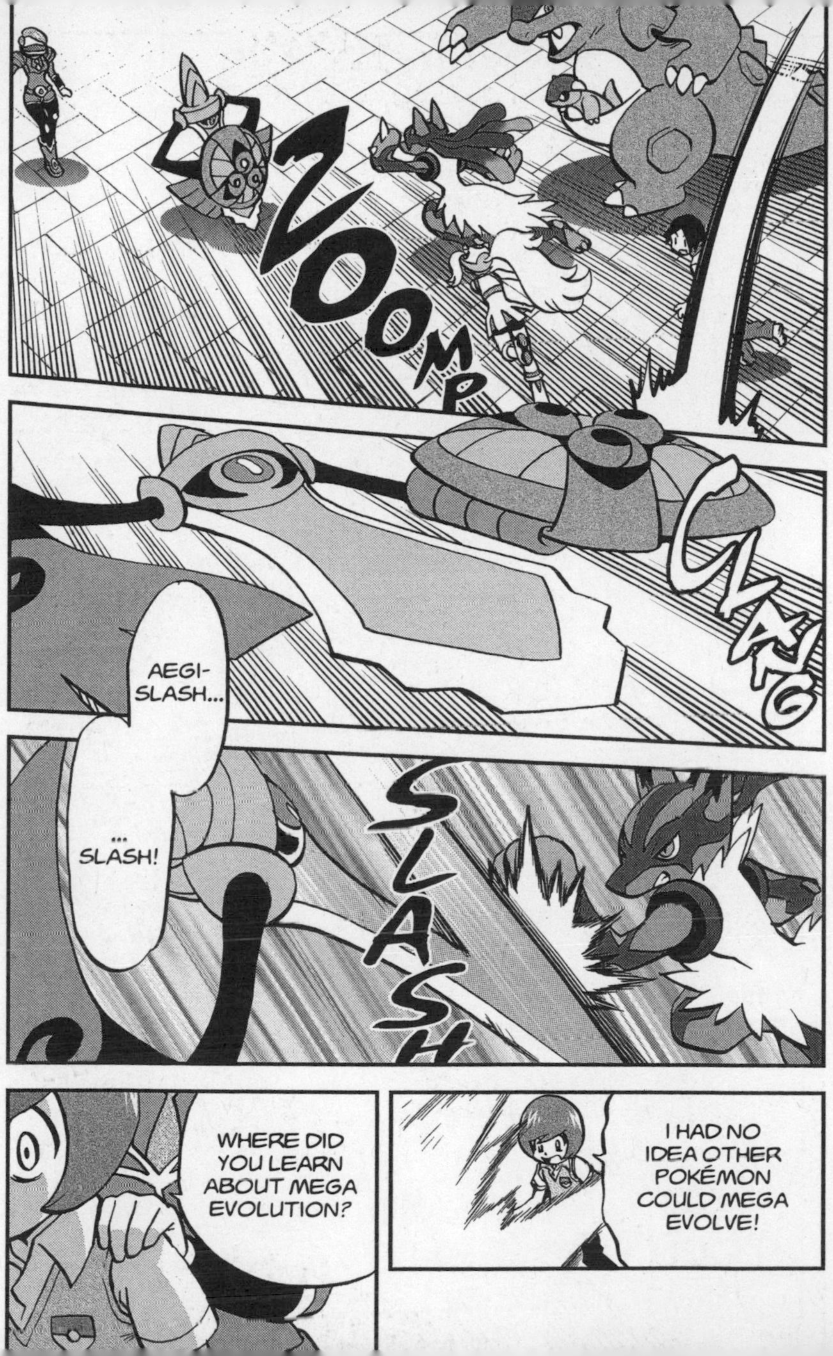
ZOOMP
AEGI-SLASH...
...SLASH!
SLASH
I HAD NO IDEA OTHER POKÉMON COULD MEGA EVOLVE!
WHERE DID YOU LEARN ABOUT MEGA EVOLUTION?

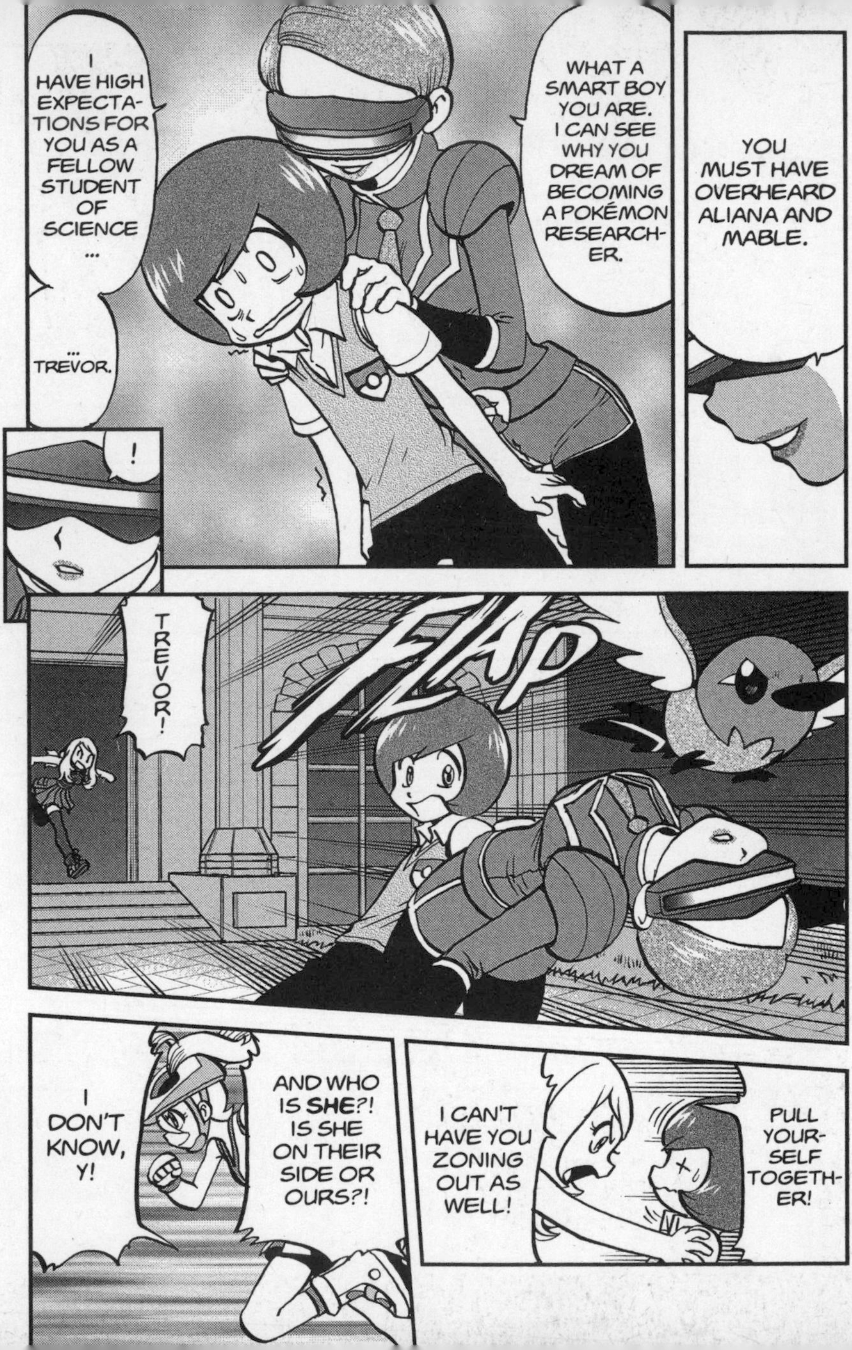
YOU MUST HAVE OVERHEARD ALIANA AND MABLE.
WHAT A SMART BOY YOU ARE. I CAN SEE WHY YOU DREAM OF BECOMING A POKÉMON RESEARCHER.
I HAVE HIGH EXPECTATIONS FOR YOU AS A FELLOW STUDENT OF SCIENCE ...
... TREVOR.
!
FLAP
TREVOR!
PULL YOURSELF TOGETHER!
I CAN'T HAVE YOU ZONING OUT AS WELL!
AND WHO IS **SHE**?! IS SHE ON THEIR SIDE OR OURS?!
I DON'T KNOW, Y!

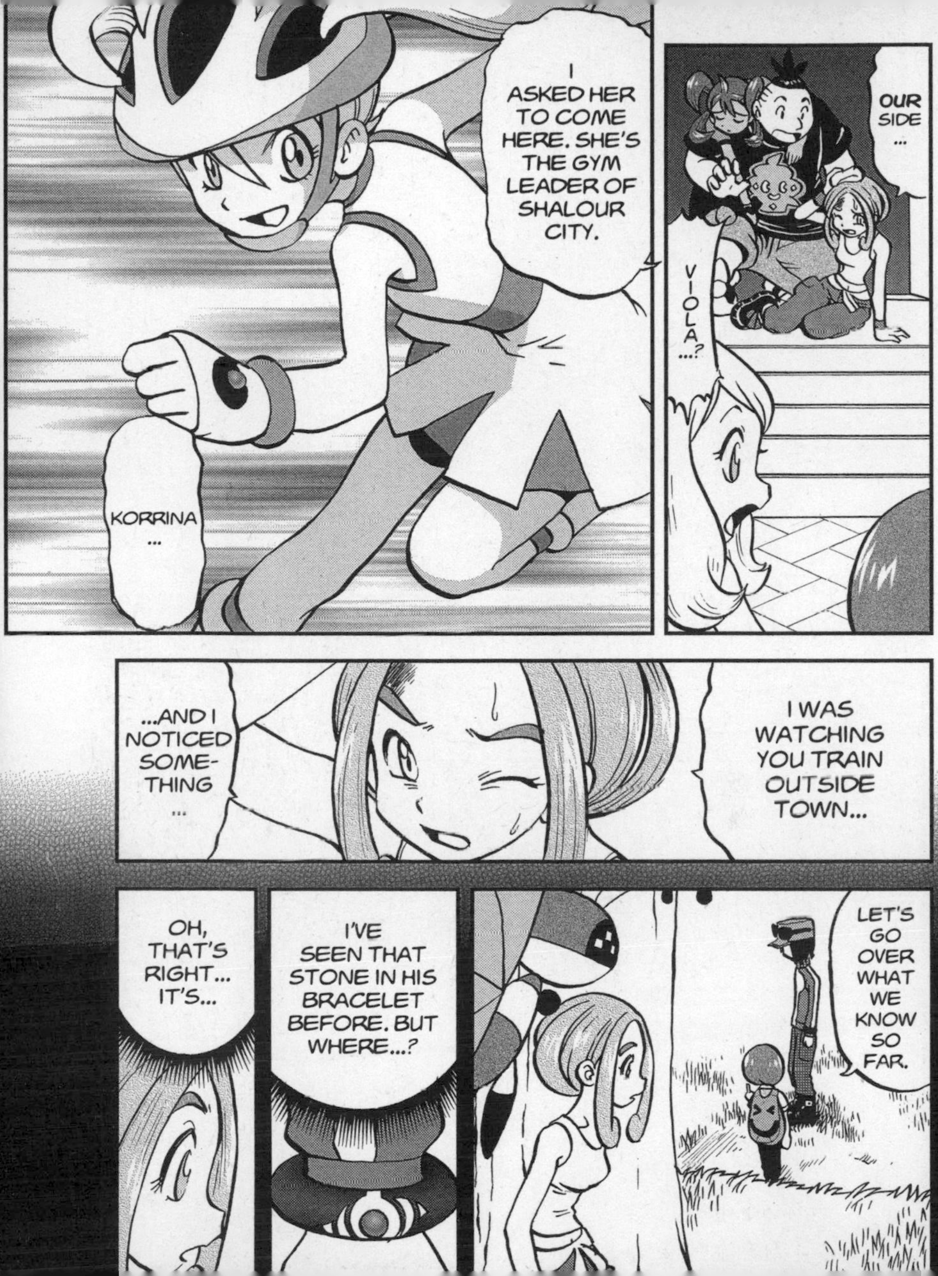
OUR SIDE ...
VIOLA ...?
I ASKED HER TO COME HERE. SHE'S THE GYM LEADER OF SHALOUR CITY.
KORRINA ...
I WAS WATCHING YOU TRAIN OUTSIDE TOWN...
...AND I NOTICED SOMETHING ...
LET'S GO OVER WHAT WE KNOW SO FAR.
I'VE SEEN THAT STONE IN HIS BRACELET BEFORE. BUT WHERE...?
OH, THAT'S RIGHT... IT'S...

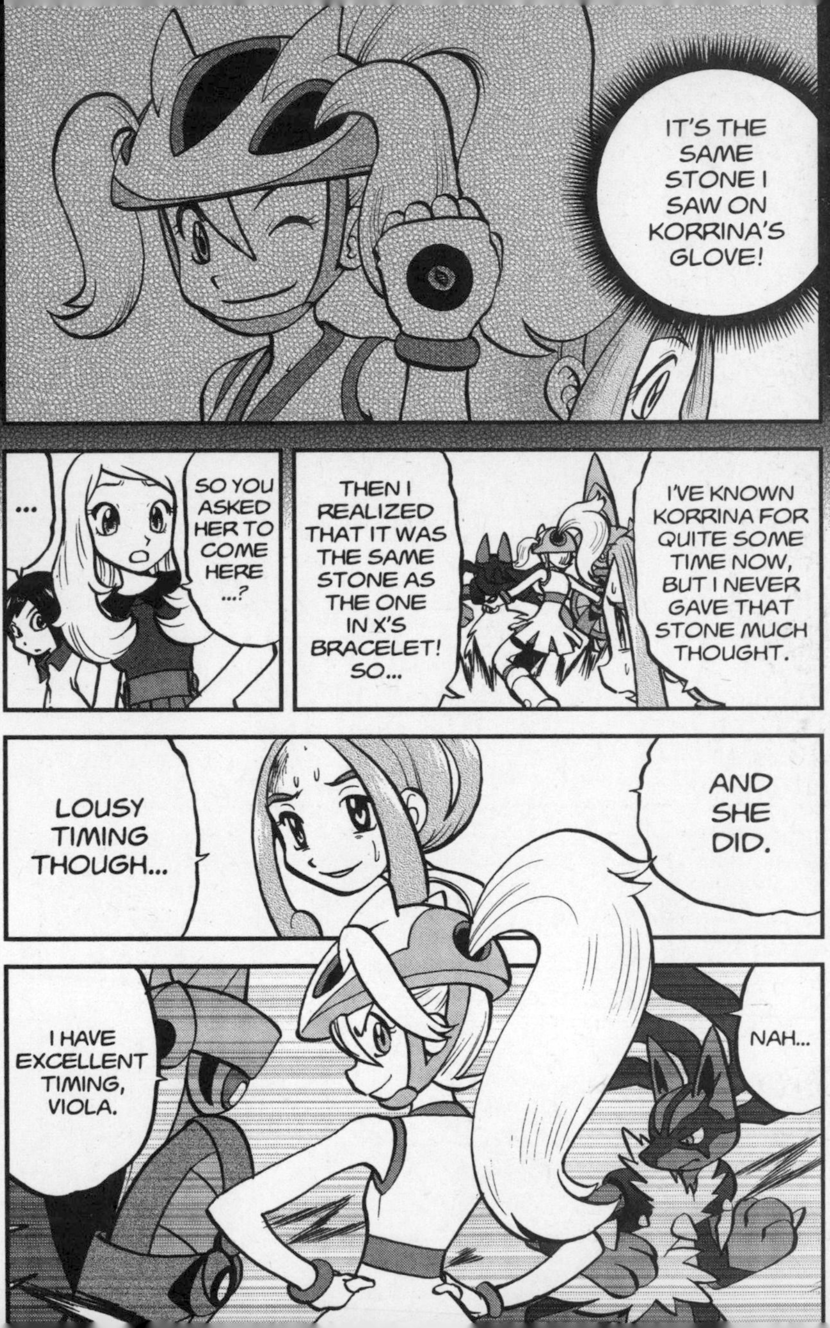
IT'S THE SAME STONE I SAW ON KORRINA'S GLOVE!
I'VE KNOWN KORRINA FOR QUITE SOME TIME NOW, BUT I NEVER GAVE THAT STONE MUCH THOUGHT.
THEN I REALIZED THAT IT WAS THE SAME STONE AS THE ONE IN X'S BRACELET! SO...
SO YOU ASKED HER TO COME HERE ...?
...
AND SHE DID.
LOUSY TIMING THOUGH...
NAH...
I HAVE EXCELLENT TIMING, VIOLA.

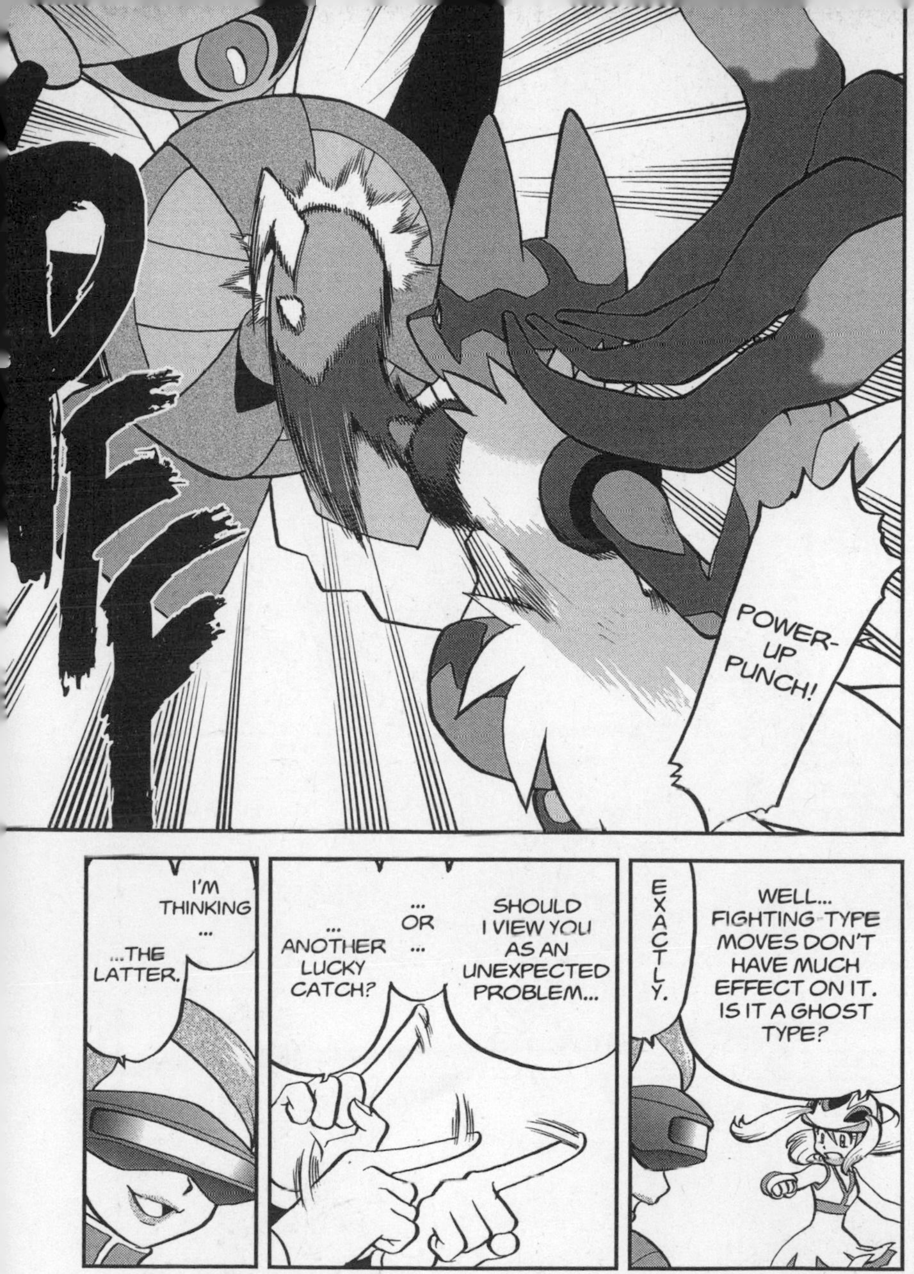
POWER-UP PUNCH!
WELL... FIGHTING-TYPE MOVES DON'T HAVE MUCH EFFECT ON IT. IS IT A GHOST TYPE?
EXACTLY.
SHOULD I VIEW YOU AS AN UNEXPECTED PROBLEM...
...OR...
...ANOTHER LUCKY CATCH?
I'M THINKING...
...THE LATTER.

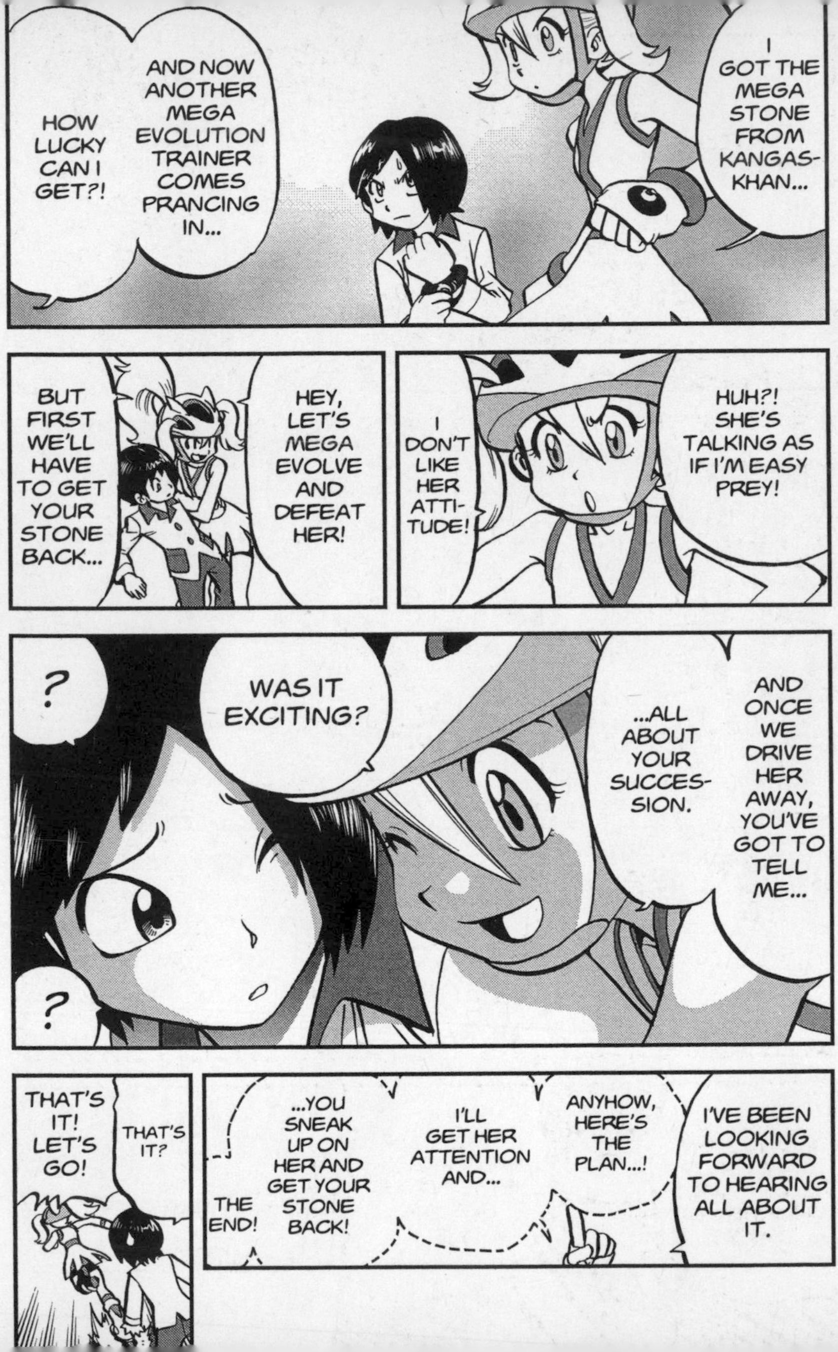
I GOT THE MEGA STONE FROM KANGASKHAN...
AND NOW ANOTHER MEGA EVOLUTION TRAINER COMES PRANCING IN...
HOW LUCKY CAN I GET?!
HUH?! SHE'S TALKING AS IF I'M EASY PREY!
I DON'T LIKE HER ATTITUDE!
HEY, LET'S MEGA EVOLVE AND DEFEAT HER!
BUT FIRST WE'LL HAVE TO GET YOUR STONE BACK...
AND ONCE WE DRIVE HER AWAY, YOU'VE GOT TO TELL ME...
...ALL ABOUT YOUR SUCCESSION.
WAS IT EXCITING?
?
?
I'VE BEEN LOOKING FORWARD TO HEARING ALL ABOUT IT.
ANYHOW, HERE'S THE PLAN...!
I'LL GET HER ATTENTION AND...
...YOU SNEAK UP ON HER AND GET YOUR STONE BACK!
THE END!
THAT'S IT?
THAT'S IT! LET'S GO!

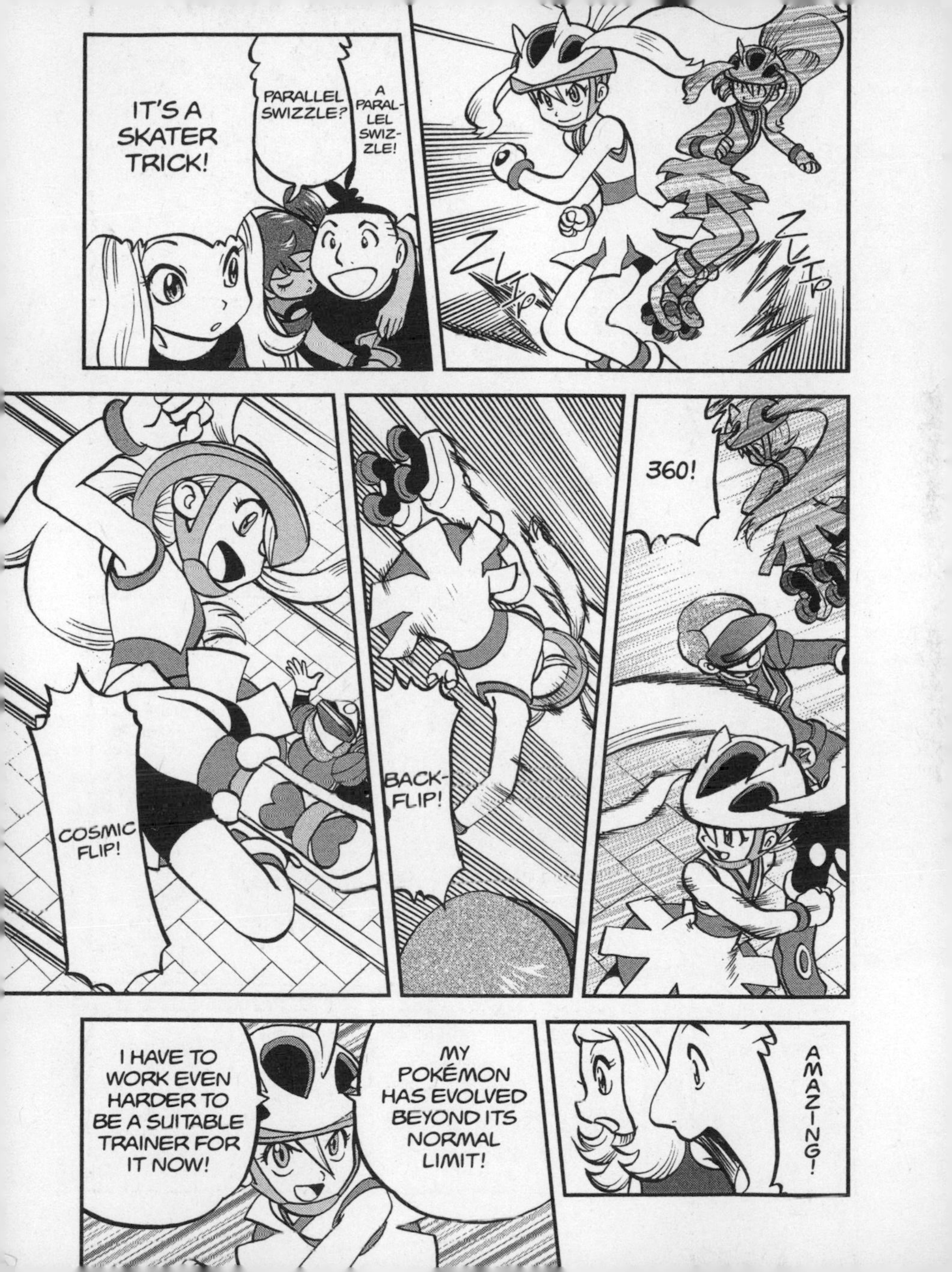
A PARAL-LEL SWIZ-ZLE!
PARALLEL SWIZZLE?
IT'S A SKATER TRICK!
360!
BACK-FLIP!
COSMIC FLIP!
AMAZING!
MY POKÉMON HAS EVOLVED BEYOND ITS NORMAL LIMIT!
I HAVE TO WORK EVEN HARDER TO BE A SUITABLE TRAINER FOR IT NOW!

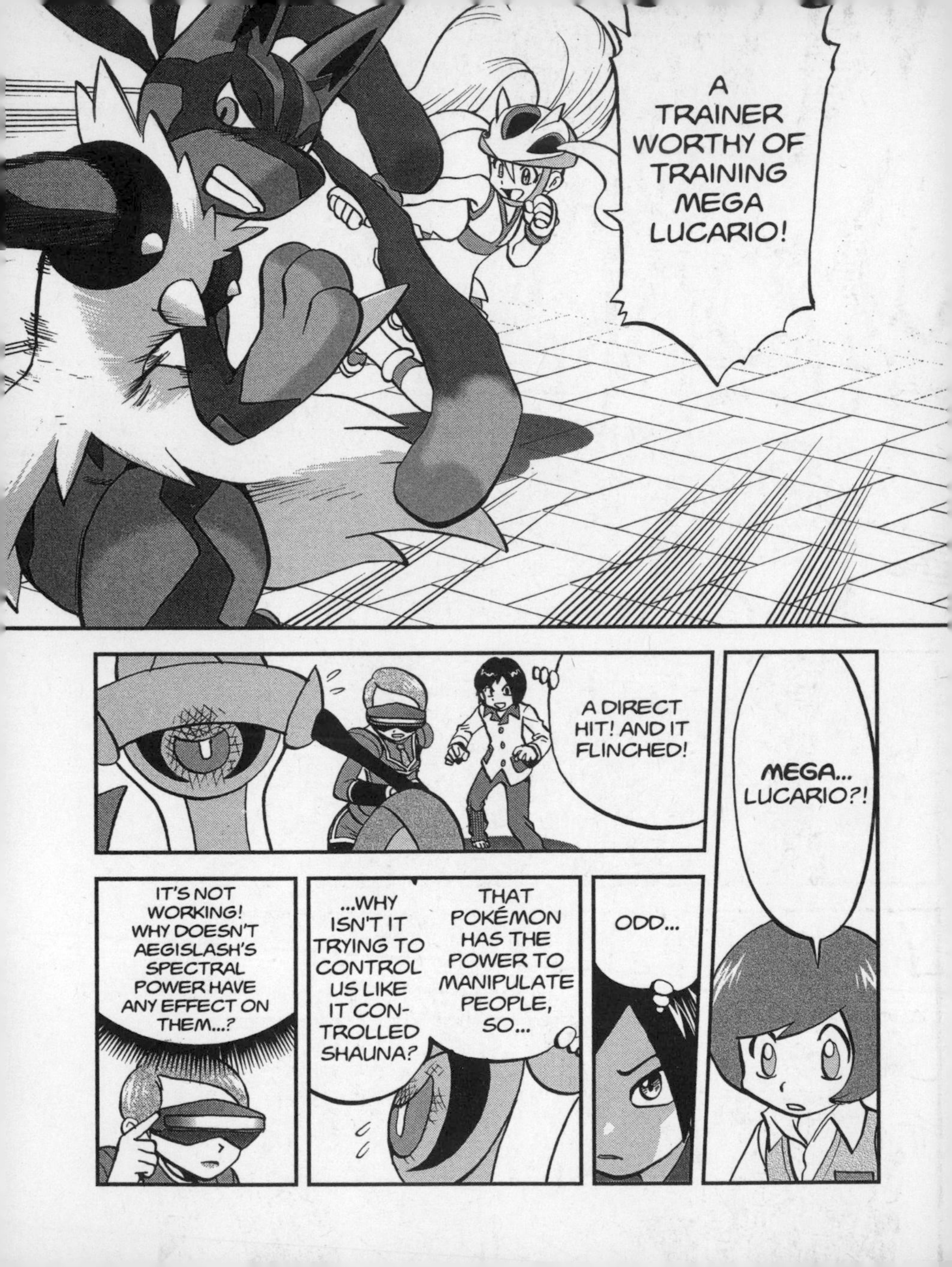

A TRAINER WORTHY OF TRAINING MEGA LUCARIO!
MEGA... LUCARIO?!
A DIRECT HIT! AND IT FLINCHED!
ODD...
THAT POKÉMON HAS THE POWER TO MANIPULATE PEOPLE, SO...
...WHY ISN'T IT TRYING TO CONTROL US LIKE IT CON-TROLLED SHAUNA?
IT'S NOT WORKING! WHY DOESN'T AEGISLASH'S SPECTRAL POWER HAVE ANY EFFECT ON THEM...?

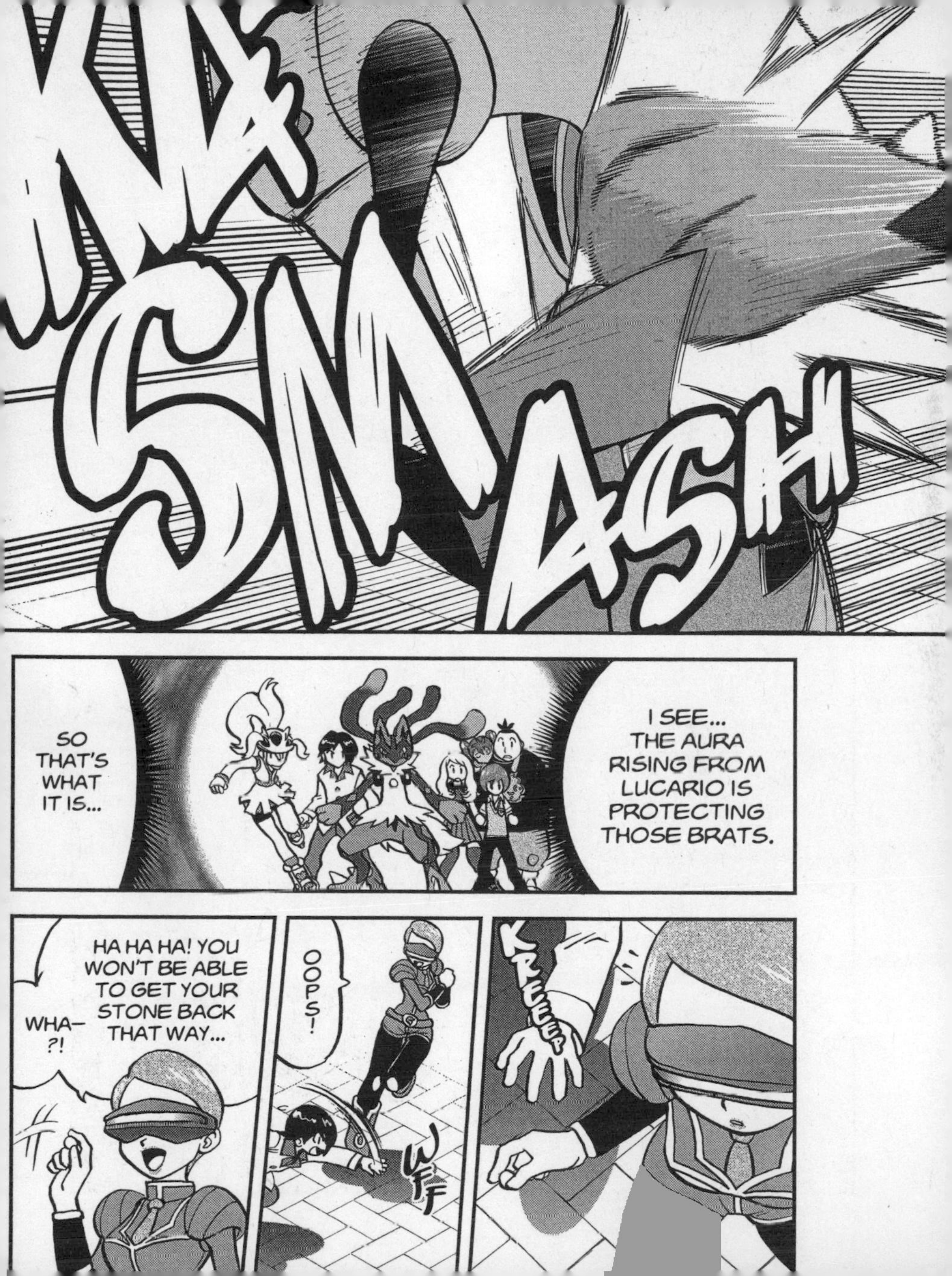
SMASH
I SEE... THE AURA RISING FROM LUCARIO IS PROTECTING THOSE BRATS.
SO THAT'S WHAT IT IS...
KREEEP
OOPS!
WUFF
HA HA HA! YOU WON'T BE ABLE TO GET YOUR STONE BACK THAT WAY...
WHA—?!

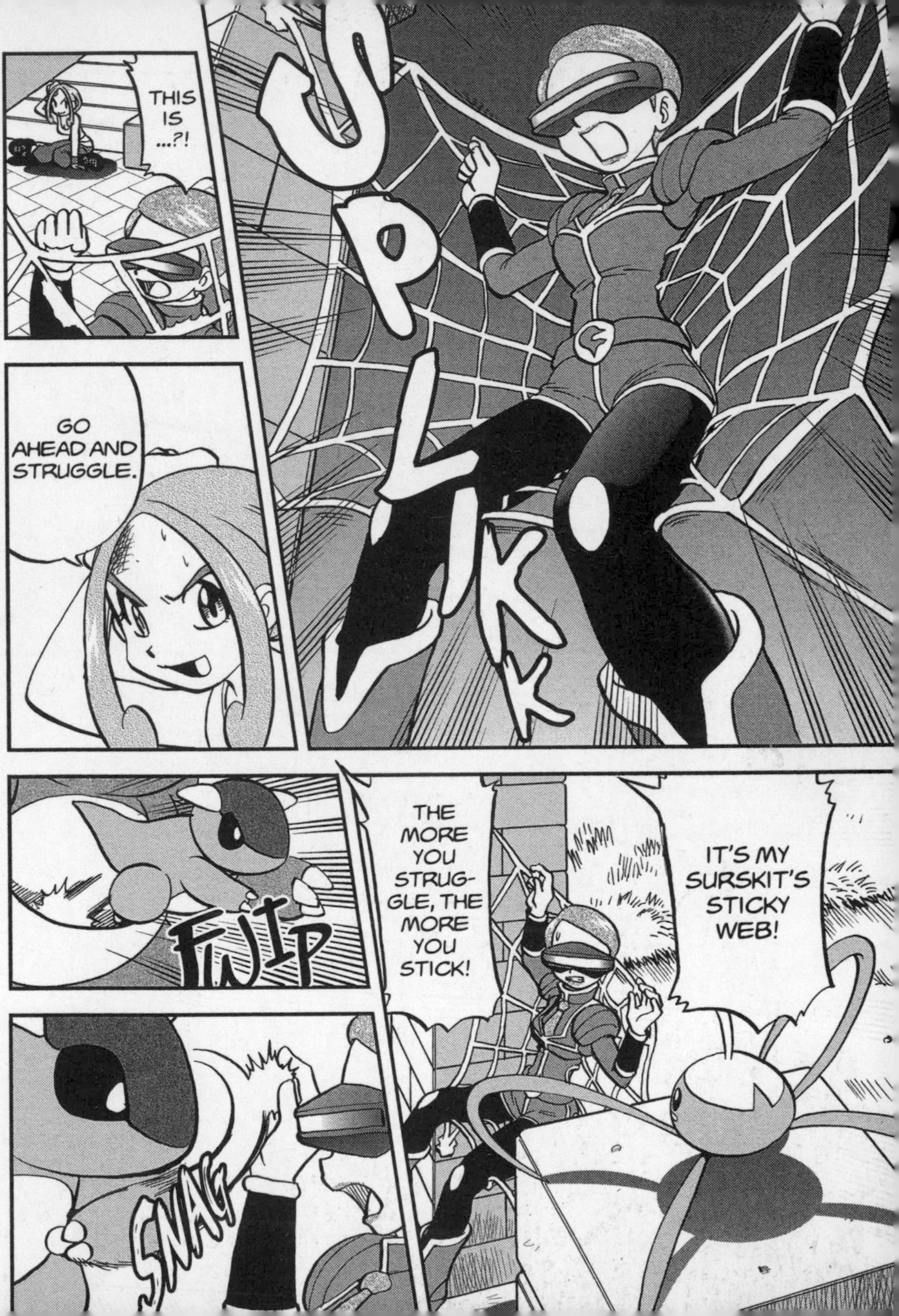
SPLIK
THIS IS ...?!
GO AHEAD AND STRUGGLE.
IT'S MY SURSKIT'S STICKY WEB!
THE MORE YOU STRUG-GLE, THE MORE YOU STICK!
FWIP
SNAG

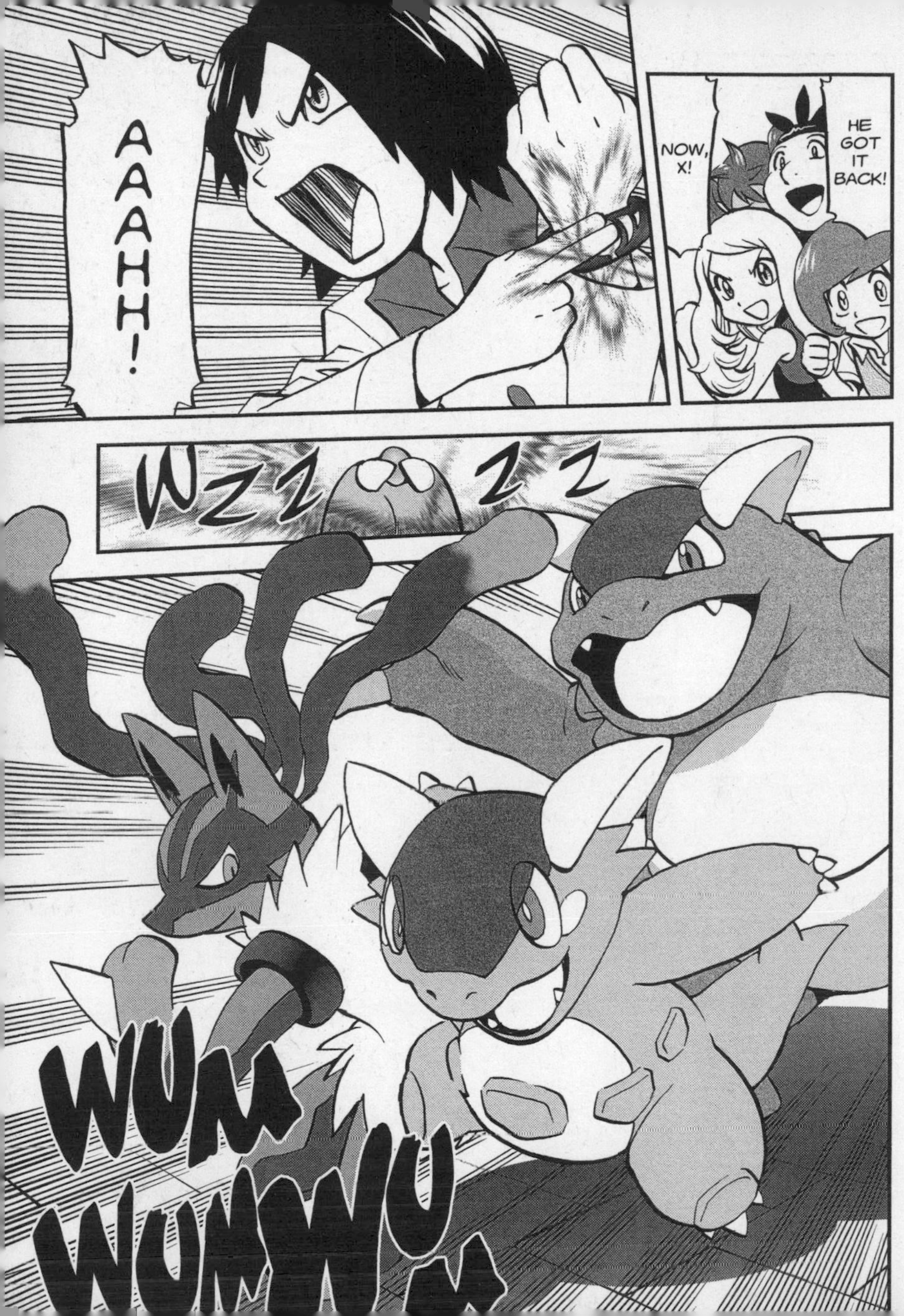

HE GOT IT BACK!
NOW, X!
AAAAHH!
WZZZZZ
WUM WUMWUM

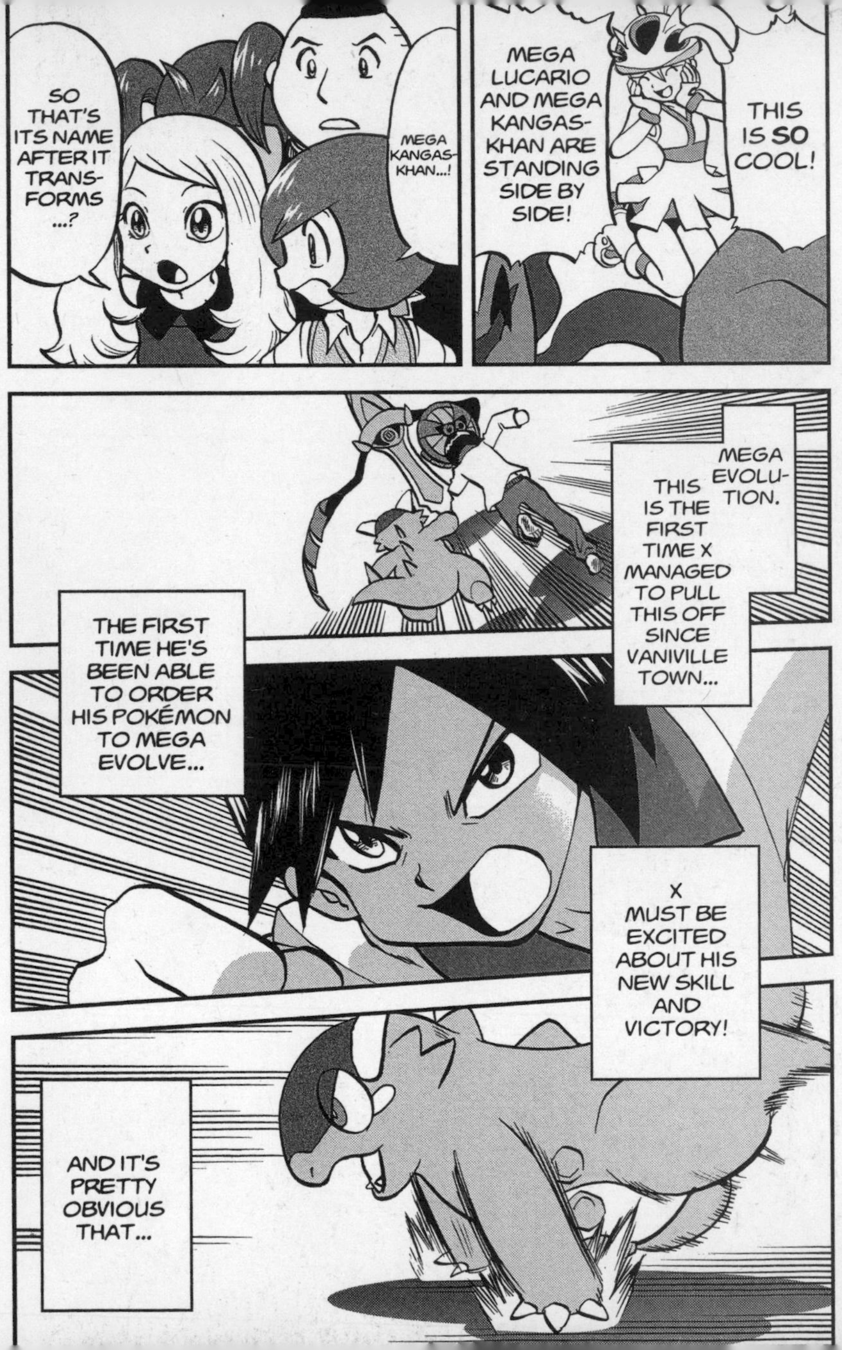
THIS IS SO COOL!
MEGA LUCARIO AND MEGA KANGAS-KHAN ARE STANDING SIDE BY SIDE!
MEGA KANGAS-KHAN...!
SO THAT'S ITS NAME AFTER IT TRANS-FORMS ...?
MEGA EVOLU-TION.
THIS IS THE FIRST TIME X MANAGED TO PULL THIS OFF SINCE VANIVILLE TOWN...
THE FIRST TIME HE'S BEEN ABLE TO ORDER HIS POKÉMON TO MEGA EVOLVE...
X MUST BE EXCITED ABOUT HIS NEW SKILL AND VICTORY!
AND IT'S PRETTY OBVIOUS THAT...

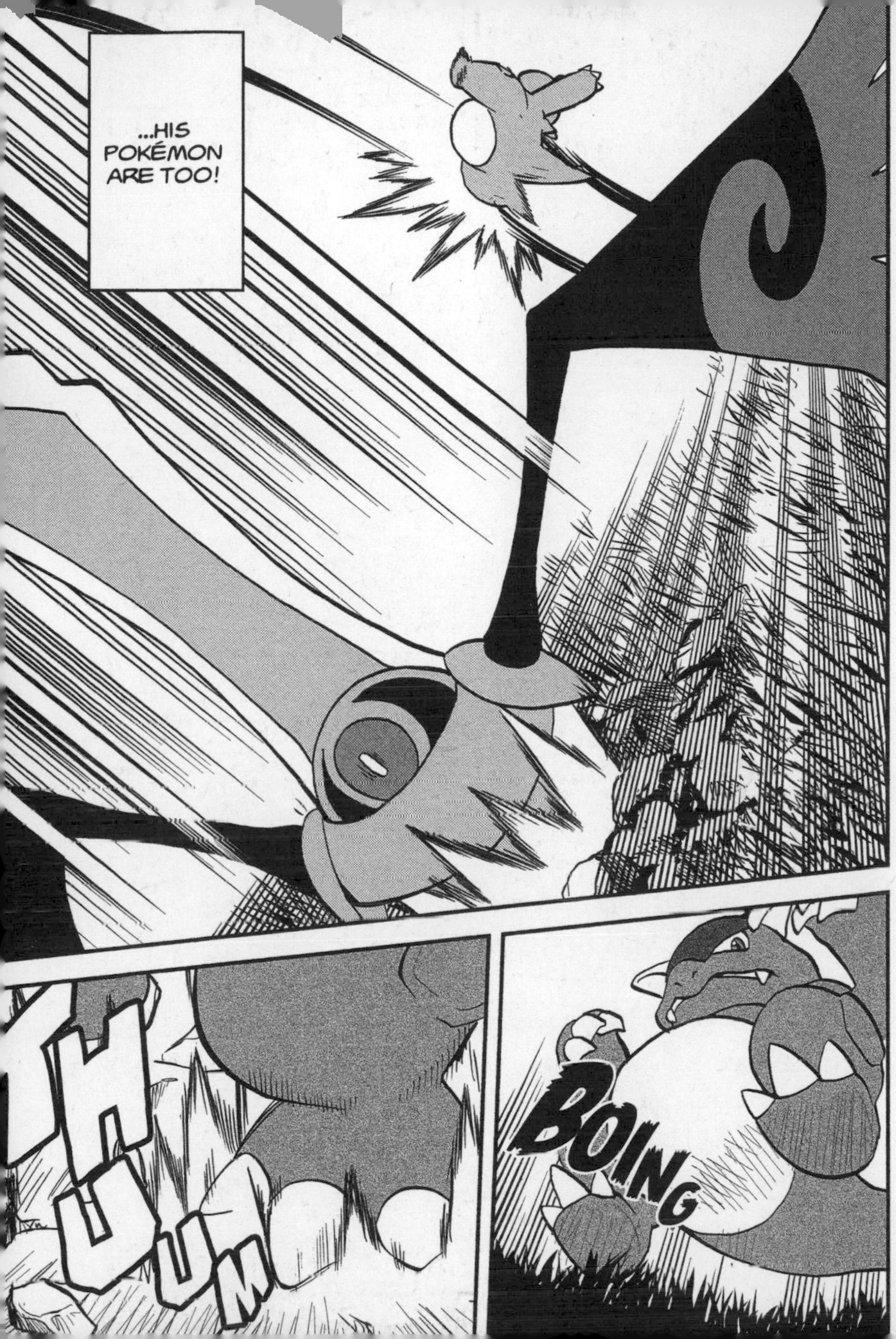
...HIS POKÉMON ARE TOO!
BOING
HUUM

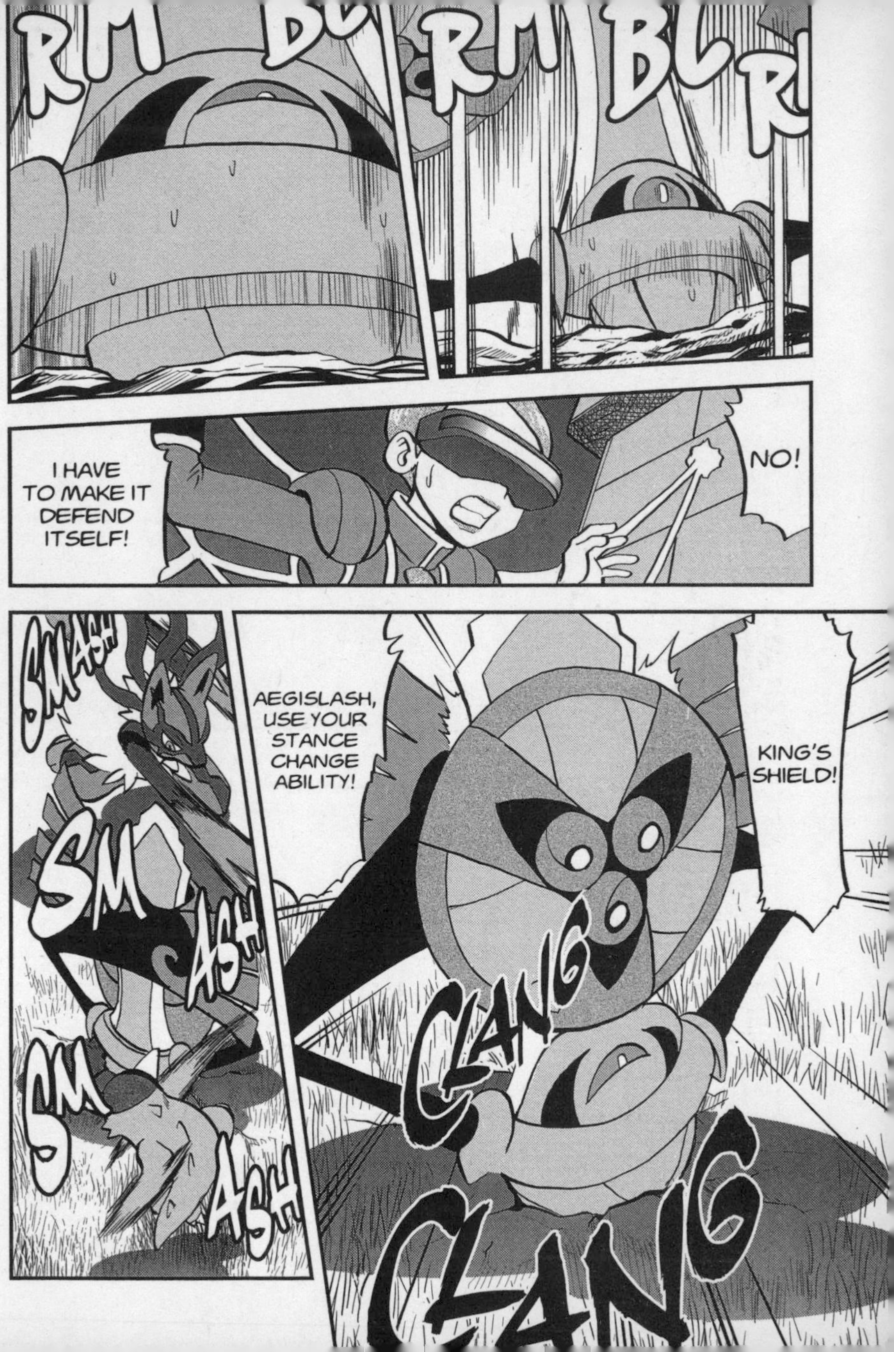
RM
BL
RI
RM
BL
NO!
I HAVE TO MAKE IT DEFEND ITSELF!
AEGISLASH, USE YOUR STANCE CHANGE ABILITY!
KING'S SHIELD!
CLANG
CLANG
SMASH
SMASH
SMASH

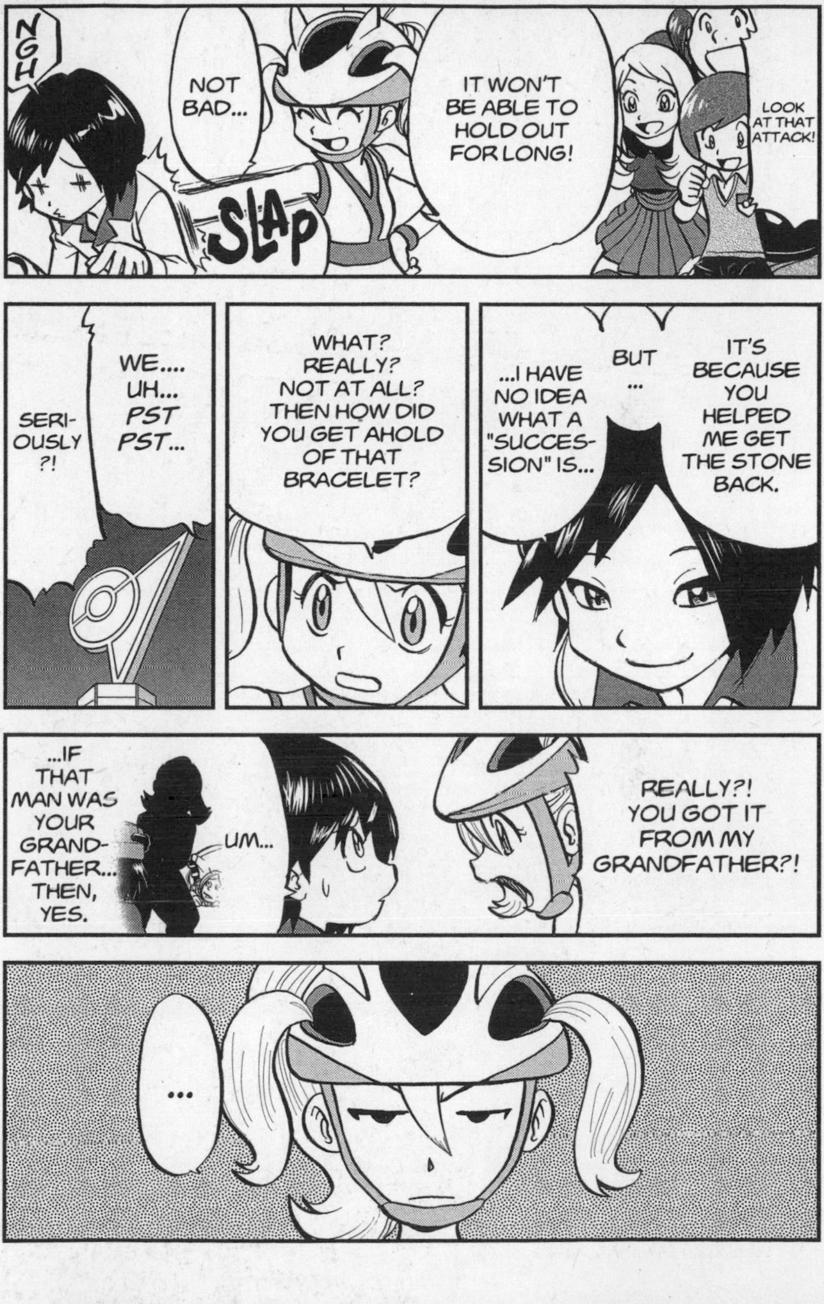
LOOK AT THAT ATTACK!
IT WON'T BE ABLE TO HOLD OUT FOR LONG!
NOT BAD...
SLAP
NGH
IT'S BECAUSE YOU HELPED ME GET THE STONE BACK.
BUT ...
...I HAVE NO IDEA WHAT A "SUCCESSION" IS...
WHAT? REALLY? NOT AT ALL? THEN HOW DID YOU GET AHOLD OF THAT BRACELET?
WE.... UH... PST PST...
SERIOUSLY?!
REALLY?! YOU GOT IT FROM MY GRANDFATHER?!
UM...
...IF THAT MAN WAS YOUR GRANDFATHER... THEN, YES.
...

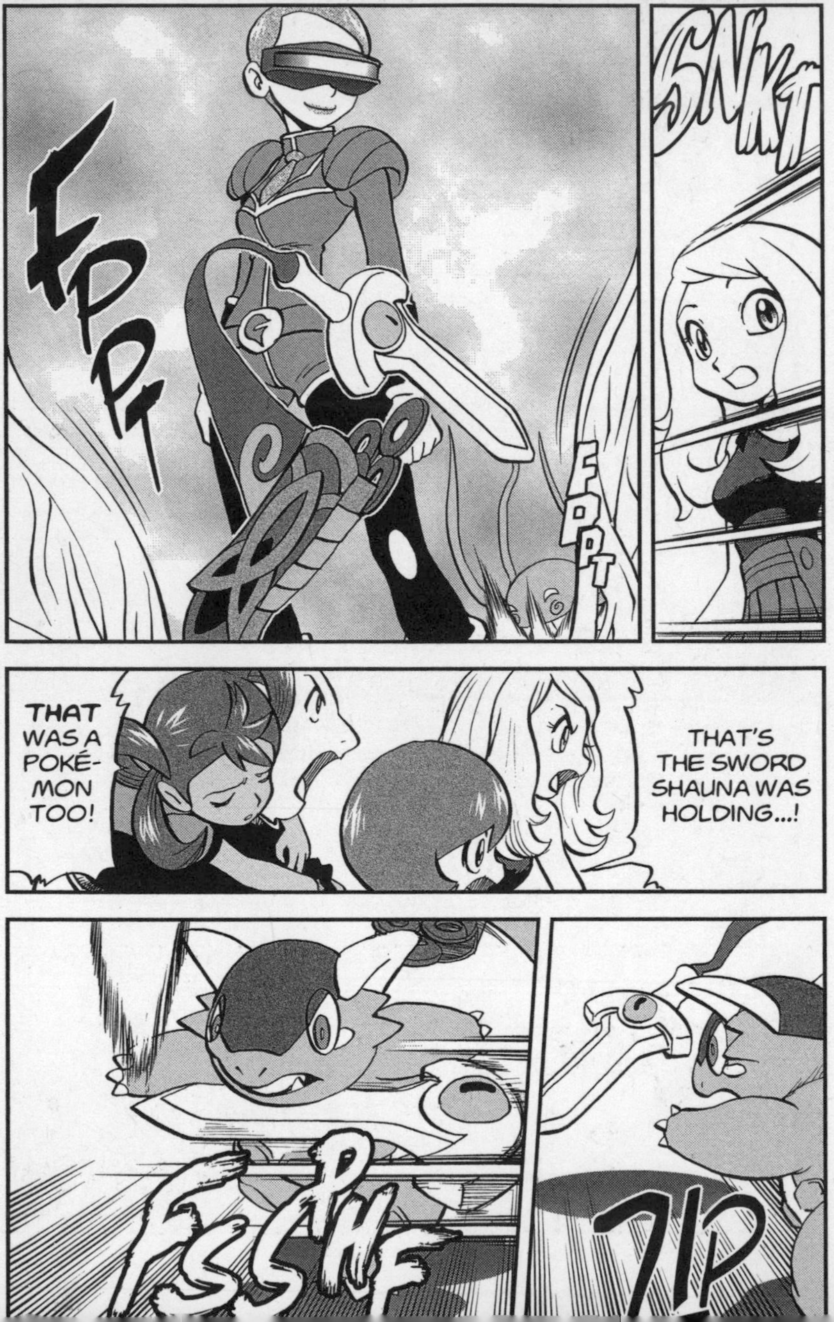
SNKT
FPPT
FPPT
THAT'S THE SWORD SHAUNA WAS HOLDING...!
THAT WAS A POKÉMON TOO!
ZIP

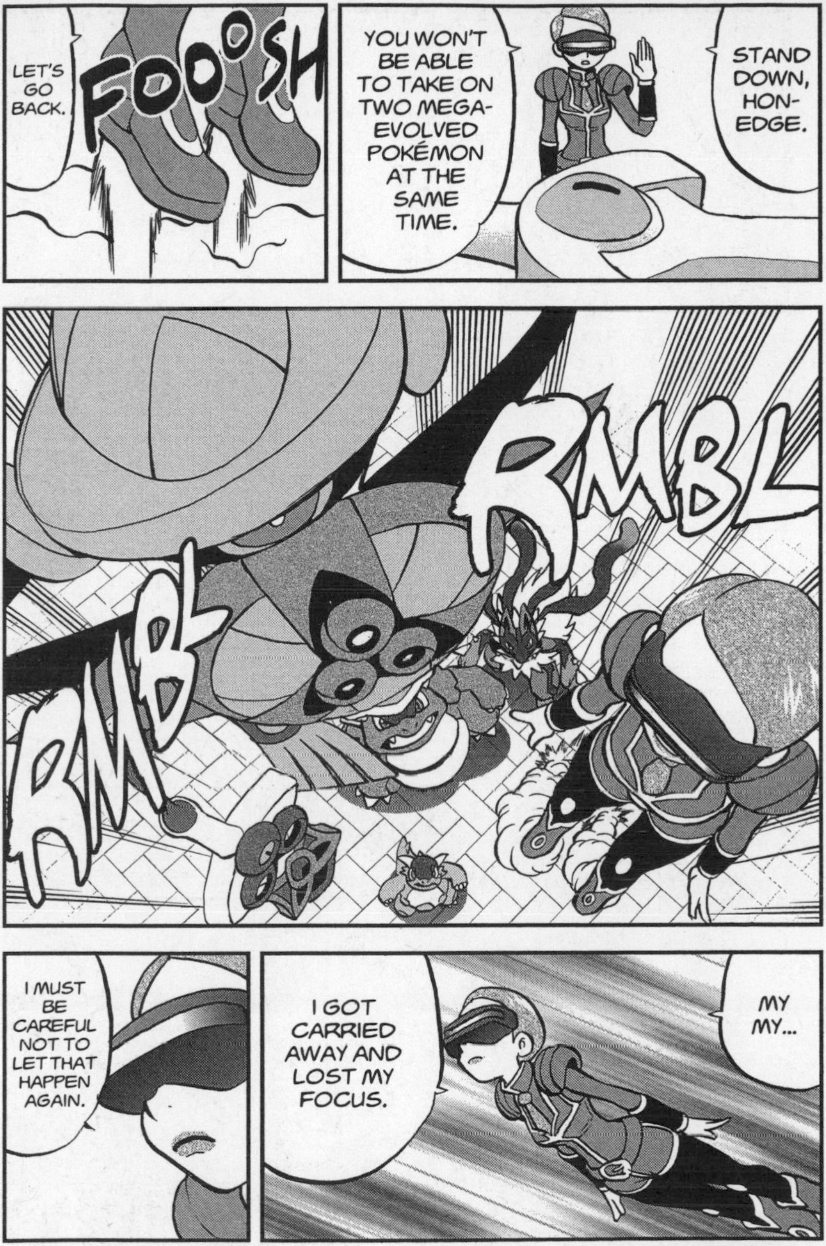
STAND DOWN, HON-EDGE.
YOU WON'T BE ABLE TO TAKE ON TWO MEGA-EVOLVED POKÉMON AT THE SAME TIME.
FOOOSH
LET'S GO BACK.
RMBL
RMBL
MY MY...
I GOT CARRIED AWAY AND LOST MY FOCUS.
I MUST BE CAREFUL NOT TO LET THAT HAPPEN AGAIN.

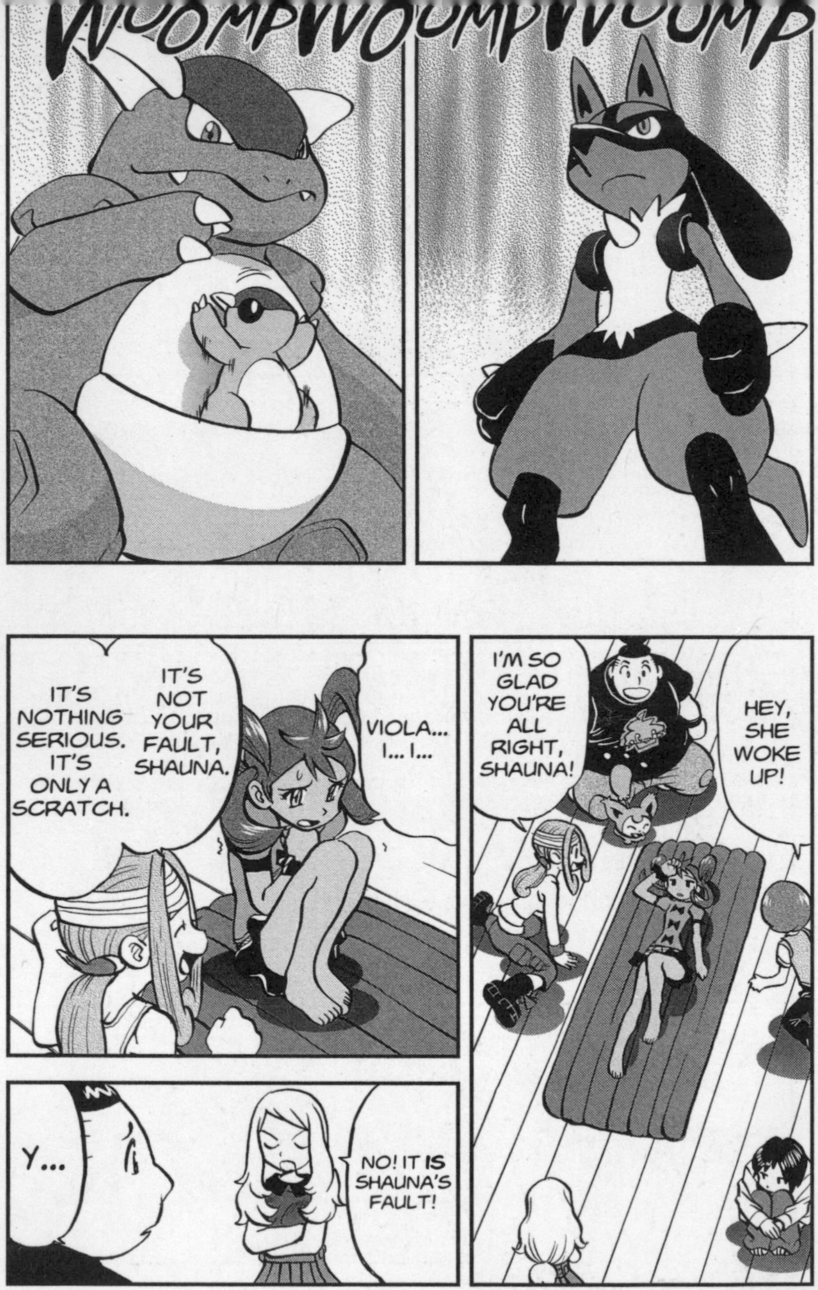
WOOMP WOOMP WOOMP
HEY, SHE WOKE UP!
I'M SO GLAD YOU'RE ALL RIGHT, SHAUNA!
VIOLA... I... I...
IT'S NOT YOUR FAULT, SHAUNA.
IT'S NOTHING SERIOUS. IT'S ONLY A SCRATCH.
NO! IT **IS** SHAUNA'S FAULT!
Y...

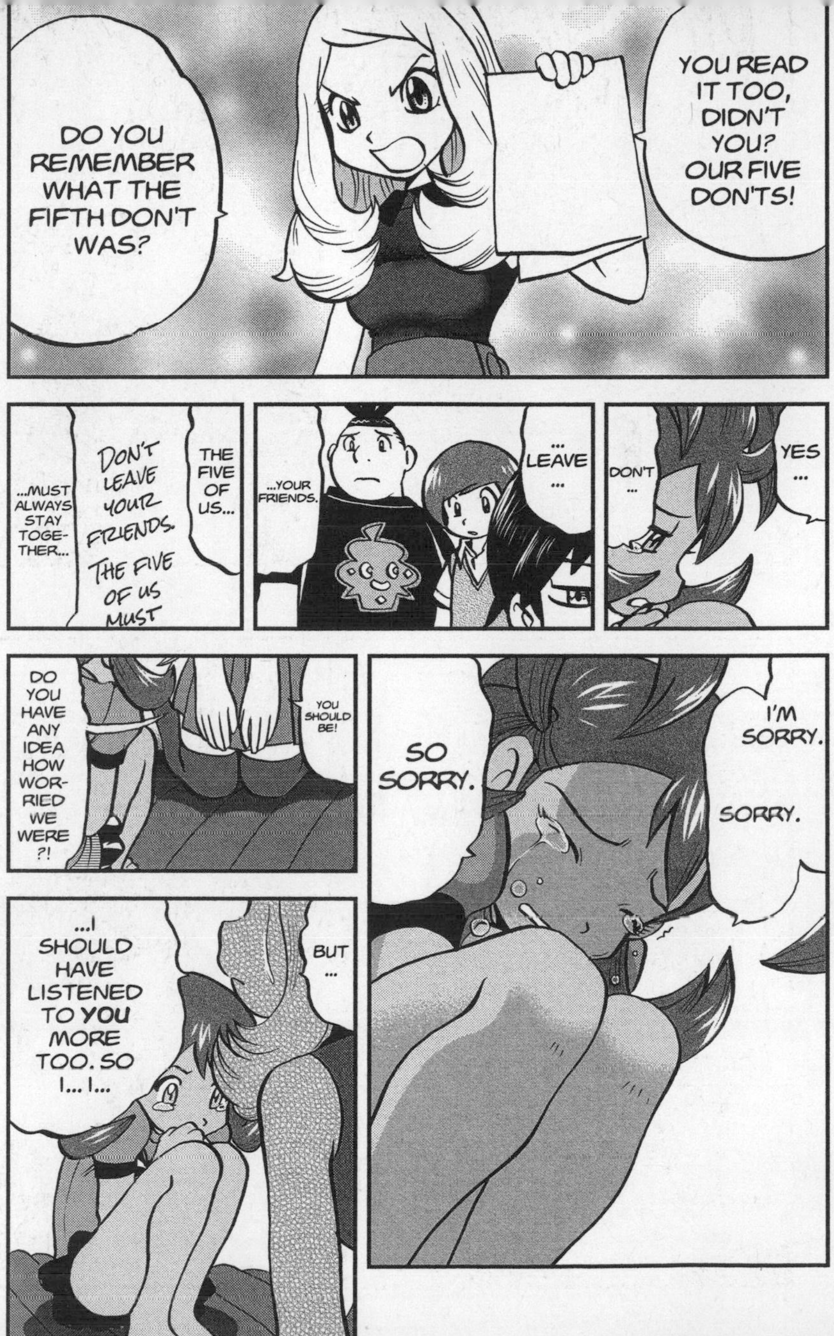
YOU READ IT TOO, DIDN'T YOU? OUR FIVE DON'TS!
DO YOU REMEMBER WHAT THE FIFTH DON'T WAS?
YES ...
DON'T ...
... LEAVE ...
...YOUR FRIENDS.
THE FIVE OF US...
DON'T LEAVE YOUR FRIENDS. THE FIVE OF US MUST
...MUST ALWAYS STAY TOGE-THER...
I'M SORRY.
SO SORRY.
SORRY.
YOU SHOULD BE!
DO YOU HAVE ANY IDEA HOW WOR-RIED WE WERE?!
BUT ...
...I SHOULD HAVE LISTENED TO **YOU** MORE TOO. SO I... I...

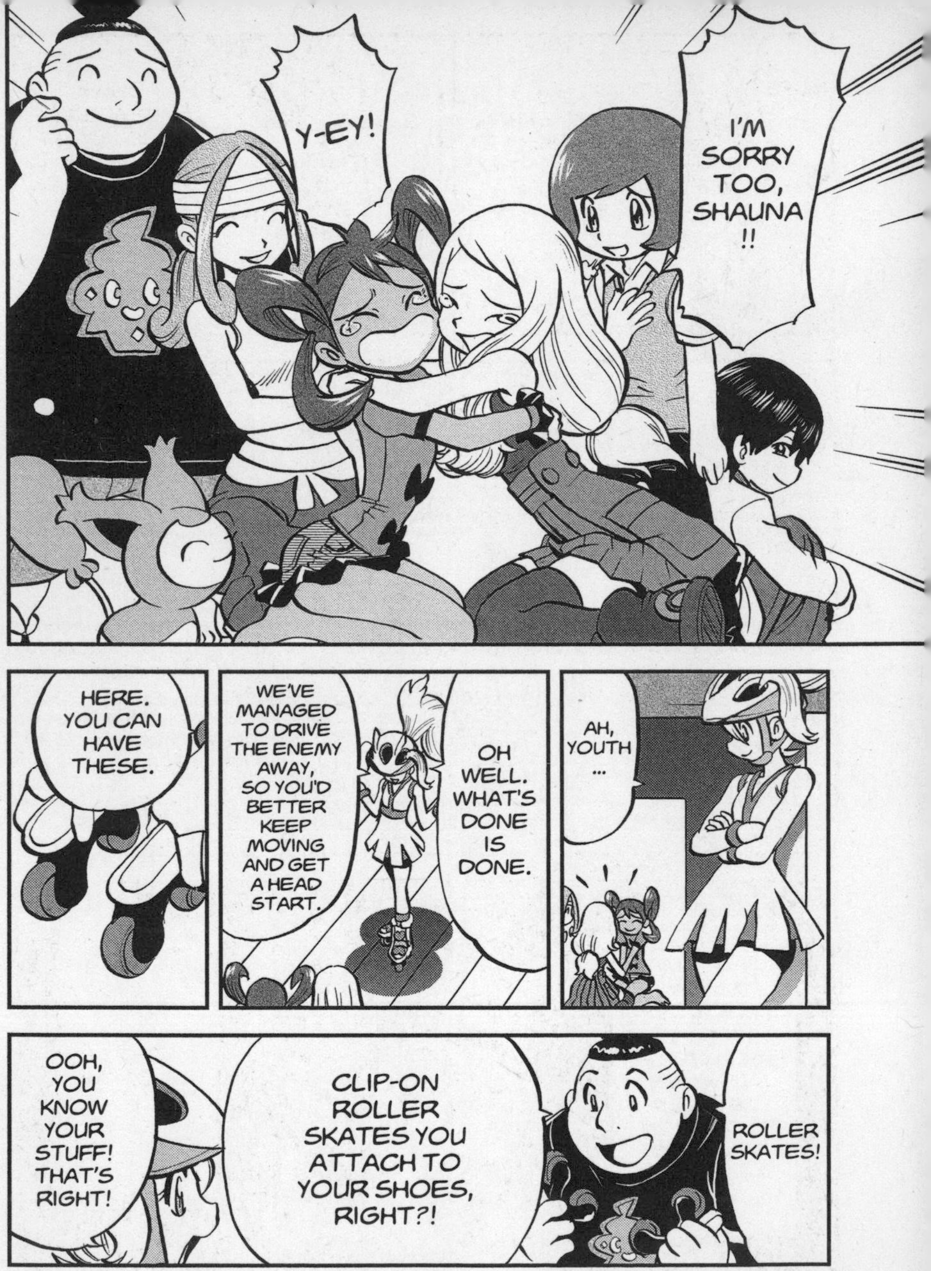
I'M SORRY TOO, SHAUNA!!
Y-EY!
AH, YOUTH...
OH WELL. WHAT'S DONE IS DONE.
WE'VE MANAGED TO DRIVE THE ENEMY AWAY, SO YOU'D BETTER KEEP MOVING AND GET A HEAD START.
HERE. YOU CAN HAVE THESE.
ROLLER SKATES!
CLIP-ON ROLLER SKATES YOU ATTACH TO YOUR SHOES, RIGHT?!
OOH, YOU KNOW YOUR STUFF! THAT'S RIGHT!

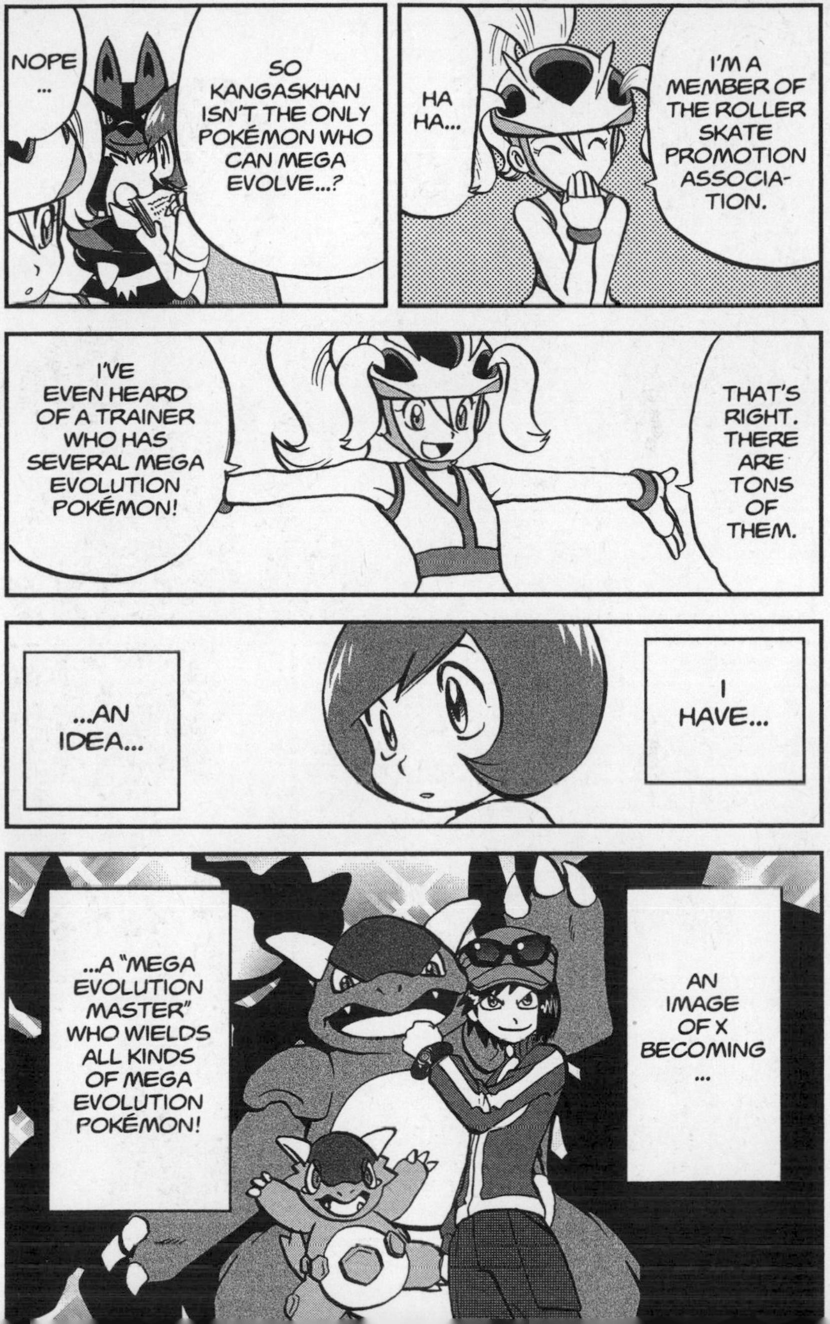
I'M A MEMBER OF THE ROLLER SKATE PROMOTION ASSOCIATION.
HA HA...
SO KANGASKHAN ISN'T THE ONLY POKÉMON WHO CAN MEGA EVOLVE...?
NOPE ...
THAT'S RIGHT. THERE ARE TONS OF THEM.
I'VE EVEN HEARD OF A TRAINER WHO HAS SEVERAL MEGA EVOLUTION POKÉMON!
I HAVE...
...AN IDEA...
AN IMAGE OF X BECOMING ...
...A "MEGA EVOLUTION MASTER" WHO WIELDS ALL KINDS OF MEGA EVOLUTION POKÉMON!

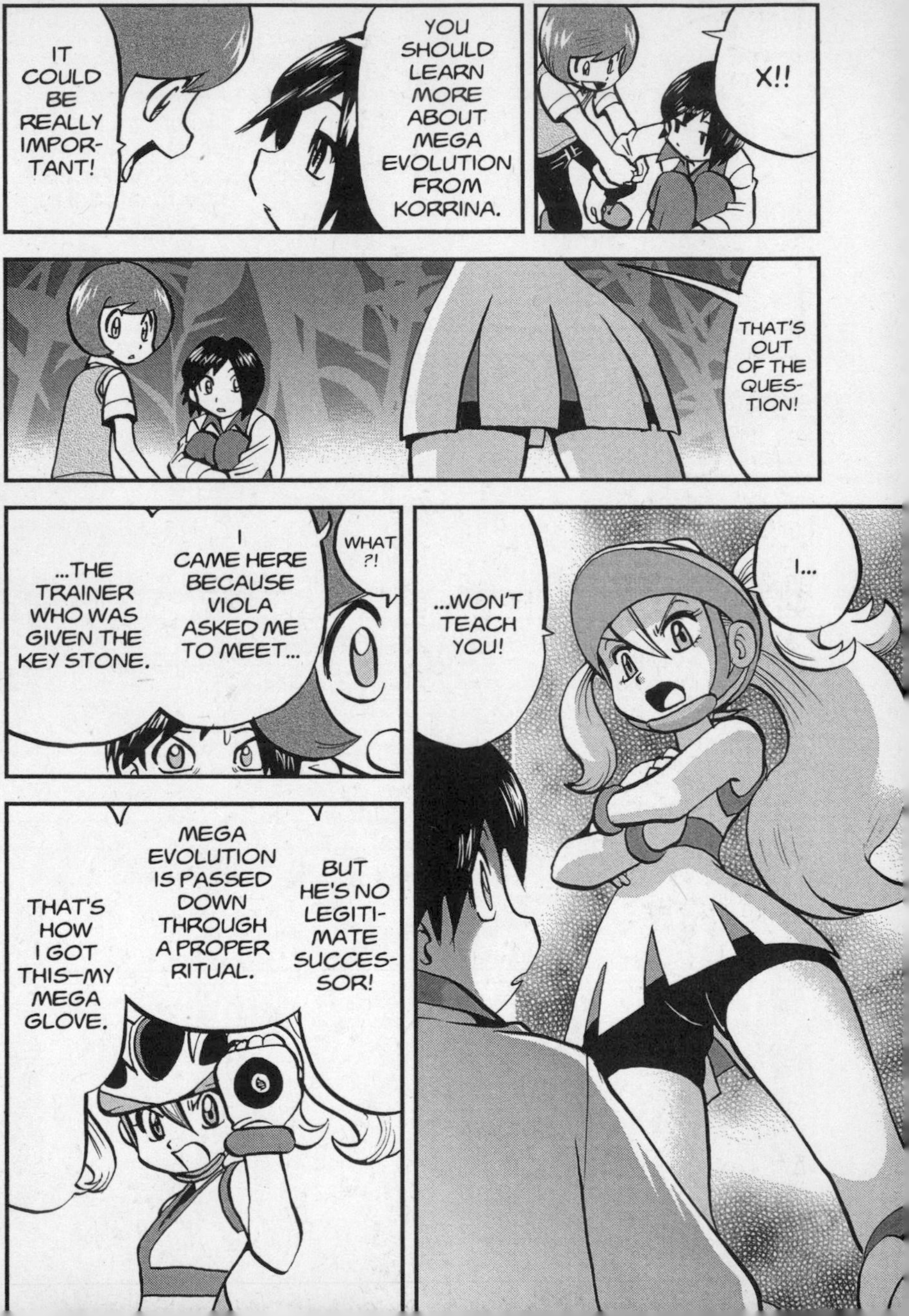
X!!
YOU SHOULD LEARN MORE ABOUT MEGA EVOLUTION FROM KORRINA.
IT COULD BE REALLY IMPOR-TANT!
THAT'S OUT OF THE QUES-TION!
I...
...WON'T TEACH YOU!
WHAT?!
I CAME HERE BECAUSE VIOLA ASKED ME TO MEET...
...THE TRAINER WHO WAS GIVEN THE KEY STONE.
BUT HE'S NO LEGITI-MATE SUCCES-SOR!
MEGA EVOLUTION IS PASSED DOWN THROUGH A PROPER RITUAL.
THAT'S HOW I GOT THIS—MY MEGA GLOVE.

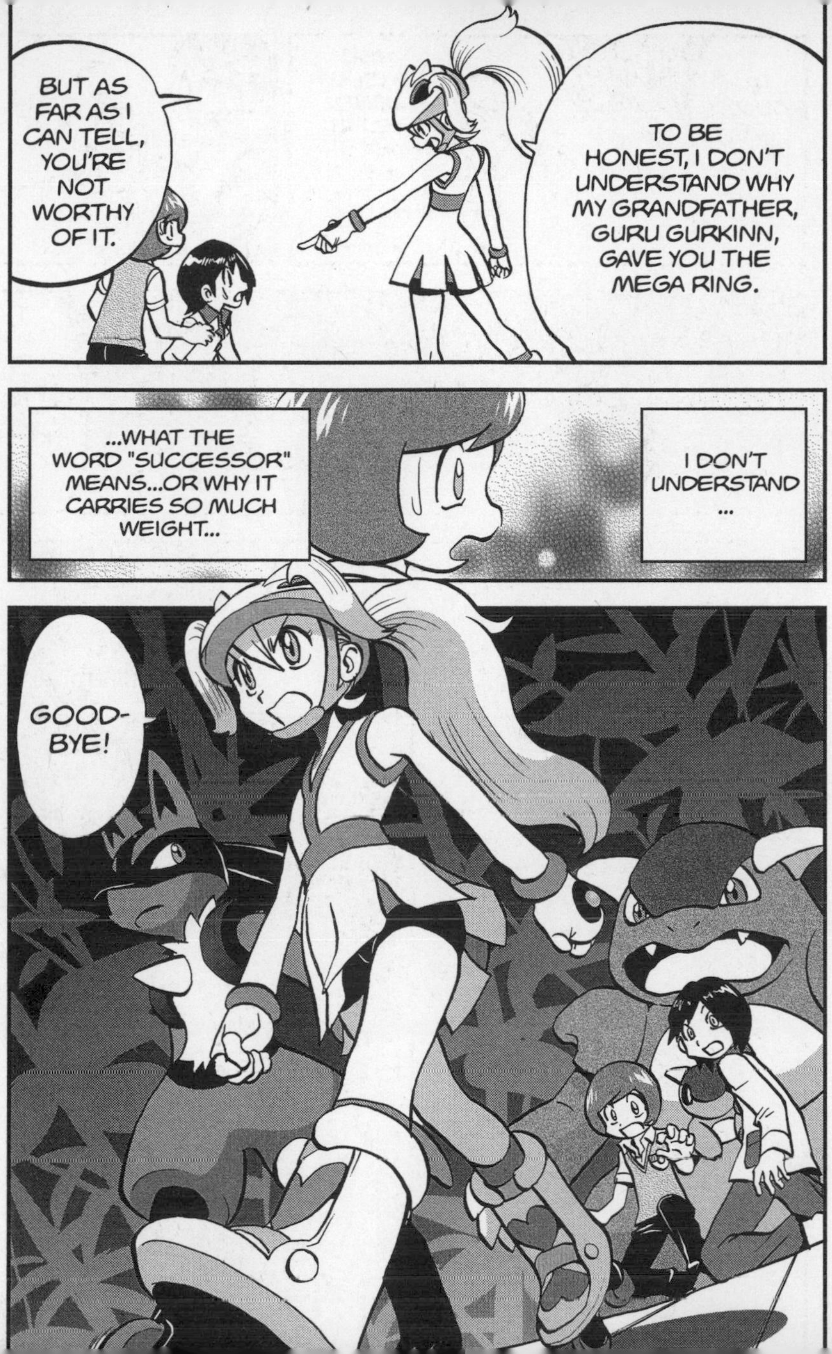
TO BE HONEST, I DON'T UNDERSTAND WHY MY GRANDFATHER, GURU GURKINN, GAVE YOU THE MEGA RING.
BUT AS FAR AS I CAN TELL, YOU'RE NOT WORTHY OF IT.
I DON'T UNDERSTAND ...
...WHAT THE WORD "SUCCESSOR" MEANS...OR WHY IT CARRIES SO MUCH WEIGHT...
GOOD-BYE!

Current Location

Santalune City

Many beginning Trainers gather in this friendly city to start a Pokémon journey.

◆ CURRENT DATA ◆

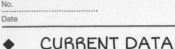

TREVOR'S NOTES

○ Mega Evolution: The phenomenon that occurs when Kanga and Li'l Kanga transform and their power increases.

○ A stone triggers Mega Evolution. The Pokémon must hold one as well as the Trainer.

○ The Pokémon's stone is called a Mega Stone.

○ The Trainer's stone is called a Key Stone. Key Stones are embedded in items such as bracelets and gloves. The bracelet with the Key Stone is called the "Mega Ring" (X has one). The glove with the Key Stone is called the "Mega Glove" (Korrina has one).

○ The stone begins to shine during battle and its light surrounds the Pokémon, transforming it.

○ A Mega-Evolved Kangaskhan is called Mega Kangaskhan. Kangaskhan isn't the only Pokémon who can Mega Evolve. Many Pokémon can Mega Evolve, but not all. Lucario evolves into Mega Lucario.

○ Although the word Evolution is included in Mega Evolution, it differs greatly from the Pokémon Evolution we are accustomed to. Pokémon don't remain in the Mega-Evolved form forever. They change back into their original form after battle.

○ Mega Evolution doesn't always succeed. Do the Pokémon and their Trainer need something other than the stones to connect them?

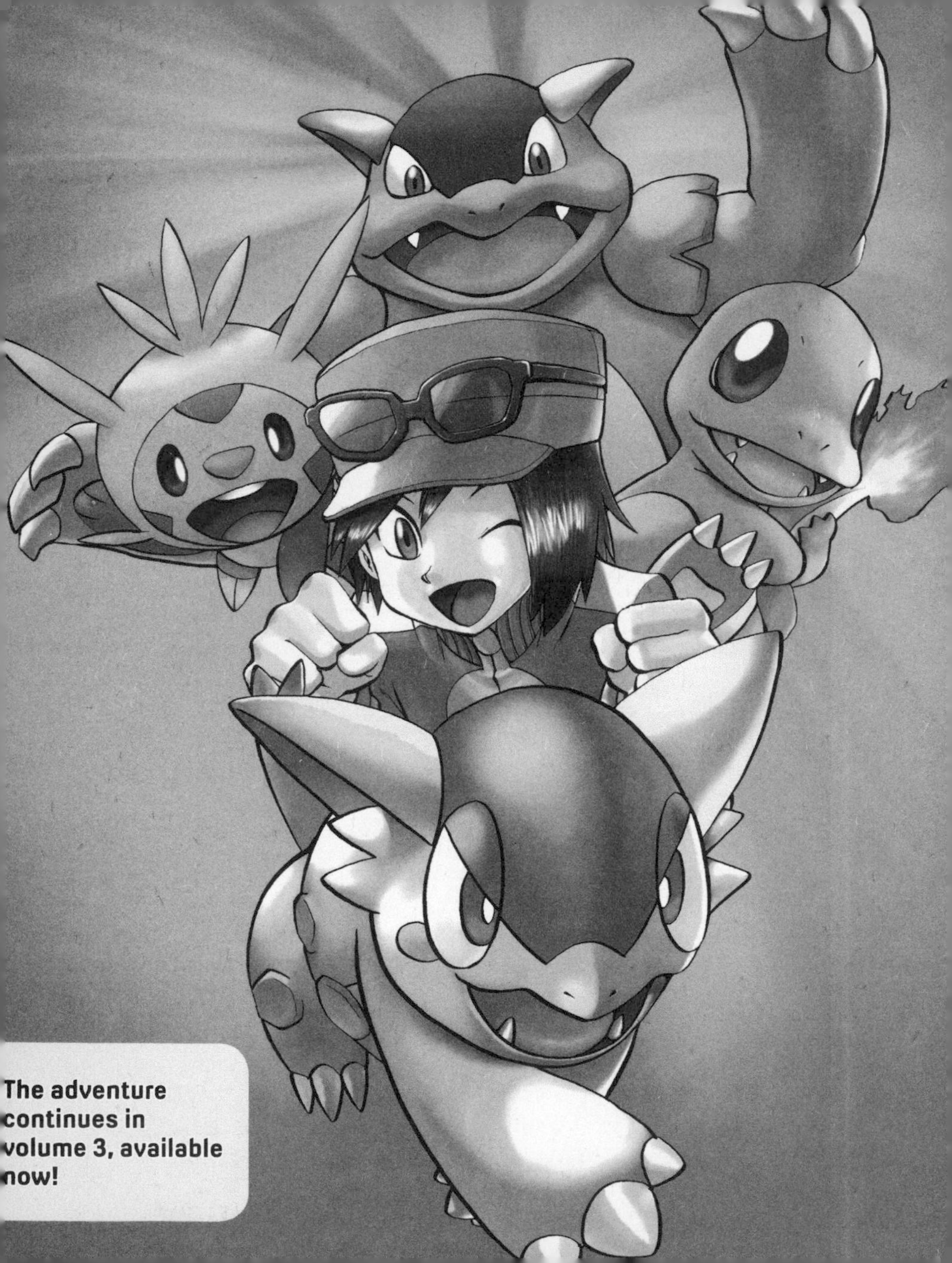

The adventure continues in volume 3, available now!

Pokémon X • Y
Volume 2
Perfect Square Edition

Story by HIDENORI KUSAKA
Art by SATOSHI YAMAMOTO

© 2015 The Pokémon Company International.
© 1995-2015 Nintendo/Creatures Inc./GAME FREAK inc.
TM, ®, and character names are trademarks of Nintendo.
POCKET MONSTERS SPECIAL X•Y Vol. 1
by Hidenori KUSAKA, Satoshi YAMAMOTO
© 2014 Hidenori KUSAKA, Satoshi YAMAMOTO
All rights reserved.
Original Japanese edition published by SHOGAKUKAN.
English translation rights in the United States of America, Canada, the United
Kingdom, Ireland, Australia and New Zealand arranged with SHOGAKUKAN.

English Adaptation—Bryant Turnage
Translation—Tetsuichiro Miyaki
Touch-up & Lettering—Annaliese Christman
Design—Shawn Carrico
Editor—Annette Roman

The stories, characters and incidents mentioned
in this publication are entirely fictional.

No portion of this book may be reproduced or transmitted
in any form or by any means without written permission
from the copyright holders.

Printed in the U.S.A.

Published by
VIZ Media, LLC
P.O. Box 77010
San Francisco, CA 94107

10 9 8 7 6 5 4 3
First printing, February 2015
Third printing, October 2016

PARENTAL ADVISORY
POKÉMON ADVENTURES
is rated A and is suitable
for readers of all ages.
ratings.viz.com

www.perfectsquare.com   www.viz.com

3 1994 01560 7317

SANTA ANA PUBLIC LIBRARY

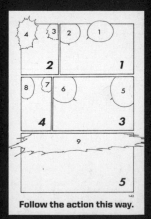

<<< READ THIS WAY!

THIS IS THE END OF THIS GRAPHIC NOVEL!

To properly enjoy this VIZ Media graphic novel, please turn it around and begin reading from right to left.

This book has been printed in the original Japanese format in order to preserve the orientation of the original artwork. Have fun with it!

Follow the action this way.